SECRET OF THE LOST SETTLEMENT

THE DUTY OF WARRIORS

OTHER BOOKS *from* VISION FORUM

SECRET OF THE LOST SETTLEMENT

THE DUTY OF WARRIORS

By John J. Horn

First Printing: October 2013

"Where there is no vision, the people perish." —Proverbs 29:18

The Vision Forum, Inc.
4719 Blanco Rd., San Antonio, TX 78212
www.visionforum.com

ISBN 978-1-934554-90-6

Cover Design and Photography by Daniel R. Prislovsky
Typography by Justin Turley

Printed in the United States of America

To my mom,

who is my constant inspiration.

Table of Contents

Characters from Previous Stories In the Men of Grit Series

Brothers at Arms:
Treasure & Treachery in the Amazon (1835)

Lawrence Stoning

Sober, scholarly, and cautious, Lawrence enjoys working at his mahogany writing desk or reading a book in a comfortable armchair. These opportunities fled when his father sent him to fetch his runaway brother and Lawrence ended up serving as a bodyguard's bodyguard in South America.

Chester Stoning

Although Chester is Lawrence's twin, similar looks are about all they share in common. Chester loves action, adventure, and excitement, all of which he found when his impulsive trip to Spain as part of the British Legion led to protecting a beautiful Spanish girl with a dangerous secret.

Pacarina Stoning (née Garnica)

Although tempered by her parents' death, Pacarina is still vivacious and sweet. The secret she carries about Inca treasure plunged her and the Stoning twins into the Peruvian jungle in an adventure laced with danger and betrayal. Lawrence feared that a romance between Chester and her would delay his return to England, but he didn't expect to become interested himself. *Brothers at Arms* ended just before Lawrence and Pacarina's marriage.

The Boy Colonel: A Soldier Without a Name (1836–1837)

Colonel Nobody

As a mysterious young English colonel in Siberia, Nobody led the 42nd Regiment of Mounted Infantry, a unique British fighting force which utilized the newest available technology and nontraditional tactics. His obedience to the king brought him a betrothed wife he did not expect, and his obedience to God led him to leave the army and become a merchant in the South Seas.

Lady Liana Halmond

Orphaned soon after birth, Liana grew up as a ward of the king. When King William gave her to Nobody as his betrothed wife she followed her new protector to Siberia and the South Seas, but their relationship was tested to the breaking point by their strange adventures on Rahattan Island.

Lieutenant-Colonel Edmund Burke

Full of wit and dash, Edmund is Colonel Nobody's second-in-command and constant companion. He has fought beside "Noble," as he calls Nobody, in Siberia and the South Seas. He is incredibly dedicated to his former superior officer and intensely opposed to anyone who may threaten Nobody, Liana, or his own betrothed wife, Elyssa.

Elyssa Bradley

Elyssa grew up as Liana's maid and best friend. She left England with Liana and was subsequently met and courted by Edmund.

Lord Bronner

As a minister of state to King William, Lord Bronner arranged for the betrothal of Nobody and Liana, largely to spite his oldest son, who wanted to marry Liana.

Lord Banastre Bronner

Lord Bronner's profligate son inherited his father's title, but not his wisdom. Gambling and greed for power are the primary driving forces in Banastre's life, but it was his interest in Liana which drove him to the South Seas, where he did all that he could to get the girl into his power.

General Lysander Tremont

In Colonel Nobody's Siberian days, General Tremont became his nemesis. Overbearing and conceited, Tremont was willing to do nearly anything to hurt his enemies, and his enemy list was topped by Nobody. It was Tremont who tracked Nobody down in the South Seas and falsely accused him of pirating a ship named *Miriam*. He tried to finish Nobody entirely with a pistol shot, but the shot only struck Nobody's shoulder, and Edmund cut him down before he could fire again.

Alexander Somerset

A reporter for the *London Times* who followed Colonel Nobody around the world to get good stories. He reversed his reputation for cowardice by helping Nobody in his final battle against Tremont.

Squad One

The most elite squad in the most elite unit in the British Army in Siberia. Its members are fiercely loyal to Colonel Nobody and Lieutenant-Colonel Burke.

Corporal William Stoning

At Squad One's head, Corporal Stoning was sometimes called the "Venerable Ancient" because of his white hair. At the end of *The Boy Colonel* he lost his life while attacking General Tremont's ship.

Patrick O'Malley

A huge Irishman with a kind heart and a disdain for all things French.

Jacques Lefebvre

A voluble Frenchman who cooks much, speaks more, and somehow maintains a close though argumentative friendship with O'Malley.

Thomas Bronner

Lord Bronner's second son and Banastre Bronner's brother. He hasn't inherited either his father's devious political acumen or his older brother's profligate tendencies. As Squad One's newest member he has much to prove, and he's doing it well.

Matthew and Mark Preston

English twins who like to speak in rhymes. At the end of *The Boy Colonel*, Mark suffered a wound to his head.

Richard Dilworth

Once the owner of a dry goods store in Massachusetts, Dilworth fell upon hard times and joined the British army.

Petr Kamenev

A taciturn Russian betrayed by his own people and firmly attached to Colonel Nobody, the man who did not betray him.

Chapter 1

"Watch your step."

The alley had no gas lamps. The few moonbeams that squeezed between the house tops barely lit a path through the piles of filth, but the smell of sour beer and days-dead fish in each heap gave warning of where not to tread.

"Did you actually live in this rubbish heap, Ed?"

"Smells wonderful, doesn't it?" Edmund said. "When you were killing Cossacks and making everyone scratch their heads about this 'Colonel Nobody,' I was organizing London street urchins."

"Which is easier?"

"Killing Cossacks, definitely."

Colonel Nobody shifted his stick to his right hand and pulled his scarf tighter against his nose. The wool filtered some of the alley's odors, though that wasn't why he hid his face.

"You all right, Noble?" Edmund asked.

"Did the urchins give you much trouble?"

"Hmm? Oh, barrels full. Frankly, being second-in-command of the 42nd was easier than collaring London's Toms, Dicks, and Harrys. Minus the fact that here there weren't any Cossacks trying to kill us."

Something in the shadows moved.

"Wot's this?" a hoarse voice called. "Who goes?"

Two men waded out of the garbage and blocked the alley.

Even from twenty feet away, Nobody smelled the stale rum spiked with sweat that clung to their bodies. He switched his stick back to his left hand.

The skinniest man stuck his hand out, palm up. "You enter Black Tom's lane, you pay toll."

"I wasn't aware the city had taken to collecting toll in alleys," Nobody said.

He paused five feet from the men.

"They're young 'uns, Tom," the second man said. "We'd best take it all."

"Go it slowly," the skinny man said. "Well, what is it, gents? Pay it easy or pay it rough?"

"Do you really wish to visit the nearest constable?" Nobody said. "I'm sure he knows your names, but I wouldn't anticipate a friendly reception."

The skinny man laughed. "I ain't thinkin' that two well-dressed youngsters prowling the alleys this time o' night wants to see a constable."

Nobody fingered the pocket-watch in his waistcoat. Threading the alleys had already taken longer than planned, and if this stoppage was prolonged he would be late.

"Move," Nobody said.

Both ruffians drew knives.

Nobody's right fingers automatically cupped and swung to his left hip, but there was nothing there. His right shoulder twitched.

"Ed, would you take care of this?"

"Gladly."

Edmund twisted the handle to his cane and revealed the sword hidden inside. With two flicks he slashed each ruffian's knife-hand, then drove them down the alley. A moment later, both men lay on their backs in a puddle of filth and stared up at Edmund with dilated eyes.

"Thank you, Ed." Nobody stepped past. "I think that's a sufficient lesson."

The *click-click* of chattering teeth faded as Nobody and Edmund plunged deeper into the alley. A Cossack was worthy of respect. At least he fought for his country. But back-alley scum like those two ruffians, hawking the streets for a shilling and ready to cut a man's throat to get it? Men without cause or country. Hardly worth the filth they made.

The last three streets were better lit, but Nobody made sure that there was no one to see Edmund and him before they skirted the walkways and made for the back of a massive brick house. Shadows hid the grout lines between the bricks everywhere except around the doorway, where a lamp shone on the bronze heraldry above the lintel.

"So, this is the house?" Nobody said.

"Bronner Mansion, London, England." Edmund knocked three times on the door. "Life is odd, sometimes. I used to run by this place once or twice a week in the old days. Didn't think much of the owners. Of course, I didn't know Thomas then."

A head peeked through the doorway.

"Justice petitioned?" a voice said.

"But what is justice?" Nobody answered.

He slipped past the servant and waited to hear the bolt clang in the lock. The sign and counter-sign were his idea.

"Lord Bronner is expecting you," the servant said.

The servant's candle only showed glimpses of the rooms he led them through, but it was enough to reveal mahogany tables, Oriental rugs, and at least one well-stocked wine cabinet.

"Lord Bronner is inside." The servant pointed to a door beneath which seeped a broad line of light.

3

The hinges scarcely squeaked, but the man inside still looked up from his desk. His left eye glared at them—no, it was only the glass ball in the eye-socket. His wig looked like a snow-capped mountain, from which dropped a small avalanche of powder as he rose. He looked older than he had in King William's throne room on Nobody's first visit to London.

"Welcome, Colonel Nobody, Lieutenant-Colonel Burke. Please, sit down."

Lord Bronner waved at two chairs in front of his desk. His bulk blocked the view, but not the sound, of the fire on the hearth behind him.

"Is your son here?" Nobody asked.

"He is not. I don't let Thomas stay here any more than is absolutely necessary, for his own safety."

"And your other son?"

Lord Bronner frowned. "Banastre has his own apartments. You can be certain that I wouldn't arrange this meeting if he were here."

"Thank you," Nobody said. "Society may have accepted him back into its bosom, but Society wasn't in the South Seas. The last time I met your son he tried to stick a knife in my chest. Our meeting ended rather abruptly when my betrothed wife put my knife into his."

"Two facts of which I am very well aware." Lord Bronner rose and paced in front of the fire, his hands clasped behind him. "I want to be very clear, Colonel Nobody. The only reason I'm helping you is because by helping you, I am helping Thomas, whom you have gotten outlawed."

Nobody bit back a frown. "In fairness, Lord Bronner, Thomas made his own decision. And it was your other son who created the need for the decision."

"My eldest son's sins are on his own head. I am in no way responsible for his actions."

"You're not responsible, but I don't think you taught him much about curbing his passions, either."

Nobody instantly regretted his words. He shouldn't be lecturing about curbing passions when he couldn't even curb his own tongue.

Lord Bronner stopped pacing. His fake and his real eye both stared at Nobody. His lips were two tight lines.

4

"You took great pride in your day of being a 'fighting colonel,' Colonel Nobody, but now you see that the fighter must come begging to the diplomat. I am risking my reputation, my influence, perhaps even my position, by pleading with Queen Victoria for your measly pardon."

Lord Bronner slapped both hands on his desk and leaned close.

"My position at court has changed. Everything has changed. If my enemies use this situation to deal my hand to the dogs and replace me, then you can be assured that I risked it *only* for my son, not some stuck-up fool of a 'boy colonel.'"

Nobody tried to squeeze his frustration into his sword cane's smooth Malacca wood. This man's son had hunted him down, tried to ruin his reputation, tried to steal Liana, and tried to kill him. A little pleading at court hardly seemed much to ask.

Edmund mouthed one word: *Diplomacy*. Right. Diplomacy. Humor the lion, pet the tiger. This matter couldn't be handled by a sword or an order.

"Why did you want to see me?" Nobody asked.

Lord Bronner re-clasped his hands and resumed pacing.

"Queen Victoria has agreed to interest herself in your case because of its very unusual circumstances. However, the queen believes strongly in justice."

"Justice?" Nobody laughed. "I followed justice when I refused to let your profligate son gain control of my betrothed wife."

"You resisted officers of the queen. The queen determines justice."

"God determines justice."

"Yes, and He gave you a queen."

Nobody rose. "This isn't productive, Lord Bronner. Why did you call me here?"

"To give you this."

Lord Bronner trapped a sheet of paper to the desk with his trigger finger and slid it to Nobody. The button of wax at the page's bottom was the Great Seal.

"Of course," Lord Bronner said, "Queen Victoria didn't write directly to an outlaw, but she has made her mind apparent regarding your case. In summary—you must provide witnesses who will swear that you did not pirate the ship *Miriam*, as accused by my son and the late General Tremont. If you can prove that, then those charges will be withdrawn and she'll also pardon you for resisting officers of the Crown."

"Witnesses?" Nobody relaxed his grip on his sword cane. "Witnesses? Lord Bronner, we're saved! I have six men from Squad One who can all attest for our innocence."

"You have six men from your 'Squad One' who are accused of the same crime as yourself and whose testimony is therefore invalid. For all the queen knows, your men would swear to holes in the sun. You need external witnesses."

"But . . ." Nobody scooted his chair out of his way with his boot and stepped back from the desk. "The only other men present were the *Miriam*'s crew." He slapped his cane against his boot. "We must find them."

"I've already tried." The leather chair-bottom squeaked as Lord Bronner sat back down. "The only ones my men have found record of have sailed on the *Miriam* to hunt whales off the Greenland coast."

"Then I'll go to Greenland."

"Do so. Find them. Bring them back, restore my son's honor, and then let me never see your faces again."

Four minutes later Nobody and Edmund were breathing cool drafts of night air.

"Quite the jolly old chap, eh?" Edmund said.

Nobody gave one last glance to the solid brick building.

"If I were to die, I don't think Lord Bronner would be interested in eulogizing me at the funeral."

Edmund laughed. "I can't say that I've ever dreamed of visiting Greenland, but I suppose it can't be worse than Siberia."

"Life can always be worse." Nobody side-stepped a broken barrel and followed Edmund into an alley. "Now we need to decide who to take along."

"We're not taking the whole squad?"

"Too risky. The more of us there are together, the more likely it is that someone will have read our stories in the papers and realize who we are. Somerset's articles have fostered good public opinion, but they've also made life more dangerous."

Alexander Somerset was a good man. If Nobody hadn't let him follow to the South Seas as a reporter, he wouldn't have been there with his crucial aid at the last battle with Tremont and Bronner. His series of articles explaining exactly what happened on board *The Hound* were quite popular in England these days. Yes, he was an outlaw himself, but the *Times* was willing to overlook a few irregularities for such fascinating stories. No doubt it helped that Somerset's father worked there.

Cluck-a-tat. Cluck-a-tat. Their boots and sword canes struck a pattern on the slick pavement, softened occasionally by the swish of their cloaks. The cold bite to the air would be a pleasant spring day in Siberia, but Rahattan Island had put too much southern warmth in Nobody's blood.

"So, who are you taking?" Edmund asked.

"We shouldn't be stronger than five."

"That leaves room for three of Squad One."

"Yes," Nobody said. "We're taking Matthew."

"Matthew? Why?"

Nobody hunched a little to his left to ease the ache in his right shoulder.

"I owe him that much."

Edmund nodded. "Who else?"

"I'm sending Dilworth and Petr to America. It's the safest place for Dilworth, and Petr can keep him out of the hands of those Yankee sharpers. That leaves Thomas, Jacques, and O'Malley. Thomas is a good man, but he's the squad's most important member at the moment. If he were to die, Lord Bronner wouldn't give a pinch of wig-powder for the rest of us."

"Which leaves Jacques and O'Malley."

Nobody smiled. "We couldn't leave them together unsupervised. They'd probably argue each other into swimming the Thames, or some such excitement."

Something clattered behind Nobody. He spun around. Two lanterns bobbed down the alley.

"That's them!" a voice shouted.

Nobody reached for where his sword-belt should be and felt the usual twinge. He knew the sneer in those tones.

"Banastre Bronner!" Edmund said. "Do we fight?"

A constable's rattle *clack-clack-clacked.*

"Run," Nobody said.

The boys raced through puddles and over bits of broken glass. Steps pounded behind them and shouts ahead told of more night-watchers answering the rattle. The houses squeezed so closely together that scarcely any moonlight shown between.

Edmund stopped. "Here's a trick from my boyhood—younger years, that is." He braced his back against a house wall and cupped his hands at waist-level.

The glassless window above him gaped into black space. Nobody thrust his right boot into Edmund's hands, heaved, and caught the windowsill beneath his elbows.

"It's a boarding house," Edmund said. "That's a hallway, leads to the steps. Quick!"

Another boost and Nobody easily crawled inside.

The lanterns cast a glow on Edmund's upturned face. Nobody reached down and locked hands.

"Pull!" Edmund yelled.

Nobody wrenched at the clasped fingers, but Edmund's weight wouldn't rise. The windowsill bit into his chest and armpits.

"Noble!"

"Ed, my arm—I can't lift."

Hands emerged from the thick glow of lantern light and vised around Edmund's legs. The strain jerked Nobody against the sill. His shoulder burned and his strength trickled from his arms.

"Noble, leave me!" Edmund said.

"We stick—'til death."

"No! Find the *Miriam*. It's my only chance."

Edmund's fingers went slack. Nobody tried to hold on anyway, but they slipped through his own fingers and Edmund fell into the waiting arms below.

Three men stood where the light bled into shadow. Two were the supposed robbers who had waylaid Nobody and Edmund in the street, and the other was Lord Banastre Bronner. His gleaming eyes met Nobody's for a moment, then Nobody's eyes blurred and he stumbled down the passageway to safety.

Chapter 2

Three skinny logs crisscrossed the hearth and spat forked tongues of fire up the chimney. The little bit of heat that wasn't playing traitor was enough to warm Nobody, and if he was warm, every single man in the room was warm. It was too small to be otherwise. About as wide as a cannon barrel's length and as long as two rifles end to end, this room was exactly like a thousand others in London, and its owners didn't care a fig who its tenants might be.

A hand tapped Nobody's left shoulder and a voice thick with Irish brogue said something.

Nobody blinked away from the blaze. The room smelled of stale sweat and tobacco. The tobacco was from its previous tenants and still showed as a black stain on the walls and ceiling. The sweat was from the six men gathered behind him.

"O'Malley? You said something?"

"I said as it t'weren't yer fault, sir. I mean, the lieutenant-colonel bein' captured, and all."

Nobody swung his legs over the chest he was sitting on and faced his men. It had been months since Squad One had gathered in a single room, for the risk was too great to take often. It was good to see their faces.

Jacques sat closest, his left leg crossed over his right, both hands lightly resting on the shiny boot at the end. O'Malley's head was cocked, waiting for the argument quivering under Jacques's mustache. It had probably been a whole hour since they'd had a friendly wit-battle. Dilworth's long nose stuck out of the farthest corner, nearly hidden by Petr's bulk on his right, and Matthew Preston's square jaw on his left. Thomas Bronner stood at ease by the door.

"All together again," Nobody said. "I'm afraid this is the last time for a long while. Your instructions are clear?"

"No, sir, zhey are not clear, because zhe lieutenant-colonel is not in zhem." Jacques flicked the tips of his mustache. "He is in prison, you say. Vell, vhat of it? So, ve storm zhe Bastille."

"Jack," O'Malley said, "there's no Basteel in Loondon."

"Fine, zhen, zhe Chateau d'If."

Dilworth cleared his throat. "If you two are actually serious about rescuing the lieutenant-colonel, then let's be practical about it. What's your plan?"

"Ve sneak up under zhe cover of night, surround zhe Tower, dash inside, find zhe lieutenant-colonel, and escape." Jacques snapped his fingers. "Voilà!"

"That's about as hare-brained an idea as I've heard from a Frenchman. What say you, O'Malley?"

"I say we use strategy. We find a woman's cloak, wrap oop Jack Frog in it, and send 'im in as the laddy's sister. In course, we'd have to shave off his nose-bristles."

Jacques cupped his hand over his mustache.

Nobody raised his hand. "We're not breaking Edmund out of prison. Listen." He rose. "The law is the law. The only way to get Edmund out of prison is to prove his innocence, and to do that, we need some of those rascals from the *Miriam*."

"Zhat is zhe problem vihz zhese monarchies. You should haf a *republique*."

"Aye," O'Malley said, "and git daily shaves from the gillotine. But, Colonel, what's the worst they can do tae the lieutenant-colonel?"

Nobody propped his left boot on the chest and stared at the fire. The flames resembled the crude drawings on *sanbenitos*, those sacks of old which the Inquisition's victims had to wear, with pictures of dragons and demons reveling in flames painted onto the wool. Edmund said that the men and women inside those *sanbenitos* were usually innocent.

"Sir?" O'Malley said.

Nobody blinked back to the present. "Edmund is considered a traitor. If he is tried before we can present our evidence, he will almost certainly be convicted. If he is convicted—he will be hung."

"Then we've got tae git him oot!" O'Malley's chair scraped as he rose.

"It's not that simple, O'Malley." Nobody turned and pointed at Jacques. "Jacques, arrange my new disguise."

Jacques untied a box and deposited five pencils, a bottle of glue, a brush, and a pile of hair on the chest. Nobody looked at O'Malley.

"Of course I want to get Edmund out. I want him out more than even you. But to break into the Tower would be against the law. I don't believe I've broken the law or committed treason, so I don't feel compelled to turn myself in, but if they capture me I don't feel justified in breaking the law to get back out. This isn't Siberia anymore. We're not at war with England."

Nobody twitched as the glue-laden brush coated his chin and the strip of skin between his upper lip and nostrils. He didn't like other people touching his face, but Jacques's skill with cosmetics was too great to ignore.

"But England's at war wi' us," O'Malley said.

Jacques held the hair against Nobody's skin and patted it into the glue. It was human hair and smelled like rancid beer. Best to not ask where it came from.

"O'Malley," Nobody said, "we're not attacking the Tower, and we're not bribing guards. Lord Bronner is going to do all that he can to save Edmund, and we must do all that we can. Now, get me my cane. No, not the sword cane, the thick one Dilworth is propping his chin on. The 'Boy Colonel' just became an old goat, so he'd best have something stout to hold him up."

Jacques handed him a mirror. "You look *magnifique*."

"I think 'decrepit' fits me better."

The beard looked natural, jutting out from the chin and ending in curls, while the wrinkles on his forehead gave him a tired, worn look.

"Excellent job on the lines on my face. They look real."

"But I haf not yet applied zhe pencils."

Nobody grimaced and lowered the mirror.

"Jacques, O'Malley, Matthew, I've told you that you're coming with me. Do you have any questions?"

Matthew nodded. "Is Greenland peaceful, sir?"

"As far as I know."

"Good. But—why would you want me, sir?"

"Why wouldn't I?"

Matthew opened his mouth, then shut it. He shrugged slightly and receded into the shadows.

"Very well," Nobody said. "Let's go to Greenland."

Chapter 3

"Aye, but it looks like another village, sir."

O'Malley took the spyglass away from his eye. His red hair writhed in the land breeze which swept off the rocks on the port bow and declared mortal combat on the whale blubber fumes clinging to the ship. It was a fierce battle, and dangerous for anyone with hair caught in the middle. Nobody kept his left hand buried in his fake beard while he took the spyglass with his right.

A scattering of long Eskimo huts bordered a bay. There wasn't any green land in sight—it was all black rock and snow—but it was Greenland. This sight was becoming familiar after weeks of searching up the Greenland coast, trying to catch up with the *Miriam*, which seemed to be somewhere up ahead. Ten or fifteen natives stood where the beach shelved into the bay and watched the ship with hands cupped above their eyes to shade from the sun.

Nobody worked through groups of bare-chested sailors, carefully hunching his shoulders and nursing the supposed limp in his right leg. His disguise had been successful so far. The captain, a middle-aged sailor with a coating of two-day stubble perpetually on his cheeks, met him in the stern.

"Taking some air, old man?"

Nobody filled his chest with oxygen and talked as he exhaled, making his voice sound as old as his face.

"There's an Eskimo village abreast of us, Captain."

"Not surprised. This is where they make Eskimos."

"I'm requesting a boat-crew to take us ashore."

The captain scowled. "We've been ashore half a dozen times in as many weeks. We're here to catch whales, and I never seen a whale in an Eskimo village."

"With respect, Captain, that was our agreement. I'm paying you to set me ashore whenever we see an Eskimo village so that I can ask about the ship I'm tracking. Trust me, I didn't come out here to smell the blubber."

"Then why did you come?"

"That's my business."

"Humph," the captain said. "There ain't hardly blubber for you to smell. We should've been here long since, and the beasts ain't blowin'."

Nobody clamped down his impatience. He didn't need to be reminded that it had taken absurdly long to get out here. Every day was another that Edmund had to spend languishing in the Tower.

"I'm sorry, Captain, but you can't hold me responsible for storms, leaks, or whale swimming patterns. I've paid you my money faithfully, and I need you to fulfill your part."

The ship's boat could have fit three squads with a little squeezing, so there was plenty of space for the rowers, Nobody, his three soldiers, an interpreter, and a harpooner, who spent the entire trip looking back at the ship and muttering that they were sure to sight a whale now that he was gone.

The Eskimos were wearing shore-clothes—smooth black seal skins dried, scraped, and rubbed by hand. The whole village poured out of the houses and swarmed over the sheet of snow to the bay, waving at the sailors as they pulled up to the shingle and jumped ashore.

Nobody remembered to grumble as Jacques and Matthew helped him out of the boat. He had worn many disguises in his time, but that of the grumpy old man was the second most enjoyable of them all. Nobody pointed the interpreter toward an intelligent-looking Eskimo with a bird-dart in his hand. The dart was six feet long, with a barbed spike at one end and four jagged strips of bone sticking from the shaft. A skillful thrower with that weapon would outclass the best swordsman.

The interpreter made his usual inquiries. The hunter returned a string of Eskimo syllables.

"I think we have something," the interpreter said. "He says that some weeks ago the spirits of the waters raged and swallowed up a 'great kayak' not far from here. Most of the 'Kablunets,' the white men, died, but some came here in a boat."

"Where are they?" Nobody said. The words were out before he realized they were in his normal voice. He watched the interpreter's face. The sailor seemed too busy asking the question of the Eskimo to notice the mistake.

"They're not here anymore," the interpreter said.

Nobody squeezed two handfuls of cloak. From what he had picked up at the villages they touched at, the *Miriam* was sailing up the coast a few weeks ahead of them. If a storm had wrecked a ship some weeks ago, it could be her.

"Where did the sailors go?" Nobody asked. "Did a ship pick them up?"

"That's what I'm trying to get out of him. He doesn't seem to want to talk about it."

The Eskimo just leaned on his dart, shook his head, and stared at the ground. Jacques, O'Malley, and Matthew wandered up.

"Have ye found anything, sir?" O'Malley asked.

"Something, but the fellow won't talk."

The Eskimo's head shot up and his hand raised as if he was about to speak. Nobody watched the interpreter. The Eskimo stood still a moment, then grabbed something from his hair, snapped it between his teeth, and tossed it away with a laugh.

Jacques shuddered. "Zhe savage has lice."

"Try him again with these on the table," Nobody said. He pulled a handful of nails and sewing needles from his pocket.

The Eskimo's eyes glimmered like those of a drummer boy being praised for bravery by his colonel. He reached for the treasure. Nobody closed his hand.

"Tell him it's a trade, not a gift."

"He says he'll talk if you promise not to be angry," the interpreter said.

"That depends on what he tells me."

The Eskimo started talking. His face and arms twitched as he spoke, and he waved his spear towards the interior.

The interpreter turned to Nobody.

"I'm a little confused. Best I can make out, they headed inland. It seems there was an angekok—that's the Eskimo name for a wise man, or a sorcerer—and he got some ideas into his head and took these sailors along with him."

"As prisoners?"

"No, more as shipmates, best I can tell. He still won't say exactly why they left, though—either that, or I'm not quite following the lingo. He's still rather touchy."

"How many, and how did they travel?"

"Five. They went by the fjord. There's a fjord just over the rise yonder, he says, and the sailors took the ship's boat they came here in."

These fjords were something new. Huge rivers that sliced through the coastline and supposedly wound deep into the interior, most of them wide and deep enough for the largest ship to travel. This particular fjord must be a small one, because it hadn't been visible from the ship. And only five men? If those were the *Miriam*'s sole survivors, Edmund's life rested in very few memories.

"We will follow them," Nobody said.

He sent the harpooner to inform the ship and bring back his party's trunks. He also gave orders to request the captain to stop back periodically. The old mariner wouldn't like it, but it was Nobody's only way out.

The interpreter presented the biggest problem. Without him, there was no way to talk to the Eskimos. But, if Nobody kept him, the ship would have the same problem. And that might make the captain angry enough to forget to come back. No, the interpreter must leave when the harpooner returned with the trunks. Nobody would have to manage his tracking expedition with sign language.

The Eskimos seemed happy to learn that four of the "Kablunets" were staying with them. They expressed their pleasure by the means of hugging, which is always rather annoying, and which gains a new flavor when the opposite party smells like the seal fat, whale blubber, and other unmentionables in which they lived.

"Colonel!" Jacques said. "Help! *Ouste*! Murder! Zhe dirt—zhe lice—I can feel zhem crawling on my skin. *Peste*!"

Jacques backed out of an Eskimo embrace with such abruptness that he tripped and plopped into a snowdrift. O'Malley folded his arms and stood over him.

"Aye, that's a good idea, Jack Frog. Meself was aboot to suggest ye swallow some snow. Shame on ye fer complainin'. Ye should feel at home in this place. Tiny pipsqueaks o' fellows wantin' to hug ye at every turn and chattering like monkeys—why, overlook the snow and ye'll think ye're back in France."

Nobody was glad that his beard hid smiles. O'Malley was right in saying that the Eskimos were tiny. Most of them were under five feet tall, making Jacques stand out at his five feet two inches. O'Malley, a foot taller, looked like a young Goliath come to visit the Davids.

The trunks arrived, and Nobody asked the interpreter to arrange for some guides to follow the angekok. The Eskimos seemed hesitant.

"They say they don't dare to go," the interpreter said.

Men who attack polar bears with spears and risk drowning if their kayaks flip rarely lack daring. There must be something out of the ordinary about this expedition—which was probably why the angekok could only get Kablunets to go with him, not his own people.

Nobody unlocked his trunk and ran his fingers over the various trade packets until he found his goal. The hatchet's blade glinted as he unwrapped the steel. The atmosphere thickened as the odorous Eskimos squeezed close.

"See if this will interest them in taking us," Nobody said to the interpreter.

The interpreter pointed at something in the trunk. "Is that a red handkerchief? The Eskimos love color."

Something about the way he asked sent warning pulses through Nobody's nerves. He looked down. The removal of the hatchet had left a space in the midst of the trade packages, and there, peeking among the brown wrappings, was one of his uniform's sleeves.

"No."

Nobody dropped the trunk lid and locked it.

"Ask them."

The interpreter displayed the hatchet and jabbered with the Eskimos.

"They still seem to think that this expedition is very dangerous," the interpreter said. "They want to know more about you. They're asking if your country is far away."

"My country is—" Nobody paused. He was an outlaw. He didn't have a country. "My country is very far," he said.

"They want to know what you did in your country," the interpreter said.

Nobody looked the interpreter hard in the eyes. These didn't sound like the Eskimos' questions.

"The boat is waiting for you," Nobody said. "I'll finish the bargaining myself."

He did. The hunter and a couple others knew some broken English, so between that and signs they agreed to go with Nobody in exchange for the hatchet and some more iron. Spending the night in the village was an option, but there was still plenty of daylight left, and Nobody didn't want to waste an hour. Besides, it would take a direct order to get Jacques inside one of those smoke-spewing huts.

O'Malley opened his trunk and lifted out something long wrapped in red fabric.

"I say, sir, noow that we're on this place wi' naught but savages, don't ye think as we can wear these?"

Nobody re-opened his own trunk and fingered the green shawl that hid his sword. It was Liana's shawl, her last gift before they parted on the way to England. Nobody unwrapped the thin fabric and tucked it carefully back in the box.

"Do you feel threatened, O'Malley?" Nobody asked.

"Nay, sir, but my waist jist don't feel the same wi'out something dangling from it."

Nobody smiled.

"Then, arm."

He slipped his sword-belt under his cloak and strapped it in place. The drag, the bottom of the scabbard, tapped against his boot, and the familiar weight pulled at his left hip.

"Do ye think we could wear our uniforms, sir?" O'Malley asked.

Nobody stopped smiling. "Outlaws aren't entitled to wear the queen's uniform."

He waved for Jacques.

"Off with this beard. From here on we are ourselves, and that's a hard enough role without complicating matters by pretending to be someone else. Let's go."

Chapter 4

"So, you big Irish *boeuf,* do you still like ships so much?" Jacques asked.

"This is no ship, Jack Frog. This is a boat."

Jacques grunted as he dug his paddle into the fjord.

"Zhe blisters on my hands say zhat if you like ships so much, you should paddle for zhe bohz of us."

"Arrah, so noow yer blisters are spayking, are they? An' I thought as only yer mouth was bad enough."

Nobody shook his head. He probably shouldn't have put those two in the bow together. Their paddles sent ripples scurrying until they collided with those from the Eskimos' kayaks and made tiny white wave peaks on the blue fjord. Cliffs rose high on either side, mostly blanketed in white, but darkened occasionally by jags of black rock.

"Do you have any complaints to add, Matthew?" Nobody asked.

Matthew uncorked his square jaws.

"No, sir."

His jaws locked again.

Nobody thrust his paddle into the fjord with his left hand while he balanced the end of the shaft with his right. Even so, the ache in his shoulder was persistent. He looked sideways and found Matthew staring at his shoulder. The soldier looked away instantly, but Nobody knew what he was thinking. It had been Matthew who was assigned to work on Nobody's shoulder after Tremont shot him during the battle on *The Hound*, and it was Matthew who had accidentally done something wrong and left Nobody with a disabled arm.

Matthew hadn't been cheerful since.

The hunter had been out scouting around the next bend in the fjord, and was now paddling back at full speed. It looked like he had news.

"Ah!" Jacques said. "Perhaps he has found a place to camp."

"It's only midday," O'Malley said.

The hunter's approaching kayak dashed a wave against the boat's side and splashed fjord-water in Nobody's face. The hunter pointed at the curve he had just come from. Nobody shrugged his shoulders. The hunter pointed to his kayak and held up one finger, pointed to the boat, which the natives called an 'umiak,' and raised another. Had he found a kayak and an umiak? Or— Nobody squeezed his paddle shaft. A kayak and a ship's boat?

"Put your backs into it, men," Nobody said.

"Oi!"

As the boat rounded the curve, Nobody found himself shooting toward a low shore that gradually sloped up into a mountain range taller than any he had yet seen in Greenland. The snow-mounded peaks twinkled in the sunlight.

Of more interest were the objects on the shore. They were an Eskimo kayak and a regular ship's boat. The three Eskimos beached their kayaks about a hundred yards before Nobody's umiak, but no one descended the slope to greet them.

Nobody gave a last pull with his paddle, dropped it next to his seat, and let the boat's way take them into shore. His boot heels sunk two holes in the pebbly shore but he was three steps away before the fjord had time to seep into them. A ring of stones marked the site of a campfire, but the ash in the pit had all blown away. It was old.

A piece of canvas draped over the ship boat's stern and showed an inch or two of lettering. Nobody gripped the canvas in both hands, forced his teeth together, and lifted.

M.

The boat's stern was dreadfully scraped, probably by rocks, and all but the first letter of the name had disappeared into a crisscross of splinters and missing chunks. The first letter could stand for *Miriam*—or *Mary*, or *Marielle*, or *Magnificent*.

"Vell?" Jacques watched Nobody from the other side of the boat. "Has zhis been a vild chase of gooses?"

"I don't know. Whoever the geese are, they seem to have flown the coop." Nobody pointed to the mountain. "Did they go there?" he asked the Eskimos.

The Eskimos stuck their heads into a triangle and babbled. They seemed to be debating who should be the spokesman. Finally, the hunter straightened to his full height of nearly five feet and raised his empty arms to the mountain.

"What's that all aboot?" O'Malley asked.

"It looks to me zhat zhey vorship zhe mountain," Jacques said.

The hunter dropped his arms and pointed to the umiak. He wanted Nobody to get back in.

Nobody shook his head and pointed at the mountain. What were these Eskimos doing? They knew he was following these sailors, and it was clear that the sailors had landed here and walked off somewhere. The only place they could have gone was up the mountain.

The hunter shivered and backed away from the mountain. The other two were already next to their kayaks.

"Why, it looks like a mutiny, sir," O'Malley said. "Shall we clap 'em in irons?"

"I'm afraid it's not that simple. There's something peculiar about this mountain, but I don't know what."

Nobody tried to communicate his ignorance by shrugging and letting his arms dangle by his sides. The hunter clicked his teeth. Finally, he dragged his two comrades away from the kayaks and knelt in the snow. They heaped four piles of snow—one tall, one short, and two medium.

"Arrah! Those are supposed to be us!" O'Malley said.

The Eskimos flung their arms and began circling the piles with jerky steps. The hunter uttered an eerie moaning, which the others picked up, and as the wail loudened, their steps quickened.

"Zhey look like devils," Jacques said.

"I think that's the idea," Nobody said.

The song stopped. The Eskimos poised each on one leg, then flung themselves on the piles of snow and tore them to slush.

Jacques grasped his mustache. "I do not like zhat. I very much do not like zhat."

The Eskimos slipped into their kayaks and pointed once more to the umiak. Nobody shook his head.

The hunter shrugged, thrust his kayak into the water, and paddled away. In five minutes they were around the bend, and the only signs of life in the vast wilderness were an Irishman, a Frenchman, an Englishman, and Nobody.

"What's it all mean, sir?" O'Malley said.

Nobody scanned the foreboding rock heaps that loomed above them.

"They think the mountains are haunted by demons."

"So, what are we going tae do?"

Nobody pushed his sword-hilt behind his hip.

"We climb the mountains."

Chapter 5

"Now, you put your pinky here, hold it like you'd hold a hammer—not that you hold hammers—draw back, forward, and then let it slip out and into the target."

Five pistols cracked at half-second intervals a few yards to the right, where a group of London gentry in their shirt sleeves were trying to bury bullets in wooden targets. Lawrence told himself to concentrate on something other than the noise. Something like the acrid smell of the smoke accumulating inside the long, open building.

"You need to stop blinking every time a pistol goes off, Law," Chester said.

Lawrence forced a smile. At least he no longer closed his eyes every time he pulled the trigger. Better yet, he occasionally hit the target.

"And, throw," Chester said.

The knife-handle stuck quivering out of the target. Chester hooked his thumbs on his sash.

"Not bad, eh?"

"Beautiful, Chester. But I thought I was here for sword lessons, not knife-throwing."

"Right. I'm just showing you how to start evening the odds if four or five fellows all decide to see the color of your insides at the same time."

Chester took two swords from the table which held his knives and handed one to Lawrence.

"Spanish steel." Chester whisked the air with his blade. "Bad tempers and good swords are about the only things the Dons make well. And Pacarina, of course, though she's part Inca. Are you ready?"

Lawrence tried to put his feet in two places he could remember them and held his sword in Chester's direction. He didn't even ask if Chester was worried about being accidentally cut.

"*En garde.*"

Something flashed and Lawrence switched from looking down his own blade pointed out to looking down Chester's blade pointed in. He stepped back and tried to rub off the memory of the point's kiss on his Adam's apple.

Chester frowned. "I think we'll be here for a while. Why didn't you at least try to knock my blade away?"

"I didn't see it."

"Were your eyes open?"

Lawrence lifted his sword again. "Remember, you promised I can read any book I like to you for an hour in exchange for this."

"Did I say I would stay awake?" Chester grinned. "*En garde.*"

First, the blade was the problem. Then, when Chester's directions about how to hold it finally made half-sense, Lawrence's feet got out of order. By the time they were untangled his sword was pointing east, and Chester was standing in the north. Someone laughed.

The rich young fellows at the targets were watching Lawrence and Chester with smiles smeared on their faces. One of the oldest, a man with a red nose and tight skin, pointed at Lawrence.

"I think he's practicing for the circus," he said with a loud voice. "One of those farces where fellows make fools of themselves and everyone laughs."

They were hardly worth the effort of ignoring. Lawrence reset his feet, pointed his sword, and tried a lunge. Something happened—his right foot caught, the world spun, and he was lying on his back with his sword and sword arm trapped beneath him.

Chester looked down and scratched his chin.

"I say, how did you do that?"

The same man laughed again.

"You won't get any women with swordplay like that."

Lawrence stood up, his cheeks hopefully not as red as they were hot.

"I happen to have already 'got' a woman, as you call it. She's my wife, and she values an unsullied honor more than a little skill with the blade, Lord Bronner."

The skin on Banastre Bronner's face tightened. One of his companions started laughing, but stopped when he saw Bronner's face. Lawrence turned away, signaled Chester that the day's lesson was over, and slipped into his waistcoat while Chester gathered the knives from the target.

A hand tapped Lawrence's shoulder.

His muscles contracted. He wouldn't fight a duel with Lord Bronner or anyone else, but he had made an unwelcome insinuation about the fop's character, and Bronner might demand an apology. Lawrence wouldn't apologize for hinting at the truth. He turned slowly and saw—no one.

"Mr. Stoning?"

Lawrence looked down. A boy with a cap slanting over his pale forehead stared up.

"Here's your note," the boy said.

"I beg your pardon?" Lawrence said.

"You asked me to bring you a note when the room was done. You are Mr. Stoning, aren't you?"

"I am Lawrence Stoning, but I'm afraid you've made some sort of mistake. I've never seen you before."

"But you just stopped by the inn this morning, and Master had you talk straight to me. You couldn't have forgot."

"Is there a problem?" Chester was back from the target with an armful of knives.

The boy jerked back.

"Ah, so you've brought the note." Chester pried a piece of dirty paper from between the urchin's fingers.

"But—I thought—" the boy pointed at Lawrence.

"No need to let your teeth drop out, boy. We're twins. Run along, now." Chester turned to Lawrence. "Are you still in love with your fancy balls, and masque parties, and all?"

Lawrence frowned. "You know that I abhor this constant round of parties. I wouldn't be at any of them if I weren't trying to honor Mother."

"Right, well, I've danced the quadrille a few times too many myself, so I've been doing some thinking. Collect your gear and Pacarina and meet me at the Golden Hind. I've got plans."

He was gone before Lawrence could say a word. *Plans*? This sounded dangerous.

Pacarina was in the milliner's shop next door with a rich yellow capelet around her shoulders. Apparently, the hat-makers also sold a few pieces of outer clothing.

Pacarina smiled when she saw him. "Don't worry, Law, I'm only trying this on. I've already made my purchases."

"Did you get one of those?"

"No, I still have that nice brown one your mother gave me."

Lawrence frowned. His mother had only given that away because she thought it looked ugly. He took a few coins from his pocket and snapped his fingers at one of the shop girls.

"We'll take this capelet."

"Oh, Law!" Pacarina gave the fabric a little swish with her shoulders. "Do you like it?"

"Nearly as pretty as its owner," Lawrence said. "Now, Dear, I'm afraid that I have some bad news. Chester has plans."

"Plans for what?"

"I don't know, that's the problem. But, please, make me promise you that we won't take any hare-brained scheme he has."

Pacarina slipped her arm under his and grinned. "As if you would let Chester go anywhere by himself."

They had to pause outside the door to let a woman and a small boy pass. Pacarina squeezed Lawrence's hand and nodded at the boy. He was marching like a taller version of a tin soldier and seemed immensely proud of himself. He had probably just been breeched. The practice of keeping boys in skirts until they were six, or seven, or sometimes older, seemed slightly absurd. Lawrence had been breeched too early to remember the indignity, but he distinctly recalled Chester rushing around the house with his toy sword raised to the ceiling and his skirts sweeping the floor behind.

Pacarina waited until the mother and son were out of hearing, then laughed lightly.

"I think he's proud to be out of skirts." She sobered. "Law, do you think we'll make our boys wear them?"

Lawrence pressed her elbow close to his side. After nearly three years of marriage, God hadn't blessed them with children, and he knew their absence left an ache in her heart just as it did in his own.

"Our boys won't," Lawrence said quietly.

The pale boy at the Golden Hind Inn ushered them into the private room in the back. Chester met them at the door with that dangerously excited gleam in his eyes.

"Are you ready for this, Mr. and Mrs. Stoning?"

"I doubt it." Lawrence followed Pacarina and stopped just inside the door.

A five foot square map of the world north of the equator was tacked to the wall. In the right corner a harpoon and a stubby paddle leaned across each other, the harpoon's arrow-shaped head pointing at the ceiling. On the table, a three-masted model ship rode a thick book, the spine of which read *The*

History of Greenland. Three bowls of steaming something lay between forks and spoons.

"What do you call this?" Lawrence asked.

"I call this the beginning of an adventure." Chester ushered Pacarina to a chair, scooted her in, and waved Lawrence to a second. "What do you think?"

"No. I have no idea what you're about to propose, but the answer is 'no.' Peru was enough adventure to last me at least half a life."

"That was three years ago," Chester said. "Three years and nothing more exciting than learning how to ride two horses at once. I'm tired of waiting for adventure to come knocking. I'm going to yank its beard and see what happens."

"The whole idea of surviving an adventure is so that you can get back to peace and quiet, which is normal. Normality, Chester."

"Peace and quiet, eh?" Chester tapped the table with a whalebone knife. "In other words, you can't think of tearing yourself away from the balls and parties of London high society."

"Not exactly. We don't all dance and jest as well as you, Chester."

"Yes, well, I've had my fill for the moment. Three nights from now, Mother has us scheduled for that ball put on by the Viscountess of Hereford." Chester shuddered. "I can't stand her daughter, that Maria girl. Her eyes are as batty as a vampire cave."

"I think," Pacarina said, "that she admires you."

"That's why I want to be gone by night three." Chester spooned some frothy white liquid from his bowl.

"Where do you intend to go?" Lawrence asked.

Chester rose and slammed his knife into the top section of the map. "There."

"Did you buy or rent that map?"

"There probably aren't any natives willing to fight, but the weather itself will be an excellent challenge."

"I don't think that map's owner is going to appreciate a hole in Greenland."

Chester growled. "You're missing the point." He sat back down and leaned close. "Listen. I was talking to Lord Bronner—no, not that rake Banastre, but his father, the adviser—at the ball two nights ago. He's the one with the splendid glass eye. Well, he was telling me about some odd soldier from the little skirmishing they were having in Siberia."

Lawrence slid his bowl close enough to smell. It had a faint fishy odor, but it wasn't exactly a bad smell. He sliced through a half-inch layer of froth and struck bits of meat buried below.

"What is this?"

Chester shrugged. "It's a special dish I showed the kitchen how to make. I'm calling it 'whale blubber' in honor of our mission. But, back to my story. This Siberian oddity—well, he's actually English—actually, they don't know what he is." Chester held up his hands. "Forget the nationality. The point is that this colonel is named 'Nobody,' and he's called the 'Boy Colonel,' because he's extremely young, but nobody—er, no *one* knows how young he is or anything about him."

"Yes, I remember reading the story from the *Times* to Pacarina."

"We're going to find him."

Lawrence blinked. "I beg your pardon?"

"He's been off in Greenland looking for witnesses for a while now, and the queen has finally given an ultimatum that if he isn't back by a certain date they'll go ahead with the trial for his lieutenant-colonel. I think she's being pressured by some of Banastre's friends at court. Anyway, I volunteered us to go find him, tell him about the ultimatum, and help bring him back."

Lawrence swallowed reflexively and sucked a half-chewed glob of meat into his system. "You volunteered *us*? Chester—" Lawrence massaged his sternum around where the meat felt stuck, "—I appreciate your heart to help this poor colonel, but you need to go back to Lord Bronner and unvolunteer us. I can't go gallivanting around the world anymore. I'm a married man."

"Of course you're married. It's not as if you were making moon eyes at Pacarina *before* you were married. But you don't have any children to worry about, so—" Chester stopped. "I mean . . ."

Lawrence looked down and swirled the soup with his spoon. Pacarina's hand rested on his knee beneath the table.

"No, we don't have children to care for. Just each other." Lawrence put his arm on Pacarina's chair-back and wrapped some of her hair around his index finger. "What does my wife say about this wild idea?"

"She says that she will do whatever her husband thinks best."

Chester hunched forward, his eyes eager. The tip of a knife hilt peeked between his shirt and cravat. It hurt to disappoint him, but it must be done.

"I think it best that we not go," Lawrence said. "I'm sorry, Chester, but I don't see how this is any of our business."

"Nothing is our business until we make it so." Chester pushed *The History of Greenland* to Lawrence and grasped the harpoon. "You tell me what to expect and I'll show the Eskimos something they're *not* expecting. Come with me, Law."

"No, Chester. I'm sorry."

Chester tapped his top teeth with the harpoon head. The knife still stuck in the great glob of land called Greenland behind his head, like the marker of some monarch of old claiming his next conquest. The soup had stopped steaming.

"Very well," Chester said. "If you won't go, then I won't. I wish you could see how noble the cause is, but if you can't, I'm not going to break up our threesome just to do it." He rubbed his chin. "Since you won't go with me to Greenland, though, you must promise to come with me to the Hereford ball."

"I'm afraid Mother hasn't given us a choice."

Three nights later, Lawrence sipped punch and watched the dancing couples flit by, each girl vying with every other girl to attract just as much attention as was deemed appropriate. They all looked like balloons which had been squeezed in the middle and puffed out at the bottom. Thankfully, Pacarina's style was simpler. She could walk into a room without dusting both door posts, and her waist didn't look like she was trying to fit a finger ring over it.

"Has Chester seen Maria yet?" Pacarina asked.

"No, but I'm sure she's seen him." Lawrence searched the waltzing crowd for any particularly tall headdress. "Have I ever thanked you for not being a forward hussy?"

"There he is now, and he has a girl with him. But it's not Maria."

"Hello, lads and lassies," Chester said. "May I introduce to you the Lady Liana, betrothed wife to Colonel Nobody, formerly of His Royal Majesty's 42nd Regiment of Mounted Infantry."

The girl's cheeks dimpled into a sad smile. "It's a pleasure to meet you."

Lawrence bowed. This was a real lady. A classic on a shelf of penny dreadfuls.

"I hope," Lawrence said, "that my brother's words have not raised unpleasant memories."

Lady Liana shook her head. "It's a pleasure to think of my betrothed husband. He has done nothing shameful. The only smear on his honor is the machinations of his enemies, and, frankly, the disregard of an ungrateful government."

Chester rubbed his hands. "Since you don't mind talking about him, perhaps you could explain why he's in disgrace right now? I've read the articles in the papers by that reporter named Somerset, but of course you would understand it better than even him."

"It is simple," Lady Liana said. "General Tremont and Lord Banastre Bronner falsely accused my future husband of pirating a ship called *Miriam*. They were going to take Nobody back to England in irons. He would have gone with them, but then they said that I would also have to go, and Nobody wouldn't agree to put me in their power. So we fled—they followed—we fought—and he is called an outlaw."

"Thank you, my lady." Chester waved at Pacarina. "I think that you two girls— pardon the familiarity—will get along famously. For that purpose, I'm leaving you together. Come along, Law."

Chester grabbed Lawrence's arm and led him away from the refreshments. His sash looked out of place, as usual, but at least he didn't have any pistols in it. He halted.

"'Bout face."

As Chester swung Lawrence around and marched him back toward the refreshments, Lawrence glimpsed the feathered headdress of Maria, future Viscountess of Hereford.

"I know what you're doing, Chester," Lawrence said.

"Yes, I'm running away from that horror." Chester peeked over his shoulder. "Do you think she saw me?"

"If you wanted to be less conspicuous you should remove that sash, but I'm not talking about Maria. I'm talking about Lady Liana. You want Pacarina to befriend her, and then try to convince me to go to Greenland for her betrothed husband."

Chester ducked into a niche. "Law, think of it this way. If you were in this colonel's boots, and Pacarina were Lady Liana, how would you act?"

"I would probably be doing what he's doing, working my hardest to prove my innocence so I could marry her."

"And how would you feel about a man who helped you?"

Lawrence sighed. "I think I would feel that it wasn't his business unless I asked for his help."

Chester shook his head. "No, you're thinking like Professor Lawrence. You need to put yourself in his red coat and think his thoughts."

"I'm a scholar, not an actor, Chester."

"Hist." Chester frowned at something behind Lawrence. "The impudence!"

Lawrence turned. A young nobleman stood talking with Pacarina and Lady Liana. Something about him, whether his slightly too colorful clothes, or his stance, or the experienced way in which he held his wineglass, breathed caution, but the red nose on his profile when he turned was what made Lawrence click his teeth.

Lawrence cut a corner by threading two pairs of waltzers and approached Banastre Bronner's back. Lady Liana saw Lawrence coming, and her eyes showed relief.

"Perhaps you would like to talk with this gentleman here," she said to Bronner.

Bronner didn't even turn. "No, thank you. The delights of conversation with you make all others pale." He stepped right and turned slightly, edging Pacarina and Lawrence away from the conversation.

Lady Liana stepped the same way. "Mr. Stoning, may I introduce to you Lord Banastre Bronner?"

"Stoning?" Bronner looked at Lawrence, then Pacarina. "So this is the girl you got. Not bad. Are you sure you gave your name when you proposed? She might have thought she was saying 'yes' to that knife-throwing twin of yours."

"The 'knife-throwing twin' is present," Chester said. "If you knew what shame was you'd be feeling it right now, Lord Bronner. How can you have the impudence to come lurking around Lady Liana after the scurrilous way you've treated her and her betrothed husband?"

"Meddler! If you had honorable blood and the slightest fashion in clothing I might consider teaching you a lesson with rapiers in some nice secluded corner, but as it is, I wouldn't sully my boots on you."

Lawrence stepped between Lord Bronner and Lady Liana. "If anyone here was insulted, I believe it would be myself."

"You?" Bronner laughed. "I wouldn't duel you. I could just say 'boo' and you'd trip onto your own sword. Do you have any children?"

"No."

"Good. The world is probably a better place. You see, I don't believe that anyone too inept to fight for a girl deserves to marry one."

Lawrence locked eyes with Bronner. He was stung by the words. Fine, let the braggart blow air, he didn't care what he thought—but he cared what Pacarina thought. But Pacarina loved him, Pacarina wouldn't care—but she had heard the words too. Lawrence fought with a pen, but a man like this wouldn't understand that. But Lawrence didn't care about Bronner. But Pacarina—it always came back to Pacarina.

The fierce urge to prove himself to Pacarina and help anyone who was an enemy of this man entered his heart.

Lawrence smiled. Not the smile he gave Pacarina when she smoothed his hair. Not the smile he gave Chester when he joked. Not the smile he gave his books when they called to him from the shelf. A cold smile. He made his voice gentle.

"Goodbye, Lord Bronner. We're escorting Lady Liana back to her lodgings, and then we need to prepare. You see, we're going to Greenland."

"We're what?" Chester said.

"We're going to Greenland. There's someone there we need to find. Pack your knives, Chester."

Chapter 6

Colonel Nobody pushed his scabbard out from between his legs for the thirteenth time. Mountain-climbing with a sword wasn't pleasant, but it was better than being unarmed. Their rifles hadn't fit in the trunks, so swords and pistols were this expedition's only available weapons. Below him the fjord snaked away in a blue ribbon. Above him, the mountain peaks looked like sleepy Cossacks peeping beneath white fur caps.

There weren't many paths up the mountain, and a pair of scratches at this one's base showed that someone had climbed it recently. Many parts of the path were smooth, as if blasted for years by water, so it was probably a dried-up watercourse. It wasn't hard climbing at all—Nobody had ridden horses in Siberia who could have scaled the path.

"Aha!" Jacques said. He pulled at something wedged between two rocks. "I did not know zhat demons smoked."

Nobody took the pipe and showed it to Matthew, who was guarding the rear.

"Clay pipe," Matthew said. "Probably a sailor's."

Nobody pocketed the clue and continued up. They must be on the right path, but it looked like the sailors had never made a return trip. There was nowhere to go but back to the boats, and the boats were empty. Could they have all fallen off a cliff? No. They couldn't have. Nobody was going to find witnesses.

"I'm starting tae wish as that you *had* pirated that ship, sir," O'Malley said. "I climbed enough hills in the ould country. Of course, it's our luck that we have to find a boat-load of adventurers tae chase."

"There's no such thing as 'luck,' O'Malley."

"Sorry, sir."

Hours later, O'Malley held up his hand.

"What do ye take that for, sir?"

He stood in the cleft of a boulder which blocked whatever he was pointing at. The ends of the scarf he had wrapped around his neck flapped in the biting wind, which had picked up soon after they reached the snow line and was now constantly swirling snow and ice particles against Nobody's bare face. That fake beard would be a blessing to have now.

Nobody clambered over the boulder and paused by the Irishman's side. A large opening, probably ten feet high and twenty wide, gaped in the mountain. It was utterly black and utterly still.

"Vhat beasties are zhere in Greenland?" Jacques asked.

"The kind o' baysties that doon't stomach cold steel." O'Malley drew his sword. "Shall we be entering, sir?"

Nobody's sword rasped against his scabbard as he drew. Something was odd. This was where the path led—this was where the sailors must have entered—but what had been strong enough to convince a bunch of bandy-legged jack-tars to sweat up a mountain to get to a cave? Nobody had matches, but no torch to burn, so he entered the cave's twilight with only his naked sword in hand.

O'Malley coughed.

"Don't ye think as I should go first, sir? That is, it's not as if ye're not capable, and all, but it's just that—well—" he nodded at Nobody's right arm.

Nobody ran his left thumb over the grooves in his hilt.

"I'm leading, O'Malley."

The floor was smooth, but there was still no trace of whatever ancient water had carved it so. The quiet inside was eerie after the constant gusting outside.

The light from the entrance faded as Nobody slowly advanced, scouring the rock in front with his blade in case there was a hole or drop-off.

"Do you zhink it is a mammoth cave?" Jacques whispered. "I vould like to cook mammoth."

Nobody motioned for silence. The cave had curved, and the light was gone. Jacques's breath steamed the hairs on Nobody's neck, while O'Malley's breath ruffled his hair. Matthew was somewhere in the back.

"Hist," O'Malley said. "I can see me hand agin."

He was right. The darkness was dissipating—the few inches of blade now visible gleamed dully. Firelight? No, that would be more red. This was daylight. The cave curved hard to the right. The light was strong now, so strong that the path was totally visible.

On the other side of a corner of rock a huge hole in the wall gushed light, just like at the entrance on the outside. Nobody stepped through the hole and stood in a glare of sunlight.

An incredibly green valley was sunk far beneath a rim of colossal mountains. Forests on the floor and bottom slopes looked like little bunches of shrubbery poking out of a green patchwork quilt. Green-land, indeed. Something else stood out from the green, though, and it wasn't more trees. Nestled close to the mountains on the right was a rectangular brown patch with lines through it. It looked like—houses?

Something struck Nobody's sword from his fingers and a blow smashed his right shoulder and dashed him to the ground. He tried to blink away the haze of pain and sunlight and see who the dark form above him was.

"*Vive la republique!*" Jacques shouted.

There were three more thuds, then a jumble of legs, arms, and scabbards piled onto Nobody's prone body.

Deep voices spoke rapidly in a foreign language. Jacques's leg jerked away from Nobody's face and gave him a clear view of their attackers. Half a dozen men in helmets and armor stood with their backs to the cave entrance. In their hands were curved rectangular shields and six-foot spears.

Something about their words was naggingly familiar. Something . . . something . . . Nobody wrapped his left arm around Jacques, heaved him off, and sat up.

45

"*Salve*," Nobody said.

The men in armor sprang away from him as if he were a leper.

"*Tu loquerisne Latine?*" one of them asked.

"*Etiam.*"

Jacques swiveled his head between Nobody and the wide-eyed men above them.

"I did not know zhat you could speak a native tongue," he said. "I zhought zhat you only knew French and Latin."

"That's all I know."

"But—"

"Jacques, I'm speaking Latin."

Nobody stared at the legionary markings on the red shields and the *gladius* in each man's belt.

"These men are Ancient Romans."

Chapter 7

The rope halter rubbed ruts in Nobody's neck as he twisted down the path, sometimes hugging the mountain with fingers and knees, sometimes sliding boots first, jamming his heels into every crevice to slow his descent. The rope through his halter led back to O'Malley, then Jacques, then Matthew, like a hemp chain gang. No, it wasn't hemp—that probably didn't grow in Greenland—but this substitute was just as scratchy.

Trying to stay alive on the path left little time for thought, but even if it had, Nobody didn't know what to think. It wasn't a dream. His shoulder ached too much for that. Besides, the only thing he dreamed about was seeing Liana and Edmund again. But if it wasn't a dream, what was it? What were Ancient Romans in full regalia doing in a remote valley in Greenland? This was 1838! Romans of this type hadn't been around for over seventeen centuries.

The six men who captured them had been replaced by at least fifteen more soldiers, some leading the way, and some guarding the rear. They all wore the same clothing and armor and gestured with the same weapons, though their faces differed, some showing amazement, some anger, and some fear.

Nobody rolled words through his brain until he remembered the right ones and strung them together.

"May we pause?" he asked in Latin.

Time to plan was crucial. The soldiers looked about to agree, but their leader waved his hand forward. He was a muscular brute, with half-inch hairs that stuck out of his skull, and some animal's fur draped around his shoulders.

Objects on the valley bottom became clearer as the group descended. The brown rectangle was actually a city, laid out just like the drawings Edmund had once shown Nobody in a history book. The houses looked mainly built from wood, though several buildings had massive stone columns. The city hugged the mountain on the right, while the rest of the valley was green fields and orchards, except for a patch of forest in the farthest right corner. A huge rock jutted out of the mountain-side and overlooked the city. On it was either a small town or a massive palace which honeycombed the mountain.

"I do not understand zhis," Jacques called. Something scraped somewhere up in the vicinity of his voice and a shower of loose stones pelted Nobody's head. "*Peste!* Ve come looking for sailors and find Romans. I ask, who gave zhem permission to be here?"

Nobody didn't ask. The bristle-haired fellow had already made clear that he didn't want to be talked to. At the moment he was arguing with the others, and the way in which he kept pointing to the empty air below showed how he wanted the prisoners to get to the bottom.

"Vhat is it zhey say?" Jacques asked.

"I think they're trying to figure out what to do with us." Nobody shook his head. "I can't catch all the words. I learned Latin to read Caesar's *Commentaries*, but I've never spoken it before. It's a dead language—at least, we thought it was."

"They doon't look very dead tae me," O'Malley said.

The argument was violent enough now to stop the whole procession. Bristle Hair seemed to be the only one advocating throwing the prisoners off a cliff, but he was advancing his side of the question with alarming passion. Most of the words they were using were familiar, except for some which might be the names of places and people in the valley, and some which were probably camp slang.

"Do you zhink ve could haf traveled, sir?" Jacques said. "Zhat is, traveled zhrough time?"

"Not through time, but through a mountain. My guess is that they don't appreciate visitors. I'm not certain if they would have let us live if I hadn't shocked them by knowing their language."

Bristle Hair concluded his argument by kicking a small rock off the mountain. It plummeted hundreds of feet and shattered on an outcropping. Nobody had seen men fall from cliffs before, and the sight at the end was a hard thing to forget. He eased the rope's pressure on his neck. If all four of them fell it would be a tangled mess all the way to the bottom.

"I'm worried about what they may have done to the sailors," Nobody said.

"What do we do if we can't find witnesses?" O'Malley asked.

"We find witnesses."

Bristle Hair lost the argument. There must be some extraordinarily strong power the soldiers were fearful of offending for them to disobey an officer's decision.

About halfway down the mountain the path began to zigzag and then ended abruptly just after a zag. The rock was scraped level for about eight square feet and a three-foot high man-made wall skirted this section and bordered the mountain's edge. Piles of stones were prepared to drop on anyone below. Four of the soldiers leading the procession were gone.

In the middle of the level area was a square depression floored by a wooden platform, and the soldiers pushed Nobody and his men onto this. Wood squeaked and the floor lowered until the view of the valley disappeared and the outside became one square of light in the roof. Was this a dungeon?

Light burst from around their feet and they were slowly disgorged from the perpendicular tunnel. Apparently, it was just part of the path. The missing guards were at the bottom with four new guards, and these kept Nobody and his men at sword-point until the rest of the procession descended the dumbwaiter. It was an incredibly defensible position, but it was backwards. Why build fortifications and pile stones at the top of the tunnel? That would help an invading force. It was as if these soldiers were here, not to keep people out of the valley, but to keep them in.

The new guards gawked at Nobody and his men as they filed by. Jacques tilted his nose.

"Zhey look at us as if ve vere monsters, but zhey zhemselves are zhe oddities."

"Actually," Nobody said, "they're calling us barbarians."

"Barbarians?" Jacques nearly slipped off the mountain. "Zhey call us barbarians? Zhe indignity, zhe outrage, zhe—how dare zhey? To zhink zhat a Frenchman, a soldier, a one-time citizen of zhe great Pairee, should be called 'barbarian' by a flock of second-century sandal-vearing buffoonish—"

"O'Malley, stop him."

O'Malley clamped one hand over the Frenchman's mouth and gripped the back of his neck with the other. The soldiers watched the pair with narrowed eyes. Thankfully, Jacques couldn't speak Latin.

Bristle Hair glared at Nobody.

"We will take you to Little Caesar," he said. "He will decide your fate."

"What is the name of this place?" Nobody asked.

Bristle Hair spread his massive right palm over the valley.

"Vallis Deorum."

Vallis Deorum. Valley of the Gods. Apparently, the Eskimos weren't the only superstitious men around.

Chapter 8

Night was nearing when Nobody reached the path's bottom. Even the climate was different. Gone were the cold winds, and, though it certainly wasn't the South Seas, there was almost a hint of balm to the air.

Bristle Hair pointed toward the city ahead of them.

"Be careful, men," Nobody said. "We have to be diplomats for the moment. The Ancient Romans weren't the kindest, and I doubt they've changed much in the last seventeen or eighteen centuries."

One of the guards wrenched Nobody's arms behind his back and thrust his head into a sack. Pain bounced through the bones in his right shoulder. He was loaded into some kind of cart, which rattled first over dirt, then stone. He was unloaded, still blindfolded, and marched up a steep incline. At last the fresh air ended in a final draft as a door crashed shut.

The sack lifted off Nobody's head and the orange-tinged light of torches bathed his face. He stood in a wide hallway built entirely of smooth stone, with purple drapes hanging on the walls and torches poking from sockets every ten feet. The passages deeper inside were similar, except that the farther they walked, the more statues lined the walls. Most of these were hewn from intensely black rock, with little white pebbles in the eye sockets.

Male and female voices murmured close by. Bristle Hair pointed to the end of the hallway.

"Little Caesar," he said.

Nobody brushed his right arm against his side and felt the small bump of the dagger sheath strapped against his skin. It was well-hidden, which was why he still had it, but it was also hard to access. In quick action he would probably find himself skewered on a *gladius* before he could get his hand on the knife's handle. And even if he could get it out, how much would a knife in his left hand help against a *gladius*?

A thick curtain of ultra-white wool blocked the hallway. Bristle Hair parted this and the other guards pushed Nobody and his men through the perfumed fleeces. Jacques gasped.

The little square of black rock at the entry faded into a field of white wool which blanketed the floor and melded into the purple drapery covering the walls. Fires blazed in niches in the walls, their flames reflecting off the pebble-eyed statues that stared toward the room's center. The whole place smelled of spices and wine.

"What took you so long?" said a voice from the far end of the room.

A wide dais, or raised portion of the floor, was constructed at the back of the room and was buried under a waterfall of fleeces, blankets, and gauze draperies. A couch was planted somewhere in the middle of the billows and on the couch lay a paunchy man with wisps of black hair sprouting from his shiny head.

Bristle Hair bowed.

"Forgive me, Little Caesar. I brought the prisoners by cart."

"Delay, delay, there's always reasons for delay." The 'Little Caesar' waved his hand. "Bring them closer so that I can question them."

Little Caesar was the only one on the dais, but many more men and women lay on couches along the wall on both sides, and each couch had a table next to the head-side with plates of food and goblets. Bunches of red grapes with bright green trailers peeked through the wall-hangings.

Little Caesar looked like a happy puppy who has eaten until his stomach bloats and then collapsed in a pool of sunlight. He snapped his fingers at a slave girl, who poured a stream of red wine into his goblet.

"At last, something interesting," Little Caesar said. He propped his head on his fist. "Which of you speaks my language?"

Nobody pulled his left foot back and bowed just like Edmund had taught him those lifetimes ago in London. If only Edmund was here now.

"Well, speak!" Little Caesar said. "There's no good in knowing how if you don't do it."

Nobody cleared his throat. "Greetings, Caesar."

A scowl creased the tight red forehead.

"You may not call me that. The Great Caesar is in Rome, and I am but Little Caesar, his subject to command if he sends me a message."

A tiny wave of wine crested Little Caesar's goblet and melted into a red stain on his toga.

"But the Great Caesar can't send me a message, because we've left the land of mortals." Little Caesar squinted at Nobody. "But then where do you come from?"

"From—from a far land," Nobody said.

Little Caesar snapped his fingers at a male slave of almost O'Malley's height, who brought a scroll and unraveled it in front of them. As he bent down his open mouth revealed no tongue. The mute gripped both ends of the parchment, which showed a map of the Roman world.

Nobody pointed to Matthew. *"Britannia."* He pointed to O'Malley. *"Hibernia."* He pointed to Jacques. *"Gallia."*

"Gallia?" Little Caesar blinked. "Impossible. We have read of the Gauls, and they are giants with long flowing hair and terrible eyes."

"Vhat is he saying?" Jacques asked. "He is pointing at me."

"He—ahem. He's heard of the Gauls before. That's the name of the French before they were French."

"Vell, he had best not impugn zhe name of my honorable country, for I tell you, zhat should he do so, I vill personally demand satisfaction."

"What does the little one say?" Little Caesar asked.

"He is—er, intrigued by your attention."

Some of the wall-hangings in the farthest left corner of the room parted and a troop of dancers slipped inside. Little Caesar waved his jewel-laden hand at them.

"Take them away. I have something new to interest me." Little Caesar raised himself to a sitting posture and leaned forward. "Come, tell me about yourselves. Which is the leader?"

"I am," Nobody said.

"Don't lie to me. You are a boy. Even the little one is obviously your elder. Which is truly the leader?"

Nobody dug his boot-heels deep in the fleece.

"It's the truth, Little Caesar. I am the leader."

Little Caesar blinked, then slowly smiled.

"I don't believe you, boy. You speak our language, but you cannot be the leader of that giant." He pointed to O'Malley. "I will test you. You must command the giant to do something, and I'll only believe you if he obeys you."

"As you wish. Command him to do what?"

"Hmm." Little Caesar scratched his chin with a diamond. "Command him to grovel on the floor before you."

Nobody clenched his left fist. He hated to use his authority just to amuse some besotted pig of a Caesar, but it was crucial that they all remain in favor for as long as possible.

"I'm awfully sorry, O'Malley, but this fellow doesn't believe I'm the leader. I need you to lie down and grovel next to me."

"Ah—aye, sir." The faithful Irishman dropped to the floor and buried his face in the fleece next to Nobody's boots.

Nobody held back a glare as he looked at Little Caesar. "Does that please you?"

Little Caesar slurped some wine. "It's not enough. Tell him to chop a head off." He waved his hand at a little crowd of slaves waiting in the corner. "Any of them will do. Yes, that one is fine."

The guards pulled a young woman into the center of the room. She looked a year or two younger than Liana, with hazel eyes just like Liana's, which stared at Nobody in terror. The guards' fingers clutching her bare arms made red splotches in the white flesh. For the first time, Nobody was glad that Liana was not with him.

"The crop from the last festival could use some more thinning," Little Caesar said. "Tell your man to behead this one."

"I can't."

"What?" Little Caesar cupped his hand to his ear.

"I can't. It's wrong."

Little Caesar's cheeks purpled and a dark blue web of veins swelled on his forehead. The slave girl sunk as close to the floor as the guards would let her, and even the guards bowed their heads and planted their legs as if about to withstand a storm. Nobody slid his fingers across his shirt towards his knife.

Little Caesar opened his mouth. "You refuse to obey Little Caesar, ruler of the Valley of the Gods? You reject my commands?"

"I don't mean any offense, Little Caesar, but I don't war upon the innocent," Nobody said.

"I declare who is innocent!" Little Caesar snatched a cluster of grapes from the table and squeezed until the juice spurted in all directions. "I have the power to crush anyone!"

"God declares the innocent, not man."

Little Caesar was on his feet, shouting.

"Which god? Mars, god of war? Vulcan, god of fire? Jupiter, king of the gods?"

"Christ, the one and only true God."

Little Caesar gaped. "You're a Christian? I didn't know they existed elsewhere. I've tired of you rebellious Christians. We're about to deal with you all for the last time."

Christians? Ah, so there were Christians in Vallis Deorum. Where did they learn their faith? Was it from their fathers, who learned it from their fathers, and so on into the mists of antiquity and whenever this unearthly valley was colonized? Or was this a recent development, perhaps taught by missionaries who had found this lost civilization? Actually, it wasn't a lost civilization, because you can't lose something you never knew existed.

Little Caesar's expression changed into a curious, more gentle look. He didn't seem very stable.

"But you are from the Outside. You speak our language, so there must be something Roman out there." Little Caesar tapped his fingers on his lips. "Come, strange boy, you can answer our questions. My priests believe that our ancestors left the world of mortals when they came here and entered the world of the gods." He waggled his fingers at the luxurious throne room. "The gods live well. But what do you say?"

The girl was still a trembling heap on the floor. The guards stood expressionless above her. If Little Caesar forgot about her, her life might be saved.

Nobody hesitated. How exactly do you tell someone that the empire they think rules the world is actually just a small, armyless city?

"Many things have changed in what you call the 'Outside.'"

"What has changed? Has Rome conquered new dominions?"

"Not exactly." Nobody breathed deep. Hopefully the reaction wouldn't be too violent. "The Rome your ancestors knew is no longer. Its strength and power have faded, and the Caesars are no more."

"No more Caesars?" Little Caesar stared. Then, the spark in his eyes caught fire and his teeth gleamed above his goblet. "No more Caesars? Then I am the only Caesar in the world!"

The thought of the sudden grandeur he possessed seemed to speed the effect of the wine on his brain, and Little Caesar's cheeks pinked.

"Enough of this talk, my head hurts. I'm going to bed. You, strange boy, I'll talk to you tomorrow. What do you do in the Outside?"

"I was a soldier."

"Ah, then you can teach my Praetorians a maneuver for the festival." Little Caesar flicked his wrist at the slaves. "Carry me to my chamber."

The feast ended and in five minutes Nobody and his men were standing in their newly assigned chambers.

"I zhink ve can make zhis vork," Jacques said.

Nobody leaned against the doorframe of one of the rooms. To the left, the hall ended in a wall, while to the right it was cut off by a metal grate and door about ten feet away. The hall opened into four luxurious rooms, each arranged exactly the same with sheep fleece for carpets, pillow-covered beds, and one black stone statue in each room.

"Put some clothes on that fellow," Nobody said.

O'Malley ripped a blanket from the bed and tossed it over the statue.

"If this here is prison, then I doon't knoow as why the boys back home are always complainin.'"

"No windows, only one way out, and that way blocked," Nobody said. "Looks like we're spending the night here. At least we're honored guests—for now."

He gathered his men in the room at the end and dropped the curtain over the doorway. The lamp hanging in the center gave the only light.

"All right, men, here's our position."

Nobody sat down on the bed and crossed his arms.

"We've somehow wandered into an Ancient Roman settlement that no one knows exists. I know the language, but I know little about their culture. I suppose it's quite something, since our schoolboys get it drilled into their heads, but that's not the important point. The important point is that we confirm the *Miriam*'s sailors came here, and if they did, we get them and leave."

"Vhat if zhese barbarians do not vant us to leave?" Jacques asked.

"The Cossacks didn't want us to do a number of things, but we did them. If necessary we'll use the same methods here."

The grate rattled. Nobody sprang to the doorway and pushed through the curtain. At the end of the hall a guard unlocked the door, pushed four figures inside, and locked it after them.

Jacques snorted. "Vhat, do zhey haf prison-crowding here, too?"

"We are here to serve you," the first figure said.

It was the slave girl who Little Caesar had wanted chopped up in his throne room. She wasn't trembling anymore, but she was still pale. The three girls behind her murmured agreement, but she seemed to have been elected leader. Nobody translated her speech to his men.

"Ridiculous." Jacques pinched his mustache. "Do zhey zhink zhat a Frenchman cannot adequately serve himself and zhree ohzers? Does she zhink zhat I did not serve an entire squad of ungrateful vretches—" he looked at O'Malley, "—for years, vihz absolute success? I need no barbarian girl to help me. I can make any food in zhe vorld!"

"Except tea," Nobody said.

"I speak of food. Tea is not food. Tea is vhat happened one day vhen an Englishman dropped a leaf in a puddle."

Nobody turned to the girl. "Thank you, but we can take care of ourselves."

The girl's eyelashes widened into two big black rings around her hazel eyes.

"But we must," she said. "Little Caesar commanded that we serve you. We cannot leave."

Nobody groaned. Where was Edmund when he needed him? How was he to explain to these girls that their presence wasn't desired? Liana he could understand, and she understood him. Even Elyssa, Edmund's betrothed, could be sensible, but beyond them females made no sense. Maybe that's what happens when you grow up without a mother.

"We appreciate the offer, but we don't need servants," Nobody said. "Please, call the guards to let you back out."

"We can't. Little Caesar commanded us to serve you. The door is locked until he calls for you again."

"Oh." Nobody scratched his chin. "In that case, we're rearranging rooms. Jacques and O'Malley, you take this second to last room, and no arguments longer than half an hour. I want to get some sleep tonight. Matthew, you and I will take this last room, and you girls can take the one closest to the door."

The girl hesitated. "You—you mean it?"

"I mean it. I forget what the Roman expression is, but good night."

The slave girls filed into their room and Nobody scanned his men's faces.

"Matthew? Anything to say?"

Matthew shook his head. He didn't have much to say these days.

"Stay alert," Nobody said, "but sleep well. I'm afraid that tomorrow may be one of the most fascinating days in our lives."

Chapter 9

Nobody knelt on a swath of grass the next day and tied the leather thongs on his sandals. O'Malley knelt beside him.

"I thought as that you wouldn't put on a uniform, sir."

"Not an English uniform," Nobody said.

"I'm sorry, sir, but—doesn't it seem traitorous somehow? That's to say, putting on the enemy's uniform?"

"I'm not an English soldier anymore, O'Malley." Nobody yanked the thongs. "Technically, I'm not English anymore." He tied the loose ends into a bow and stood.

Jacques wound a black scarf around Nobody's neck and helped O'Malley hoist the armor onto Nobody's shoulders.

"I also do not like zhis, sir," Jacques said. His mustache quivered in the light breeze whisking down the mountains. "Could you not shoot togehzer at a target, or somezhing?"

"They would have to invent a rifle first."

Nobody buckled his belt. The apron of metal-specked leather strips bounced on his thighs. The armor felt incredibly different from the familiar trousers and coat he was accustomed to wear into battle. The metal strips rattled against each other as he moved, and the air blowing through the openings in his sandals made his bare feet feel vulnerable.

"Are you ready, boy?"

Bristle Hair stood on the training mound, his *rudis*, or wooden sword, slashing patterns in the air.

Nobody eyed the rough grain of his own *rudis*. It was a clumsy toy compared to the trusty blade that should be hanging from his side, nicked by a hundred fights, but sleek, perfectly balanced, and razor sharp. A year ago he could have bested that braggart on the hill even with this awkward weapon, but now? He shook his head.

"The boy is scared!" Bristle Hair said. He slapped his massive arm-muscles. "I don't blame him."

The watching circle of Romans laughed. Jacques made as if to charge them, but O'Malley grabbed his neck-scruff.

"Please, sir," O'Malley said, "let me fight the fellow. I don't even need a sword, jist let me plant one good fist on the end of his arrogant nose and we'll see how the braggarts laugh."

"This is my fight, O'Malley. All you can do is pray."

The hobnails in Nobody's sandals gripped the ground as he slowly stepped toward the mound. Bristle Hair guffawed.

"Look how the barbarian boy walks. He knows he comes to his doom. He wishes now that he never pretended to be a soldier to Little Caesar."

Nobody kept the same pace. "How many men have you killed, Praetorian?"

Bristle Hair growled. "Found your tongue, young one?"

Nobody stopped at the bottom of the mound, which was probably thirty feet across and sloped up like a cone into a level battleground.

"I walk slowly because I no longer find warfare appealing. I've killed more men than I like to remember. I'm glad this isn't a fight to the death."

"Oh, yes, he's very glad," Bristle Hair said. He gave his comrades an enormous wink. "But you still won't feel very good at the end."

Nobody gripped his shield with his left hand and raised his sword with his right. The throb started in his shoulder. He was at the top now, higher than everyone else except the man who had arranged this 'test.' The semicircle of Romans shouted their champion's name, their ranks broken only by the little square of ground distinguished by O'Malley's red hair, Jacques's mustache, and Matthew's square jaws.

Bristle Hair spat on his sword, sneered, and charged. His shield crashed against Nobody's and threw him back, but Nobody managed to angle his feet behind him and stay on the mound.

Bristle Hair's sword swung over Nobody's shield. Nobody tried to raise his arm to block the blow but his arm wouldn't move, and the blunt edge jammed his helmet just above the right ear guard. Nobody staggered back, a hazy picture of blue sky skewered on white mountains whirling in his brain, then another blow dented his right side and knocked the shield from his hand.

"Colonel!" someone called.

Nobody tried to clear his eyes, tried to step toward his enemy, but wind whistled again and flames scorched through his right shoulder as another blow struck home. He screamed every whisper of air in his lungs and collapsed down the side of the mound.

The grass brushed his face, the dew mingling with his sweat and tears of pain. It smelled wild.

"Sir!"

Fingers fumbled with his helmet strap and wrestled the metal off his throbbing head. A sleeve wiped matted hair off his forehead.

Bristle Hair's laugh floated down. "So, this is what the barbarians call a soldier?"

Nobody blinked through the haze at the figure of the Roman posed on the mound. His comrades pounded their shields.

"'He'll teach you new maneuvers,' said Little Caesar. 'He'll prepare something interesting for the festival.' And he has! I've never seen *that* maneuver before." Bristle Hair pointed to where Nobody lay prone in the grass and laughed.

"Help me up." Nobody groped for the helping arm near his head. "Help me up!"

He couldn't push off with his right arm, but he slid his legs under himself and, with O'Malley grasping his left arm, managed to stand. The ground trembled.

O'Malley and Jacques were at his side, but Matthew was gone.

"Where is Matthew?" Nobody asked.

O'Malley pointed to Nobody's shoulder. "He couldn't bear tae watch."

"Give me my sword."

O'Malley held up his hand. "Sir, ye can't fight! Not noow. Let me take the scoundrel, I'll wring his neck, I will."

Nobody reached his right leg out, then his left, trying not to wobble. He stooped and clasped the wooden handle in his left fingers.

O'Malley blocked his path. "Sir, ye can't do this. Ye're not a match fer him."

"Move, O'Malley." Nobody pushed the Irishman's hands away. "This is my fight. Move. That's an order."

O'Malley covered his eyes and stepped aside. Jacques, somewhere in the shaky world behind, sobbed. Nobody climbed the mound, each step strengthening his will. He couldn't match strength with the Roman's toughened muscles, but that wasn't unusual. His opponents were usually stronger. Beat strength with skill—but he had no skill with this short sword. Dexterity, speed—they were fantasies in this armor, and even if he had them and he could close with the Roman he didn't have strength to strike a blow.

"Come back for another beating, eh, boy?" The Roman leered as he stepped back to his side of the mound. "I think you've forgotten your shield."

Nobody bent his legs, ready to spring. He clenched his right arm against his side and swung the sword with his left. The chunk of wood wobbled like a child's top as he tried to trace a pattern in the air. The pounding blood in his head echoed the legionaries' shouts.

Bristle Hair yelled an insult and charged. Nobody dodged the rush and tried to swipe at his enemy, but his sword clunked off the shield. Bristle Hair turned and rushed again, but Nobody dodged around the mound, dancing here and there as the swift chops sliced the air. Bristle Hair had stopped trying to thrust and was simply aiming for Nobody's weak arm, trying to crush the aching bone.

"Had enough?" Bristle Hair said.

Nobody paused, panting.

Crash. The *rudis* struck once more and Nobody rolled down the mound, clasping his arm.

"Welcome to Vallis Deorum," Bristle Hair said. "That's how men fight. Tonight you get to feast your gut and tomorrow you teach us maneuvers." He spat. "Little Caesar will want us to dance for him next."

Jacques's hands were busy with the buckles on Nobody's armor, easing the pressure and letting air into the boy's pumping lungs.

"Sir, are you all right?" Jacques whispered.

Nobody didn't answer. He was not all right.

Chapter 10

Something cold sucked the brain-mists through Nobody's forehead. Swirling shapes faded into solid black. His boots were missing. Fabric kissed his knees. He reached for his sword-hip and found a sheet in the way.

"Please be quiet," a voice said.

Nobody's skull felt like a South Sea islander had been using it for a tom-tom. Hands cupped beneath his head and raised it a few inches to slip another pillow underneath.

"Jacques?" Nobody said.

"No, it is I."

The voice stirred no memory.

"Who is 'I'?"

"Open your eyes."

Nobody hesitated. If there was any light on the other side of his eyelids it would pierce his pupils and stoke his headache. He fluttered his right eyelid. Little light. He lifted both eyelids. The room was only lit enough to reveal the dim outline of a girl and two hazel eyes looking into his.

"Liana?" Nobody said.

"My name is Ennia. You saved my life."

The eyes moved to the right and the light from the candle hanging from the ceiling outlined a profile. It was the slave girl Little Caesar assigned him. Then he must be in the palace, probably on his own bed. Yes, there was the blanket-draped statue in the corner. And the headache was from . . . the fight.

The Romans' laughter still twisted with the throbs pulsing in his right temple. Of course they laughed. Who wouldn't laugh at a self-proclaimed soldier groveling in Greenland grass? Raw recruits were better fighters than him.

"Who is Liana?" Ennia asked.

Nobody's brain flickered back to the present.

"Liana? Liana is one of the many people and things I've had to leave. Just like my regiment. My island. My country. Edmund. And Liana. But you wouldn't understand."

Ennia held out a goblet. "You are lonely?"

"I'm accustomed to it."

The goblet was heavy metal. The dim light showed no color, but it might be gold. He held the rim to his lips until the smell of fruit stopped him.

"What is this?"

"Wine."

Nobody handed it back. "Thank you, but I don't drink wine."

Ennia's eyes tried to mirror the size of the goblet's mouth.

"But, everyone drinks wine. Do they not have wine on the Outside? It is a liquid crushed from grapes and fermented over time, which settles the stomach, and eases the mind, and calms the nerves."

"And does a few other things as well. I know what wine is, and that's why I don't drink it."

She shook her head. "But you must drink it tonight with Little Caesar."

"We'll discuss that when the time comes." Nobody willed his head off the pillow and slowly sat up. "How long do I have until I see your Little Caesar?"

"Perhaps half a mark on the sun-dial."

"Then I'd best prepare. Please call Jacques—he's the little one with whiskers—to help me tidy up."

"Oh, but I can help." Ennia lifted the sheet off his legs, knelt, and slipped the mouth of a boot over his right foot.

Nobody pointed to the door. "Thank you, but I asked for my man's help."

She knelt there at the end of the bed with the curve in the boot touching his toes and an odd look in her eyes.

"You mean—you don't want me here?"

"Precisely. Trust me, it won't be the first time that Jacques has helped me recover after a battle."

She gave him the narrow-eyed, head-cocked expression of a curious kitten, but left without more words.

That night, the throne room sparkled with lights. A long table ran perpendicular to the dais like the blade of a dagger run crossways through a hilt, littered with plates of meat, loaves of bread, twisted vines with red and green grapes, and vases of wine covered with pictures of men, women, and animals. Guests lolled on couches along each side of the table, while Little Caesar lay on the dais next to the head table and tossed grapes into the mouth of a crouching dog.

It didn't make sense. This wasn't just some barbarian king living in splendor. This was the full opulence of a Roman emperor somehow transported to the interior of Greenland. Nobody paused in the open area before the table, unsure what to do, until Little Caesar saw him and snapped his fingers.

"Come at last, Outsider? Well? Do you want to be a dancer?"

A dancer? What does he mean? Nobody shook his head.

"Then come sit down," Little Caesar said.

Little Caesar glared at a man lying close to the head of the table, who instantly tumbled off his couch and motioned for Nobody to take it. Slaves melted out of corners to lift swaths of fleece off the floor, leaving black rock beneath, and a distant padding swelled into the pitter-patter of bare feet as a group of

73

dancers scurried in. Nobody eased his aching body onto the couch and turned his back.

"The barbarian looks pale."

Nobody looked up. Bristle Hair stood beside the dais with his arms locked across his chest. A leer creased his face.

Little Caesar held a grape to his mouth and sliced it in half with his front teeth.

"You were teaching my men a new maneuver. Have you finished?"

"Not quite. We spent today—er, getting acquainted." Nobody eased himself farther up the couch to ease the pressure on his right arm.

"Don't take long, for the festival comes soon. I want something fresh, something new." Little Caesar waggled five jewel-encrusted fingers at the courtiers. "They all say the same thing, and think the same thing, but what they say and what they think are *not* the same thing. Eh, Horatius?"

A smooth-faced twenty-something lying two couches to Nobody's left sat up.

"My lord, I assure you—"

Little Caesar waved him down. Webs of red veins scarred the whites of Little Caesar's eyes.

"Now, boy, I want to talk of something fresh. New. Who are you? Where do you come from?"

"My name is Nobody."

Little Caesar blinked.

"I don't think you had that word right. That word means nothing. 'Nonexistence,' my eminently boring philosophers would say. Try a different word."

"I meant to use that word." Nobody forced a smile. "Men in the outside world think it as strange a name as you do, but it's my name. Who am I? I led soldiers, then was a merchant."

Bristle Hair's eyes laughed.

"Strange jobs for one so young," Little Caesar said. "This amuses me. Your friends, the great tall red-haired one, and the little one, and the other—were they merchants?"

"They were my soldiers."

"Even the little one?"

Jacques's mustache would quiver with rage if he were here and could understand.

"Even the little one."

"Why do you come to my land?" Little Caesar leaned forward, his smile gone. "Who are you to invade my country? Are there more of you?" He guzzled wine. "Answer me with truth or I'll fill your stomach with wine until you burst."

This inebriated tyrant was not stable. The conversation was a little reminiscent of some of Nobody's talks with General Tremont, but at least Tremont didn't have the authority to traipse around chopping off heads or bursting stomachs.

No voices spoke, no dishes clinked, no throats gulped wine. Every face pointed at Nobody, but they were unreadable, waiting to pick an emotion when the winds of favor could be forecasted. Only the pitapat of the dancers behind punctured the silence.

"I didn't know there was a country here," Nobody said. "I came searching for countrymen who I thought crossed the mountains. Have you seen anyone else recently like me or my men?"

"How dare you interrogate me!" Little Caesar threw his goblet over Nobody's head into the dancers. "Who do you think you are, barbarian scum? You want to see my torture chambers?"

Bristle Hair unfolded his arms and popped the joints of each finger, one by one, the cracks piercing the quiet like crunching chicken bones. Nobody's shoulder quivered.

"What do you want to know, Little Caesar?"

"You are spies. You've come to search out my land, to try to find a weakness, to prepare for a horde of hard-booted men with strange long swords to destroy my beautiful valley."

Little Caesar's head drooped. His fire died as the wine took effect, and great tears squeezed from the corners of his eyes and clung to his eyelashes.

"Everyone hates me," Little Caesar said. "Everybody is against me."

There was a rush of courtiers to the dais, petting him, soothing him, bowing down before him, handing him more wine, and bunches of grapes, and wiping his sweaty forehead with perfumed cloths. This was a Caesar? A nation-ruler? He was as bad as some of the whiny native brats back on Rahattan Island.

Little Caesar sniffled. "My head hurts. I want to go to bed."

Bristle Hair coughed. "What will you do with the spy?"

"Spy?" Little Caesar said. "Oh, the spy. Maybe we should torture him, find out if barbarians scream like Romans. Do we have any tortures scheduled for tomorrow?"

Bristle Hair held up one finger.

"Hmm. What do you think, boy?" Little Caesar pointed to Nobody. "What should we do to you?"

Nobody dropped his legs off the couch and stood. He was sick with fatigue, pain, and disgust, his head ached, and his mind rebelled at every detail of this unearthly land with its bloated leader and the parasites lying at the table stuffing themselves with meat, and wine, and more.

"Do what you must," Nobody said. "I'm not a spy, and I don't like your country enough to want to conquer it. I'm searching for a small group of men who possibly came here and possibly didn't. I give you my word—no one is following me. If you want to pull me in pieces or burst me with wine, then have at it, but rest assured, you can't do a thing to me unless God, Christ, so decrees."

"There!" Bristle Hair said. "Again he says he is a cursed Christian. Why not let him be the first example of your glorious new plan?"

Little Caesar held up his hand. He blinked like an owl in daylight.

"That is so—new. The way he talks, no one talks like that to me. I like this. This is new, this is fresh. I am amused." He rubbed his chin. "But he could still be a spy. Confine him for two weeks, he and his men alone. If no one follows, we know that he's not a spy. If others do follow—"

Little Caesar pointed to Bristle Hair.

76

Chapter 11

"Chester? What are you doing?"

"I'm identifying with the natives. What do you think?"

Lawrence folded his arms. Each week he decided that Chester simply couldn't surprise him again. And each week, Chester proved him wrong.

It started with the red leather boots, traveled up the sealskin breeches into the sealskin coat, and culminated in the crowning absurdity—an entire white fox pelt with its head as a hood and its rear legs and tail dangling against Chester's back.

"I don't think the Eskimos usually wear *Alopex lagopus*," Lawrence said.

"Wear what?"

"That's the species name of the arctic fox."

Chester flicked the snout. "Perhaps I'll sponsor a fashion change. I think it looks quite good."

The ship's anchor plunged into the sea's bosom and whisked dozens of feet of rope after it. One of the boats creaked in the davits, but this trip wouldn't be after a whale. The Eskimo village lying off the port bow was where this elusive colonel landed, according to the whaler they met three days ago, and Lawrence was ready to end this quest.

Pacarina came out of their tiny cabin and paused when she saw Chester.

"Good morning, Brother. I remember hearing a splash last night. Did you fall into a seal?"

Chester grimaced. "You made a good choice in a wife, Law, but she lacks clothing sense. She never appreciates my taste."

"There's a reason for that," Lawrence said. He turned to Pacarina. "We're going ashore to see if this is where Colonel Nobody landed, but there's no need for you to come."

"But I'd like to, Law."

"We're using a small boat."

Pacarina smiled. "We don't all get sea sick, Law."

Lawrence slipped his hand between his shirtfront and waistcoat and eased the fabric's pressure on his stomach. The choppy waves *sha-lunked* sporadically against the hull. Lawrence wasn't built for an adventurer. Inconveniently, Chester was, and if he was left unattended in an Eskimo village he would probably get himself killed by a polar bear or start the first English-Eskimo war.

"Let's go," Lawrence said.

The reception on shore was less excited than *The History of Greenland* had given Lawrence to expect. Either that or his somersaulting internal organs were depressing his general outlook. It took three minutes for the snow to stop heaving enough for him to concentrate on the Eskimos.

"You didn't happen to pick up their lingo, did you?" Chester asked.

"I'm afraid not, but I did come equipped to study the native phonology. I still blame myself for missing such a splendid opportunity of studying the Mayamura language."

"It's rather difficult when the people you're studying are trying to kill you. By the by, do you think this interpreter fellow knows what he's doing?"

The interpreter smiled. "Just tell me what to say."

"The usual. Wish them a good day, and a prosperous life, and all the normal rot, and then tell them that we're looking for an Englishman—I suppose he's English—who landed here some time back."

Lawrence flipped through his copy of Paul Egede's dictionary of the Eskimo language, but he couldn't catch up with the interpreter. The words were long enough to tie a shoe with. The Eskimos nodded and said a few words back, but they all looked glum. Glum, or scared.

"They say that no one has come here," the interpreter said.

"Impossible." Chester shook his head. "I may not have been to Sandhurst, but I know how to ask questions. My sources are solid. They came here. Ask again."

The answer was the same. And that wasn't the only strange thing. According to Lawrence's research, Eskimos were friendly people, happy to see Kablunets and eager to talk. These apparently hadn't been informed that they were supposed to be jovial. The men's faces were as expressionless as dry leather, while the women hovered in the doorways of their huts with something that might be fear flickering in their eyes.

"Are you ready to return?" the interpreter asked.

"As ready as I am for a cold bath," Chester said. "I'm going to pull some truth out of their frozen tongues if I have to dance a jig to do it."

"Don't translate that," Lawrence said. "Chester, I don't like this. They look like they're hiding something, and they would only need to do that if they were ashamed or afraid. Do you think Colonel Nobody has come to harm?"

Chester yanked at his wolf pelt's snout. "I didn't buy sealskin breeches so I could find a corpse. Interpreter, tell these fellows that I want to speak with their head man. I think they call him 'angekok,' or something like that."

"They say that their angekok has gone on a long journey."

Chester frowned. "How long?"

"The snow has melted much since he left."

Chester kicked a spurt of the wet powder off his right boot.

"It still has a ways to go. Ask them where he went."

The Eskimos shook their heads.

"This is ridiculous," Chester said. "All right, thank them for their lies and tell them they can go about their business. Law, Pacarina, let's powwow."

81

Hopefully the interpreter was judicious in which sections he translated. Now that Lawrence's stomach had reestablished its relationship with gravity he was able to appreciate the topography, and really, the place was beautiful. There was a kind of rocky beach, mostly snow-covered, which sloped into the water. Mountains stood behind them like a book's deckled pages.

Chester knelt in the snow and spread his wolf pelt for Pacarina to sit on. Lawrence, having neither sealskin leggings or wolf pelt, simply crouched beside them.

"They're obviously lying," Chester said. "This place meets the description that last whaler gave. Now, why would these people lie about some Kablunets visiting them?"

Pacarina folded her arms on her knees. "You seem rather suspicious this morning, Brother. Is it all concern for Colonel Nobody, or does the thought of Lord Banastre Bronner have something to do with it?"

Chester grunted. "I won't pretend to be sorry that by saving a good man I can also disappoint a ruby-nosed profligate. What say you, Professor?"

"I think the Eskimos are afraid of something," Lawrence said. "That doesn't make me hopeful about Colonel Nobody's safety. We need to prove in some manner that they were recently visited by the colonel, or at least by someone foreign. That might give us the mental leverage necessary to pry out the truth."

The Eskimos melted back to their work. Some mended kayaks, while others sharpened spears and knives. The women sat by piles of sealskins deftly slipping needles in and out of the edges.

Chester pointed at the women. "Shall I ask them to give you lessons?" he asked Pacarina. "You could outfit Law."

Lawrence stared at the workers. There must be a clue somewhere. There was a commotion by the water's edge and the sailors started pointing out to sea and shouting.

"There she blows!"

The Eskimos dropped their work, seized their weapons, and rushed down the beach. A jet of white water exploded between shore and ship. It was a whale.

The sailors jumped into the boat and waved for Lawrence and the others to join them. Another white plume spiked the atmosphere and a dark body showed for a moment above the waves.

Chester leaped up. "If we leave now we might not be able to come back."

The sailors shouted. *Think, think.* Lawrence grasped handfuls of snow. Colonel Nobody and his men couldn't have simply vaporized. This place had to be the key to the mystery. If they left, they might not convince the captain to let them return. If they stayed, the whaler wouldn't waste time sending for them. That was their agreement. They had extra clothing and supplies in their bags—but if this was the wrong place they would lose their chance to find the colonel.

The sailors had their oars out. The interpreter windmilled his arms at Lawrence. What to do? If foreigners had been here they might have left a foreign object. A kettle, an English coat, a weapon . . . a hatchet.

"We're staying here," Lawrence called.

The interpreter shrugged and the boat sliced the water toward the spot where the whale had spouted.

"You did think about that decision, right?" Chester asked.

"If you want to find Colonel Nobody, this is the place to do it. Look."

Lawrence pointed. At the back of the crowd of Eskimos stood one of the tallest men, and in his right hand, head down, was a steel hatchet.

Chester pounced. He pointed to the hatchet, but the Eskimo hugged it to his chest. Chester pointed to his eyes, then to the hatchet, then back to his eyes. The Eskimo shook his head. Chester whisked his body into some sort of contorted bow, with his head below his knees, and executed the sign motions again. The native did something with his throat, maybe laughing, maybe gulping with fear, but he handed over the hatchet.

"No Eskimo made this," Chester said. He balanced the tool on his index finger. "Would make a pretty good throwing hatchet."

"Mine—many year," the Eskimo said.

Chester grunted. "So he does know a few English words. I thought it odd that none of them knew any. But I doubt he's had this hatchet for years. It's not worn enough to have been used for long."

"Do you have conclusive proof?" Lawrence asked. "We need something solid."

"How's this?" Chester pointed to a line of raised lettering on the metal just above the handle. "Rigsby. This hatchet was made this year."

"How do you know?"

"The metal works Stanton & Co. just consolidated with another company this January, and together they're called 'Rigsby.' No hatchet made before this year would have that maker's mark."

Lawrence shook his head. "Chester, how do you know that sort of thing?"

"Does Pacarina know the names of her milliners?"

"I presume so."

"I know the names of my knife and hatchet-makers."

Lawrence turned to the Eskimo. It was obvious that the Eskimos knew at least a little English, but had been afraid to admit it because they were afraid of the English for some reason.

"We know that this was left with you this year. Where did it come from? Did you steal it? Earn it? How did you get it?"

The Eskimo's Adam's apple poked out of his lumpy neck. "No steal, no steal. Trade."

The lie was cracked. In ten minutes, Lawrence pieced enough signs and broken English together to understand that a Kablunet ship had come not long ago, and four of the men stayed. The leader was young, and one of the men was tall with red hair. That matched the description of Colonel Nobody and at least one of his men.

"Where are they now?" Lawrence asked.

The Eskimo shook his head.

"Are they dead?"

The Eskimo trembled so violently that a lice shook out of his hair.

"Demon mountain."

Lawrence looked at Chester. What was a 'demon mountain'?

"Look, friend Eskimo," Chester said, "I don't have a sense the size of a rat's nose what a 'demon mountain' might be, but I don't care if your Kablunet visitors walked off the end of the earth. We're going to find them, and you're going to take us there."

Chapter 12

It was two weeks and one day after Nobody and his men entered Vallis Deorum that a soldier entered their room and roused them. Since their imprisonment, the only person they had seen was the slave who brought their food.

"Are we believed?" Nobody asked.

The soldier nodded. "You're back into favor. Little Caesar believes your story, and he and the priests want to know all about the Outside. I'm taking you to the library to find out where our knowledge of Outside history ends, and then you'll tell Little Caesar what happened afterward."

Nobody passed gladly through the iron door and felt half-free again. This trip to the library seemed plausible, but Nobody wasn't completely convinced. There might be another reason they were being sent there. He would be on his guard.

The training mound was on the left as they strode the path to the edge of the rock. Man-made walls blocked the valley from view, and as Nobody had been blindfolded when he crossed the valley before, it was still as mysterious as when he first glimpsed the green slopes from the mountain.

The palace gate was made of foot-thick timbers nailed together and swung between two columns of solid rock. Palace guards removed the massive metal bar that held the gates together and the doors opened, first showing a sliver of sunlight, then a crack, then a rectangle, then a great bath of sunlight flooding through the doors and washing Nobody in warm light.

"*Vallis Deorum,*" the soldier said.

A vast city spread below the palace rock. It wasn't vast compared to London, but for a supposedly desolate land it was surreal. Hundreds—maybe thousands—of close-built houses lined a grid of streets, broken occasionally by spacious quarters where villas swallowed entire city blocks.

"Vhere do zhey find food for all zhese people?" Jacques asked.

"What I want tae know," O'Malley said, "is how we get oot o' this place."

Nobody motioned for quiet. "First we need to find what we came for." He nodded at the soldier. "Lead on."

The steps zigzagged down the rock, each zag protected by a barricade. It made an incredibly defensible position but also a distinct challenge for the gang of sweat-soaked slaves with provision-baskets strapped on their heads who toiled upwards. The city only occupied a small percentage of the valley, which was mostly dotted with farms. Checkers of wheat and swaths of vineyards climbed the lower slopes while flocks of sheep, reindeer, and musk oxen grazed the rich green grass.

"Colonel, I feel zhat I am in a dream such as I haf never before imagined," Jacques said.

It was dreamlike, but a dream void of Liana and Edmund, a dream subject to the whims of a drink-besotted Caesar. Hopefully, a dream that would quickly dissolve back into the grim but more predictable landscape of reality.

"Soldier," Nobody said. "What are the chances that Little Caesar will let us leave your valley?"

"How many mountains can you fit in a wineskin?"

"None."

"That's how many chances you have. But there's plenty of fun to be had here."

The soldier slapped the satchel he wore.

"My orders are to deliver you to the library and then post these proclamations throughout the city. Little Caesar hasn't ordered you to come back tonight, so you can spend the night in the city if you want. If you can, go to the play this afternoon—I hear there's a special surprise planned."

Armor clanked as the guards at the bottom saluted. More guards, and another gate like the one above. This wasn't trustful country.

A semicircle the size of a parade ground separated the gate from the first houses. This area was deserted, but a few steps along the street brought the group into the midst of a bustling scene peopled by workmen in tunics, red-cheeked little boys, women with jars on their heads, wise-faced men with fringed tunics, and many more.

The din of a hundred conversations slowly petered away as Nobody and his men advanced, until the only sound in the street was the click of their boots on the tight-fitting stone blocks. Slave and citizen alike drank them in. An elephant tramping Berkeley Square in London would have about the same effect—less, probably.

The soldier jerked his thumb at a building on the right.

"That's the library." He nodded at the street. "If you see anything you like, take it."

"I beg your pardon?" Nobody said.

"If you see anything or anyone you like, take it." The soldier winked. "Benefits of being guests of Little Caesar. *Vale.*"

The library's front wall was fifty or sixty feet high, with columns stacked on columns and statues in niches next to each of the three open doorways. Inside, the room was a semicircle with honeycombed walls, and in each cell of the comb was a scroll.

Crash.

A man in a tunic stood next to a table on the far right side of the room, a litter of pottery shards at his feet. He stared at the newcomers.

"You are—Outsiders?" he managed to say.

Nobody touched his forehead. "Greetings. Yes, we're from outside of your valley. At the moment you could call us guests at the palace. My name is Nobody—that's right, Nobody. I didn't use the wrong word. These are my men, but they don't speak your language."

Jacques bowed and O'Malley nodded. Matthew simply stared back.

"I am sorry, you—startled me." The librarian jerked from his trance-like stare. "Please forgive my rudeness, but I have never seen anyone like you before. Why are you here?"

"I think we're supposed to learn about your valley and your history. That, and the history you know about before you came to this valley."

"Ah—learn. Yes, yes, let me think."

The librarian stooped to collect the broken shards of what was once an inkstand. He was not a young man, but he was not a very old man, either. His arms were thin, his back was straight, and his eyes looked slightly hesitant, as if his eyesight was poor. He collected the shards in the skirt of his tunic and raked them from there onto the table with his fingers. The amazement slowly faded from his face. What remained looked friendly, but a certain cast to the eyes also spoke of wariness.

"You may call me Aulus. I am the head librarian. May I ask how it is that you are the only one of you four to speak our language?"

"As strange as it is to say under our present conditions, Rome in the outside world is a memory. Its power has vanished, and the City of Seven Hills is simply a city."

Aulus nodded slowly as the information percolated. It must be a shock. It would be like waking up and learning that the only thing left of the British Empire was a few blocks along the Thames.

"Please, take these chairs," Aulus said. He placed five chairs around one of the tables. "My son will bring you some fruit."

Aulus clapped his hands and a boy hobbled into the room with a platter of grapes. No, not a boy. He had a boy's height, but a man's beard hung from his chin.

"Look, Jack Frog," O'Malley said. "Ye have kin here after all. It's a dwarf."

The dwarf was hardly four feet tall, which his bowed back and wide-spread legs made look even shorter. He stopped for a moment on seeing the strangers, then deposited the fruit and retired without a word.

"Now, then," Aulus said, "I'm collecting some of my scattered wits. I apologize for my rudeness. Visitors usually do not surprise me so much."

Nobody leaned forward.

"I have one important question for you, Aulus. Have you seen anyone that looked anything like us in this valley in the past few weeks?"

Aulus's eyebrows narrowed.

"I have never seen anyone like you before. In my many years I have seen many fashions birth and die among the young ones, but I've never seen clothing like yours." He pointed at Nobody's waistcoat. "Does everyone in the Outside wear those things?"

"Eh? Er—no, we have variety."

Nobody squeezed a grape between the knuckles on his right index and middle fingers, steadily increasing the pressure to see how much the skin could stand before it burst. It reminded him of his brain. Aulus's answer was the worst possible. If this librarian hadn't seen anyone else like them, then he hadn't seen the *Miriam*'s sailors. If they *were* the *Miriam*'s sailors. Where could they be? And why should he trust this librarian's word? Somewhere between that dropped pipe on the path and this lost world was the answer.

"Do the priests know you're here?" Aulus asked.

Nobody nodded. "Yes, though I haven't seen any. I expect they would probably rather have us under the ground."

"Yes. They wouldn't like Outsiders, for they teach that we are beyond the edge of the world in the land of the gods. But—do they know that you are here at the library?"

"That's what a soldier said."

The grape burst unexpectedly and spurted juice over the table. Nobody bit his lip, sopped the juice with his sleeve, and slipped the skin into his mouth. Aulus pretended not to notice.

"Er—where did you come from?" Nobody asked. "No one on the Outside knows that there are Romans in this part of the world."

Aulus tapped his fingers on the table top. "You say you are from the Outside." It was a statement, not a question. He seemed to be making a decision about something.

"Would you like to see something that few but our scholars have seen?"

"Probably. Depending on what it is."

"And your slaves? Are they trustworthy?"

"Vhy does he point at us like zhat?" Jacques asked.

Nobody tensed his cheek muscles against the smile that wanted to come. "He thinks you're slaves."

"Slaves! Zhey knock our heads, zhey insult my skill by trying to—vhat is zhe vord—shovel a gaggle of slave girls upon us, zhey call us barbarians, and now zhey call us slaves! Vhat is left?"

"We can hope they doon't call us corpses," O'Malley said.

Aulus slipped a key from under his toga and led them through a hallway, up a staircase, and into a secluded little corner from which one rectangular window looked down into a courtyard. A vase on the only table in the passage was coated with dust. The window was far too small for a man to pass through, and its light cast a long shadow beneath the windowsill. The atmosphere felt secure and mysterious. Aulus lit a candle, unlocked a door, and led them inside.

"Some hoard precious stones, and some caress their wineskins, but here you see *my* treasures."

The candlelight showed an empty table in the middle of the room. Aulus laid the candle on this and the light washed over the farthest wall, only five feet away, which held a rack with half a dozen yellowed scrolls.

"These were saved from Londinium," Aulus said. "They are the foundation of this library and the treasures of more than seventeen centuries." He ran his fingers over the rack, not touching the scrolls themselves, which looked ready to join the dust that covered them, but fondling their resting places as a mother might smooth her baby's pillow. Not that Nobody had ever seen a mother do so.

"Tell me the story," Nobody said.

The flickering light chased shadows up and down the folds of Aulus's white toga and lit the lower half of his face, leaving the bridge of his nose, his eyes, and his forehead in darkness.

"Many, many years ago, when the whole world was Roman and the might of Rome reached the farthest isles, a barbarian queen rebelled in the island of

Britannia. This was during the reign of Nero. Do you still remember Nero in the Outside?"

"Yes, one of the world's greatest perverts."

Aulus slashed the air with his hand. "It's dangerous to say that. He is counted as the greatest Roman, and most of our Caesars model themselves upon him. It was during his reign that this barbarian queen of the Iceni rebelled against her cruel Roman governors and washed that strange island in blood."

"Yes, I've heard of that war. The Britons did well for a time, until Suetonius crushed them with better weaponry and training."

"So, Suetonius won?" Aulus rubbed his hands together. "I thought he would. We didn't know, you see, because our story diverged before the war's end. When the barbarians threatened Londinium, Suetonius withdrew his legionaries from the city. Some of the inhabitants went with the army, but some took to the sea in merchant ships."

Aulus went to another rack on the right wall which held replicas of the original scrolls. He unrolled a map of the world as the Romans knew it in Nero's reign. He tapped the ocean next to Britain.

"They sailed away from the island with what animals and worldly goods they could. There were merchants, slaves, priests, and even some deserting legionaries who passed themselves as citizens. Though they didn't think of it at that dark hour, it was all that was needed to create a tiny colony."

"And they simply sailed to Greenland—I mean, this place—and started a colony?" Nobody said.

"That wasn't their intention, but they were directed differently. A great storm rose, terrible in its might and fierce in its winds. It blew the ships far away from land, until the people thought they would perish in the boiling ocean, then they came to new land, land that was not on any map."

Aulus traced his finger up across the ocean and off the map.

"The early writers are not very clear about what happened then. They were sick of fatigue, cramped, and utterly exhausted. Somehow they came to land with their animals and goods and ended in this valley. The priests said that they had sailed out of the world and were now in the land of the gods, and that no one must ever leave this Elysium. There is a curse on any Roman who would try to do so, and the only way out is far up in the mountains and always guarded by the most trusty soldiers."

"Yes, we know about it," Nobody said. "This is all fascinating, but at the moment I'm less interested about people getting out than I am in them getting in. We were following men who must have come here."

Footsteps filled the hallway. Some scraped, as if the feet never left the ground, and some thudded like bricks. Three knocks shook the door.

"What is it, Joktan?" Aulus said.

"Balbus brings bad tidings," a hoarse voice answered.

The dwarf stood framed by the doorway for one moment before a big-muscled man shoved past him.

"B-Bishop Aulus! May Christ b-be with you." The man threw a sheet of parchment onto the table, his back to Nobody. "It is horrib-ble."

Aulus grabbed the man's shoulders. "Think, man." The whites of his eyes flashed at Nobody.

Balbus didn't even look around, but stabbed his finger into the parchment. "The pr-proclamation has c-come."

"Calm down," Aulus said. "Breathe deep and stop that terrible stutter. Now, think, is this safe to talk of here?"

Balbus sucked air like a winded war-horse. He massaged his quivering muscles until the waves of skin began to calm.

"Safe to t-talk about? It's in every marketplace. Read!"

Aulus bent over the parchment and followed the lines with his finger. He stopped midway and looked up.

"Yes," Balbus said. "The best of them for Little Caesar's use. Keep reading. There. 'This year's games will both amuse and serve the people by ridding them of those who dishonor our laws and gods.'" Balbus slapped the parchment. "'And gods,' it says. These games aren't just for malefactors."

"So the rumors are true." Aulus folded his thin arms on his chest. "After three centuries, the priests have found a Little Caesar willing to be their tool. The persecutions begin again."

"And they take the best of the young men and women for the palace," Balbus said. "They'll pick my daughter." Balbus clenched two fists the size of artillery shells.

"*Ma foi!*" Jacques exclaimed. "I can take it no longer. Vhat do zhey chatter about? Vhy does zhis big man shake his fist and slap zhe table like a crazed barbarian?"

Balbus spun. His eyebrows formed bushes in his forehead's wrinkles.

"Who are these?"

"We're friends," Nobody said. "Probably. And we may be brothers. Are you Christians?"

Balbus looked at Aulus. He made a sign on his chest, but Nobody couldn't see what it was. Aulus shook his head.

"He may be a spy."

Nobody growled. "Contrary to popular opinion, I'm not spying for anyone. Are you Christians?"

Aulus studied him. Finally, he nodded.

"There is no reason to deceive you. If you're a spy, then you've heard enough already to know what we are. We are Christians. I am the bishop."

Bishop. That was the ancient church's name for clergymen, before the Catholics stole it for their hierarchy.

"I am also a Christian," Nobody said.

Aulus slowly nodded. "I brought you in here to test your knowledge of our history and what happened after our knowledge of history ends. I believe that you are truly an Outsider, therefore I will also trust that you are a Christian."

Nobody held out his hand. "Well met, brothers."

"Poorly met for you," Balbus said. "This is a bad day to be a Christian in Vallis Deorum. Welcome to your death."

Chapter 13

Later that afternoon, Nobody and his men left the library with Balbus. The Christian Roman had invited them to meet his family and spend the night in his home, and Nobody had accepted. He wanted to see more of the valley, and as Balbus lived outside the city walls, this would be an excellent means of doing so.

"The streets are much quieter than this morning," Nobody said.

Balbus nodded. "Many people are watching the play in the theater." He pointed at a huge building on the right.

Nobody sniffed. Tinges of a very strange yet somewhat familiar smell were in the air. A thin streak of smoke rose out of the theater. A few citizens were exiting from the many portals, but they didn't look panicked.

"Balbus, is there a fire in there?"

Balbus eyed the smoke. "The play is almost over. That would be the final execution scene."

Nobody sniffed again. "But there's something about this smell. I know I've smelled it before. It's like—" he remembered.

It was the smell of burning flesh. It bonded to the air like on that long-ago day when Colonel Hayes sprayed Tremont's sailors with Greek fire and Nobody added the name 'outlaw' to his titles. The smell flashed his brain with images of burning palm trees and the memory of the touch of Liana's arm around his neck as he carried her to the bay.

"How do they reproduce that smell for the play?" Nobody asked.

Balbus frowned. "They burn a man."

Nobody stopped walking. He blinked. "They what?"

"They burn a man. It's a tragedy. The end of the play calls for a man to die, so they kill a criminal or a Dog."

"A dog?"

"Oh, that's what some of the slaves are called. They're descendants of parties who crossed our mountains in past centuries. They're darker than you."

Dark men from across the mountains? That could mean Eskimos. But—

"They actually burn a man for people's pleasure?" Nobody said.

"Yes."

Nobody simply couldn't believe it. Several of the citizens who had exited the theater had stopped to stare at him, so he picked one and strode up to him.

"What was burnt in there?"

The citizen goggled at him. "A man," he said.

The morning's meal of bread and grapes in Nobody's stomach made a leap at his throat. He grasped at the burning in his chest.

"You're saying that a man was burnt in there for your amusement?"

The man seemed to grow less afraid. "Yes, and he was a strange one, too. He was darker than almost any of the Dogs, and he wore the strangest clothes. Skins from some animal I've never seen before. It was a good show."

Nobody staggered away and grasped Balbus's arm. "I can't stand this place's death-stench. Take me somewhere clean."

As the horrible truth sank into his brain, Nobody realized something else. A dark man in strange clothes—the clothes of a strange animal—that could be an Eskimo in seal skins. The only Eskimo he knew about that might have entered Vallis Deorum was the angekok. If they had burned the angekok—what fate was in store for the *Miriam*'s sailors?

Outside the city gates, the road's tightly-fitting stone blocks turned into a layer of hard-packed gravel which clicked under Nobody's boots and scraped beneath Balbus's sandals. The ground on either side was covered with thick green grass, dotted by knolls of black rock. Stone fences crisscrossed the fields. Stone was more plenteous than wood, judging by the profusion of stone buildings and furniture in the city. Indeed, the only wood available was the spotted belts of trees on the lower slopes and the forest in the valley's north corner.

"Vhat are zhe prospects of leaving zhis accursed valley?" Jacques asked.

Nobody tried to stop thinking about what he had just seen.

"Our prospects?" he said. "Not sparkling. If that truly was the angekok, I might have been able to talk with him, and he would have told us what happened to the sailors."

"Vhere could zhey be?"

"I don't know. Maybe they're being saved for another play." Nobody struck his thigh. "Balbus, do you still have gladiator fights here?"

"They will be a part of the games at the festival."

"Who fights in them?"

Balbus shrugged. "Dogs, mainly. The slaves, I mean. There are some professional gladiators, and occasionally a love-mad young fellow will enter the arena to impress a girl."

Nobody nursed his right arm and glared at the gravel. If the sailors were hidden somewhere here in the valley, they might be being saved as fodder for the arena.

"Vhy is it," Jacques said, "zhat everyone we see looks at us as if ve vere knaves?"

"They're all lookin' at yer mustache," O'Malley said. "There's nothin' like it here. But I've been called many things worse than a knave. A Frinchman should be honored by sich a name. What say ye, Jack Frog? When I take ye back to the ould country and introduce ye tae the boys, I can say 'hallo, boys, forget the ould names ye called me by, I'm a knave noow. Call me Knave One, and little Jack here, call him Knave Two.'"

"I object," Jacques said. "Vhy vould *you* be Knave One? Zhat makes it seem zhat you are zhe leader, vhereas it is obvious zhat I am zhe more mentally capable."

O'Malley laughed. "Ye sure didn't look more mentally capable when they pulled that sack off yer hair the first night. Ye looked more like a fried rabbit's skin."

Jacques slapped his hair. "Vhy do you zhink I vant to leave, you *boeuf*? Only once have I been so disgraced, vhen a Cossack sat on me in Siberia. But I had zhe satisfaction of killing him."

"Aye, after I kicked him off ye an' gave ye back yer sword. But what aboot that little rascal as stole yer cap in Loondon and nearly got me whitewashed?"

Jacques yanked his mustache. This contemplation of past indignities wasn't to his taste.

After about fifteen minutes of walking they came to a low section of the road. A plume of steam rose from a pit on the right hand side. Natural hot springs? Water bubbled in the pit's depths. Balbus held up his hand.

"I must check the baby pit."

He disappeared into the steam. Nobody motioned his men to stay stationary and followed slowly, testing the ground ahead with one foot. He broke through the blanket of steam and found himself on a stub of rock surrounded by white. Balbus was leaning over a hole in this rock. He straightened as Nobody joined him, and something squeaked.

Balbus's hands cradled a naked baby.

The infant was half a foot shorter than a *gladius* blade, with shriveled arms, cracked lips, and tiny eyelids shut tightly. He hardly had the strength to mew faintly, like a kitten. Nobody gulped. His arms and legs felt like logs in the presence of this human speck.

"Where did he come from?" Nobody asked.

"This is another of my country's many sins." Balbus uncapped a flask and dripped milk into the baby's mouth. The infant gurgled, and a little white stream flowed down a corner of the dried lips onto Balbus's tunic. "Do the Outsiders also leave unwanted babies to die?"

"To die!" Nobody staggered.

The Romans were military geniuses, their architecture rivaled the best, every British schoolboy was taught their poetry and their greatness, but Nobody never dreamed that they were capable of the barbarism he had seen today.

"You can't mean it," Nobody said. "You're saying that this boy's parents put him there? His own mother would murder him?"

"The philosophers recommend it, the priests support it, and the rulers do it." Balbus shook his head. "We Christians save them as often as we can, and train them as our own children, which is another reason we are detested above all other religions."

Nobody shuddered. The Eskimos were right. Demons did live across those mountains.

"This poor babe is weak, but he seems healthy," Balbus said. "They're usually worse when we find them. You remember Bishop Aulus's son, the dwarf?"

Nobody nodded.

"He's not his son by blood. The bishop found him here. His mother tried to kill him before birth, but failed, so he was born with the twisted body you saw yesterday."

Balbus led the way back through the steam.

"The Romans see the body as perfection, so they look at him like they look at a flawed statue or a splotched painting, but we Christians see beauty in every life, because God made it."

Balbus carried the tiny thing in his cupped hands for miles, as they left the city behind them and eventually turned onto a smaller road. They approached a lonely house surrounded by pastures and vineyards. It was larger than the other houses they had passed, which Balbus explained by saying that he had a forge. That must be where his massive muscles came from.

"Does he make swords?" O'Malley asked.

Balbus said that he did, but only for the army.

"Tell him that I'm a soldier, Colonel," O'Malley said. "Leastways, I used tae be, and me fingers are yearnin' right noow fer the feel o' me hilt."

Balbus stopped walking. "What is that?" He pointed at his house.

A mass of bleating sheep huddled in the roadway before the house. Helmeted heads and sword blades waved above the wool. A woman screamed.

Balbus charged. Nobody raced behind him, his men's footsteps pounding in his ears. The sheep were either too tightly packed together or too stubborn to move, but Balbus dashed into the middle of them, bowling over several ewes and splitting a path between the rest.

Three soldiers stood in the street. An officer sauntered around the house corner holding a meat-bone to his mouth. On seeing Balbus he tossed it away and spat on the nearest sheep.

"Who are you?" the officer said. Nobody recognized that face. He knew without looking that a headful of short hair bristled beneath his helmet.

"What are you doing?" Balbus waved his arms. "You can't steal my sheep!"

Bristle Hair laughed. "How can a soldier steal? Stealing is against the law, and what we do *is* law. Your miserable beasts will have the honor of feeding Little Caesar and his courtiers at the festival."

"Officer!" A soldier's head stuck out of the house. "I think we've found something worth taking along with the sheep." He flashed a sly smile between his cheek-guards.

The gnarly veins in Balbus's bare arms bulged. He plunged through the sheep, but the frightened animals slowed him so much that Bristle Hair, who skirted the flock, reached the doorway first.

Nobody signaled his men to gather round. "Pick a soldier and saunter close. Try to occupy them with gestures, or something. Be friendly, but watch their swords. If you hear me shout, grab a sword and get to that house faster than Jacques can flip an egg."

O'Malley grinned. "Wi' pleasure, sir."

Nobody threaded the sheep and passed under the low doorway. The house held one wooden table, a hearth, and a few beds in the far corner. An open doorway on the right led into Balbus's smithy, where bars of iron lay on the forge. Behind the table stood a matronly woman, a red-haired young man of maybe twenty-one or twenty-two years, and a beautiful young woman with dark hair and greenish eyes which were round with terror.

The soldier who had stuck his head out the door jerked his thumb at the girl. "I say she'd make a good slave, eh?"

Bristle Hair grinned. "Maybe this sheep-raid won't be as boring as usual." He shoved Balbus behind the table with the rest of his family and grabbed the girl's arm.

The young man slapped Bristle Hair's hand away. The other soldier leveled his sword at the young man's throat.

"He's a nice strong one," Bristle Hair said. He looked at Balbus. "I doubt you want to dig his grave."

Bristle Hair slowly extended his hand and gripped the girl's arm again. The young man trembled, but the sword blade was between him and the officer. Balbus stood at the end of the table, his hands clutching the edge, his muscles quivering.

"P-please, you c-can't do this," he said.

Bristle Hair twirled the girl from behind the table and pinioned her elbows with his right arm. He bowed to Balbus.

"We appreciate your service to the country."

"Father!" The young man jerked forward but was stopped by the prick of the sword at his neck. He ground his teeth. "If my brother were here he would never let this happen."

"Unhand her."

Everyone in the room gaped at the doorway where Nobody stood with his arms crossed, his jaw set, and his mind resolved.

"I've had enough of your bloody and perverted ways," Nobody said. "Take your hands off that girl, pack up your miserable flock of stolen sheep, and get back to that blood-dripping city you love so much."

Bristle Hair laughed. "Why, it's the warrior boy who taught us the best way to fall down a hill. I'm surprised you found enough strength in your legs to walk out here."

"You probably haven't heard of a word called 'chivalry,' but I'll tell you about it. It's a concept from the Bible, where men war to *protect* women, and nobility is judged by justice, gentleness, and courage, not the circumference of your muscles." Nobody returned Bristle Hair's impudent stare with hard eyes. "Take your hands off her."

"Or . . . what?" Bristle Hair twirled a strand of the girl's hair around his finger.

Nobody swallowed. Tinges of the fighting fury crept through his bones.

"Don't tempt me, Roman," he said.

"Ha. You know what I despise about you? Not only are you a weakling, but you talk as if you could do something. You can't, boy. You're helpless. As helpless as this girl."

Nobody unfolded his arms, but even this gave his right shoulder a twinge. In days past, he spoke hard so that he didn't have to follow his words with actions. Now, this Roman hound was right. There wasn't anything behind his words.

"Out of the way, boy," Bristle Hair said. "It's a profitable day—now we march to the palace to enjoy our rewards."

Nobody smiled. He might be helpless himself, but God was never helpless, and God had given him three men with loyal hearts and shoulders that didn't throb at the thought of a sword.

"The 42nd!" Nobody called.

The Romans looked at each other. Outside, shouts interrupted the bleating and footsteps crunched toward the door. Nobody stepped aside to let in Jacques, O'Malley, and Matthew, each with a newly acquired *gladius* in his fist.

The Romans blinked.

"Don't be too ashamed," Nobody said. "You're in good company. We English have a knack for surprising our enemies. Just ask the French."

Bristle Hair let the girl go and charged with the second soldier at his heels. The doorway darkened with the bodies of the other three soldiers, who must have recovered from their surprise.

Nobody dodged Bristle Hair's first blow. "O'Malley, take the door—you others take these."

"But sir," O'Malley said, blocking the door and slashing at the first soldier. "I've a wish tae take the big one meself."

"No fear," Jacques said, "I vill cut him down to size."

Steel scraped steel.

"Don't kill them," Nobody said. "We can't risk it yet."

He hustled the girl back to her mother's side and turned to Balbus, who was watching the fight with open-mouthed wonder.

"Do you have rope?" Nobody asked.

Balbus waved a limp hand at the forge.

Nobody pointed. "Girl, get the rope. You—" he tossed a staff into the young man's hands. "Knock those fellows down from behind."

Balbus broke from his trance. "Stop! Y-you c-can't fight soldiers. They're— soldiers. Th-they're the law."

Nobody smiled bitterly. "No fear. I have practice fighting governments. Now, knock those fellows down."

"No!" Balbus grabbed his son's arm. "We c-can't resist Little Caesar. If we d-do, he'll have us up to his t-torture ch-chambers."

The girl was back with a coil of rope.

"Balbus," Nobody said, "if you don't resist, then your daughter becomes a slave of those monsters, and how do you think she'll fare then? The threat of future horror can't delay present duty."

The young man dashed into the fray and felled the Romans with one blow each. He had good form. O'Malley had already decked one of his men with his hilt, and he now stepped back, letting the two remaining soldiers inside. Jacques and Matthew overpowered them and pinioned them against the wall while O'Malley and Balbus's son bound them with the rope.

"These fools have niver fought fer their lives before," O'Malley said. "Some o' the bloows they tried—ye'd think they learned how tae fight from the plays."

Balbus shook so hard that the plates on the table he was holding rattled.

"Wh-what do we do now?"

Yes, that was the question of the hour. Nobody looked at his empty hands and tried to fight the feeling of helplessness. It was his fault that his men were outlaws—it was his fault that Edmund lay in prison, awaiting hanging—it was all his fault, and he couldn't even use a sword in his own defense. He—Colonel Nobody—had to channel his fighting fury into terse orders to men who had strength enough to clang steel on steel. *Oh God, help me!*

Nobody looked at the glowering soldiers pinioned against the wall and echoed Balbus's question in his brain. What was he to do now? Little Caesar liked him momentarily because he wasn't a foot-licking flatterer, and because he could talk about the Outside, but the tyrant's appreciation of the novelty probably wouldn't extend to pardoning Nobody for trussing up his Praetorian Guard.

What would Edmund say? 'Diplomacy—drop the fighting colonel bit and try the ambassador.' Yes, he would probably say something like that.

Nobody knelt next to Bristle Hair. "We'll say that was the first part of the maneuvers I'm supposed to teach you."

Bristle Hair spat a warm glob onto Nobody's cheek. Nobody's fist clenched automatically, but he forced the fingers to un-tense. 'Turn the other cheek,' Christ said in Matthew. That was a hard command for a soldier to swallow, and one which Nobody had little practiced. He wiped the spittle off with his sleeve.

"Look, Roman, both of us want something the other can give. I don't want this girl going to the palace as a slave, and I don't want Little Caesar knowing that I've tied you fellows up. You want your freedom, and you also don't want Little Caesar knowing that you've been tied up, as it doesn't speak highly for your fighting abilities."

Bristle Hair growled.

That probably wasn't the best tack to use. Nobody tried a conciliatory tone.

"Let's think about this like reasonable soldiers. I'll release you and not say a word about what happened here if you don't bother the girl and also remain silent. Agreed?"

Bristle Hair looked at his bound hands, then at his men. Their faces were sour, but hopeful.

"Why should I believe you will keep your word?" Bristle Hair asked.

"Because it's in my best interest."

Bristle Hair held out his hands.

O'Malley slipped a knife from his boot and handed it to Nobody, who sliced the captives' ropes.

"You're coming to the palace with us," Bristle Hair said as he stood up and rubbed his arms. "Little Caesar has been asking for you. And as for you—" he sneered at Balbus's family. "You haven't gained anything. You had better be at the festival next week, and when Little Caesar chooses the best for his palace I'll make sure he sees your girl."

"I will accompany you in five minutes," Nobody said. He waited for the soldiers to stalk out of the house and turned to Balbus. "What were you doing? Your duty is to protect your family."

"But—we're to honor our leaders," Balbus said. "It's against the law to resist soldiers."

Balbus's son glared at the closed door. "When the state is god it defies liberty."

"When the state is god it *defines* liberty," Nobody said. "Look, Balbus. We're to give to Caesar what is Caesar's, and to God, what is God's. Your family is not Caesar's. Now, I've just risked my life and the lives of my men for you, and my trials aren't over yet. You'd best wear a sword from now on if you value your family."

Balbus bowed his head. "Citizens aren't allowed to own swords. Only soldiers are. And I *have* resisted before." He raised his head and met Nobody's eyes. "I had two sons and two daughters before last festival. My son—not this one, but his brother—did resist, and what happened? He's either dead, or, what's worse, in the mines, and my daughter was taken all the same."

An angry shout came from outside.

"I must go," Nobody said. "I will pray for you, and I ask your prayers for me. We all have much to fear from this coming festival."

Chapter 14

"So much for an exciting trip," Chester said.

Lawrence dug his paddle into the water and smiled. Chester would have been content if a family of polar bears had attacked them, or a water dragon had popped its head out of the fjord and invited them for lunch. As it was, the trip had been beautiful, uneventful, and an unspeakably pleasant change from London's hot ballrooms.

"I signed on to rescue a missing colonel, not take a holiday." Chester glared at the steep cliff on their left as if he blamed it for not trying to fall on him.

"I," Pacarina said, "have thoroughly enjoyed our trip. It's colder than Peru, but I don't mind that, and it's wonderful to be together and exploring again, just the three of us."

Chester grunted. "What do you call them?" He pointed at the three Eskimo guides who led the way in kayaks.

"They hardly speak English, so it's as if there are only three of us. Besides, I think holidays are nice. Don't you enjoy our company, Brother?" Pacarina grinned at Chester.

"At least you're not as bad as you used to be. I about gave up hope for Law after he married you. Love-struck? Why, Love used a sledgehammer on the

Professor. People expect us jolly fellows to get a bit dolly-eyed around the wedding time, but I think it's the dull quiet ones that get bit the worst."

"Oh?" Pacarina said. "And you say he loves me less than when he first married me?"

"No, he doesn't love you less—probably more, actually—but he also realizes that there's a world out there populated by additional human beings."

Lawrence coughed. "I think this would be an excellent time to adjust the topic. Do the Eskimos seem agitated to you?"

"Hmm. They do look rather as if a colony of crabs were playing hopscotch in their trousers."

The guides were jerking their bodies and pointing to the shore ahead with every evidence of uneasy consciences or unsettled stomachs. The boats were just rounding a bend in the fjord and heading toward an unusually low shore which sloped into a mighty mountain range.

"Take us in, good fellows," Chester said, pointing ahead.

The Eskimos shook their heads and stopped paddling. Although Lawrence had made excellent progress in studying the foundations of the Eskimo language, he wasn't proficient enough to really speak or understand, so the conversation was limited to gestures. The Eskimos did not spare these, but chopped the air with such a flurry of hand motions that it was obvious they were in mortal terror of the mountain.

"I say," Chester said, "there's a boat on shore there. Do you think this could be the spot our no-named friend was heading for?"

Lawrence nodded. "I think we take to the land from here, and I also think this is where we bid adieu to our Eskimo friends."

Lawrence called their guides in for a last payment of iron and sent them skimming back down the fjord. The shoreline was dotted by a number of bumps, which, as Lawrence's boat approached, turned out to be a kayak, an umiak, a regular ship's boat, and several wooden trunks.

Chester splashed into water up to his boot tops and sloshed ashore to take Pacarina, who Lawrence handed over the bow. The boats and trunks were deserted, and there were no tracks in the vicinity. Chester knelt next to one of the trunks and rattled the padlock.

"I'd say this is one of the soldiers' trunks," Chester said. "There used to be a mark down here on the bottom right corner, but it's been burned and shaved off. Was probably 'forty-two,' which was the number of their regiment, but they didn't want to be found out when they were hiding." He banged the padlock against the wood.

"That's not our trunk," Lawrence said.

"You always were an observant chap, Professor. But—" Chester searched inside his waistcoat for eight seconds and produced a thin metal strip. "If I'd known there were many locks in Greenland I would have stowed my jemmy in a more convenient spot." He jiggled the metal in the lock until the padlock clicked open.

"Chester," Lawrence said, "you're breaking into another man's property."

"In a way, yes, and under normal circumstances I wouldn't do it. But it's a little like found property, and anyway, I need to make sure that we really are following the right fellow." Chester held up a scarlet uniform with epaulettes. "And, we are. Now we're ready for some mountain-climbing. Are you sure you can manage it, Pacarina?"

Pacarina wrapped her capelet around her shoulders and grinned.

"I won't be huffing the worst of we three when we get up there."

Chapter 15

Loud laughter and the clinking of cups attested that the feast in the throne room had already begun. Nobody paused before the door-curtain in the hallway and listened. Little Caesar's whiny voice piped over the other sounds, complaining that his wine tasted strange. The soldier guarding the doorway stood motionless with his eyes focused on the near-distance and his right hand on his *gladius* hilt.

Nobody drew a deep breath and pushed through the curtain.

"Why, it's our bold young Outsider," Little Caesar shouted. "Come, join us."

Little Caesar's face was pocked with sweat, his eyes were hungry, and his toga was already spotted with wine. Outside, the night-chill had begun to bite, but the throne room was unpleasantly warm from five fires in hearths along the wall facing the dais. They looked dangerously close to the thick fleece that carpeted the floor, but no doubt the sweaty slaves tending them would smother any sparks.

"Now you will have a true chance to test my hospitality," Little Caesar said. He motioned Nobody to an empty couch close by the dais. "Tonight we have a party."

"What is the occasion, Little Caesar?" Nobody asked. He tried to keep his face from frowning as he laid down to eat. It felt slovenly.

"The occasion? Hmm, yes, why do we feast?" Little Caesar looked at a cringing slave girl who hovered next to his couch with a fan.

It was Ennia. "You—the party is in honor—" her eyes roved the room. "It is in honor of the stranger, my lord."

"Ah, yes, good thought." Little Caesar raised his goblet to Nobody. "We drink to you, strange stranger."

A slave leaned over Nobody's couch and poured a goblet of wine large enough to drown a cat in. The footsteps of dancers from Little Caesar's harem beat a steady accompaniment to harps and drums sounded by unseen players.

"Drink, young speaker of bold words," Little Caesar said. "I want to see how the Outsiders act when Bacchus unlooses their tongues and frees their heads."

This was what Nobody had feared. The first test was come.

"Thank you, Little Caesar, but I'm not very thirsty at the moment."

Nobody bit into a strip of dried lamb. Now that he thought of it, he hadn't eaten since early morning, and even that was a meager meal. Had that really been today? Each event, from the horrid play, to the baby pit, to the fight in Balbus's house, seemed like its own day.

"Drink, boy." Little Caesar pointed to Nobody's goblet. "You look too serious. I don't like it. Drink away your cares and float away to Elysium."

Judging by the amount of sweat pouring down Little Caesar's head and shoulders, he had already begun floating. However, that was a voyage in which Nobody would not join.

"No, thank you," Nobody said. He bit into another piece of lamb.

Little Caesar slammed his goblet on the table. Conversation ceased.

"You will do what I say! Drink until you vomit."

"I'm sorry, but I don't drink wine, either here or in the Outside."

Little Caesar blinked. "You don't drink wine?" He acted as if Nobody had said that men don't breathe, or women don't cry.

"It's a matter of personal conviction," Nobody said. He almost added 'if you know what that means,' but thought better of it. "I think drunkenness is a sin, and I don't drink wine at all so as to not present a temptation."

Nobody might as well have been speaking English. Little Caesar blinked some more, and rubbed his balding head, then apparently remembered that his order had been refused.

"I don't care what you want, boy. You will drink my wine until you laugh louder than—than Junius."

One of the courtiers, a stripling with plucked eyebrows who was evidently the one called Junius, giggled like a girl and buried his mouth in a goblet. *God must have a sense of humor*, Nobody thought. *I get chided for being tight-vested in 19th century England, and now I'm plopped in the middle of an Ancient Roman feast run by a fellow who wants to be Nero.*

"Little Caesar," Nobody said, "I respect your authority as ruler of this country, but that doesn't give you the privilege of dictating my eating and drinking habits. I'm not drinking your wine."

Little Caesar snapped his fingers at the guards. "Pour it down his throat until I tell you to stop."

"My lord!" Ennia was on her knees next to Little Caesar's couch. "Please, show him mercy. He is not used to our ways."

Little Caesar knocked her into the carpet and leaned back on his couch, waiting for the show.

Nobody didn't wait. He sprang off his couch and landed mid-boot in the carpet. Two of the Praetorian Guard flexed their muscles while a third took a tight-mouthed wineskin from the table and untied the cords that bound it shut. Nobody opened his mouth to shout for the 42nd—but what was the use? Jacques was somewhere in the bowels of the palace arguing with the cooks about how to cook mutton, O'Malley was with him in case the cooks got angry, and Matthew was probably brooding in his room. A yell wouldn't get far past the curtains.

Nobody struck at the first man with his left arm but the guard caught the blow and dragged him down. Guards pounced from all directions and crumpled him into the carpet. They stretched his arms out, sat on his legs, and pulled his head back until his jawbones popped and the nerves in his shoulders crunched like springs.

"Drink to Bacchus!" Little Caesar said.

A wave of bitter wine submerged Nobody's mouth. He tried to close his throat, but a hand gripped his Adam's apple and he swallowed convulsively. After that he couldn't stop the flow. The liquid burned his chest and seeped into his fingertips and toes. His thoughts muddled. His sight blurred—Little Caesar was a big blob of white with a pumpkiny head.

"You won't obey me, eh?"

The words were from far away, like an echo down a long tunnel. Nobody's stomach curdled, his innards groaned, his legs were iron logs, he felt that his soul would retch. Instead, his stomach retched, and the weight left his legs as guards flung themselves right and left.

"I say—we're not here to rescue *that*, are we?"

The voice was strange. It spoke English. Good English. Natural English. Nobody gazed up through the fog at a pair of trousers and a waistcoat.

Chapter 16

Lawrence rubbed the sweat line beneath his neckerchief. Two of the five roaring fires would have heated this room nicely.

He was still recovering from the shock of being captured at sword-point by a soldier with armor and weaponry dating to the first century A.D. The obvious path up the mountain had terminated in a tunnel showing signs of water erosion, and on passing through the tunnel they had met the soldiers. Chester had almost gotten his knife into one of them, but he was knocked down from behind. Then they had marched, dreamlike, down the slopes of this fertile valley, up a mass of rock, and into this pen case of a palace.

"That's beastly," Chester said.

He pointed to the body of a man lying next to a slave girl on the fleecy carpet. Its face was barely visible through the fleece and vomit, but the clothes were unmistakably English. He looked young. And Lawrence was looking for a young Englishman.

"You don't think that's Colonel Nobody, do you?" Lawrence asked Chester.

"I very much hope we haven't sailed across the ocean, gotten manhandled by a costume party, and been dragged into this masque just to rescue *that* drunk. But then again, there isn't exactly a surfeit of Englishmen around."

A fat man in a toga half-rose from his couch and pointed at Lawrence, Chester, and Pacarina. He said something in a strange language. And yet—the language really wasn't so strange. Lawrence had conversed with his tutor in this language for hours. It was no dream. He really was standing in a Latin-speaking Roman settlement.

"Greetings, Caesar," Lawrence said in Latin.

The fat man's jaw fell. So did Chester's.

"Law!" Chester said. "It's impossible—how on earth can you know this fellow's language?"

"It's Latin."

"Latin? But—" Chester threw up his hands. "I give up. When we were in Spanish-speaking Peru I said that we'd never again go somewhere where you knew the language and I didn't. So what do we do? We take a trip back to Ancient Rome."

"Who are you?" the fat man asked. "Do you know this boy?"

"Possibly, Caesar," Lawrence said. "We happened upon your country in search of a countryman of ours, but I can't quite tell if this is the one."

"I am Little Caesar," the fat man said. "Wipe off his face."

A slave wiped the Englishman's face and revealed skin so ghastly white that a crisscross of tiny scars which would usually be invisible showed red against the skin. His eyelids were half shut, and his breath came in pants.

"He enjoys my hospitality," Little Caesar said. "Perhaps he should have had a little less wine though, eh? Is this the man you're looking for?"

"That depends," Lawrence said. "What is his name?"

"He doesn't have one. Not a real one." Little Caesar gurgled his wine. "He said his name was nothing."

"Colonel Nobody," Lawrence said.

The figure gasped something that was gibberish, but it was English gibberish.

"That's our man," Lawrence said.

"Then why—" Little Caesar slammed his goblet on the table and staggered to his feet. "Why are you here? Am I a Caesar, or do you think I run a *caupona* for all wandering Outsiders to come and eat my scraps?"

"A *caupona*? Excellent!" Lawrence rubbed his hands. "The historians are so conflicted. Is a *caupona* just a kind of tavern for people of ill-repute, or, as I think, does it really serve as a lodging-place for the higher classes as well?"

Little Caesar rubbed his eyes.

"Stand the boy before me!"

Guards hoisted Colonel Nobody onto his feet and held him there.

"Liar," Little Caesar said, "you told me that no one was following you! You said you were alone. You said that you weren't spies. What are these?" He pointed at Lawrence. "They talk your language and wear your clothes. You lied to me, and for your lies you will die. Now, I just have to decide how to kill you."

His courtiers were full of suggestions, each more horrible than the last. Lawrence felt himself paling. At last, Little Caesar raised his hand and stopped the flow of barbarities.

"Nay, we shouldn't be selfish with him, should we? Of course not. He will die long and slow, but he will be an example to all my subjects, for he will die at the festival!"

"What's it all about?" Chester whispered.

Lawrence gripped Pacarina's hand. "We're brilliant, Chester, just brilliant. We're the colonel's death-warrant."

Colonel Nobody seemed little affected by his fate, but he might have been too drunk, or just too dazed, to understand. His right hand fluttered by his hip, and his chin drooped to his left clavicle—what Chester called the 'collarbone'—but that was all.

"But," said a courtier with disgusting eyebrows, "why let him slurp my lord's wine and gnaw his sheep? Let him work his lies away in the mines until the festival."

The rest of the courtiers shouted their approval.

"Then take him to the mines, and take that slave girl with him. Begone, all of you." Little Caesar wiped his sweaty forehead on the back of his hand. "What's that abominable stamping noise? Whip them out."

A pair of guards whipped a stream of dancing girls out of the corner and into the hallway, much to the merriment of the courtiers. Chester's hot breath tickled Lawrence's ear.

"I've never seen a pig I wanted to knock down more," Chester said. "Banastre Bronner is a prude compared to this beast."

Lawrence agreed, but didn't translate. Perhaps it was God's blessing that He kept sending them to lands where Lawrence was the only one of them who could communicate.

"Wait!" Little Caesar held up his hand. "What is this?" He pointed at Pacarina.

Lawrence swung his arm around Pacarina's waist and pulled her to his side.

"This is my *wife*."

Little Caesar shook his head. "She looks like a queen."

"Yes, she does, and I'm her king."

Lawrence felt a tremor pulse through Pacarina. She couldn't understand the words, but a woman with far less sense than Pacarina could read the look in Little Caesar's eyes.

"Yes," Little Caesar said. "Yes, I think so. I need a new consort. I've been married too long now, how long? A month! Yes, I'll have a divorce and wed this strange beauty on the second day of the festival. Ah, but this will be the best festival in history!"

Lawrence tried to control his voice. "I don't think you understand. This is my wife. We're married. She's not available."

Little Caesar shrugged. "Then I'll have you divorced too. Guards, take her away. I don't care about the men—but no, they must be worthy to be related to that beauty. I still want to hear more of the Outside. Send them into the city for now."

Lawrence nodded at Chester.

"If you've managed to keep any knives hidden, now is the time to use them."

Chester ripped his cuffs and, reaching up one arm after the other, produced two eight-inch knives. Lawrence and he swung back to back, with Pacarina between them, and faced a crowd of startled guards. Colonel Nobody gave a kind of hollow laugh.

Little Caesar giggled. "You Outsiders are strange people. Any Roman would bow down in gratitude at the honor I bestow on your wife, and here you pull knives which you sneaked past my guards." He frowned at his guards. "Nonsense, I'll give you both new wives, and you'll forget all about this one."

"Lawrence," Pacarina said, "what's happening?"

"I'm afraid, Dear, that I'm not going to live long enough to give you children." Lawrence kissed her forehead. "I love you."

The guards rushed. Lawrence tried to remember Chester's lessons, tried to keep the knife firmly in his hand, point raised, ready to slash or stab, his left hand guarding his heart and throat, but a blow swung under his guard and sent him gasping to the floor. His lungs groped for the breath that would not come. A sack imprisoned his head and cords bound round his wrists and ankles.

"A Stoning! A Stoning!" Chester shouted.

His battle lasted a minute longer, but what could one man with a knife, even Chester, do against a dozen armored guards? Two separate roars vouched for chinks in the armor, but such an unequal contest couldn't last long. Breastplates clashed, Chester's war cry became a muffled groan, and the thuds ceased.

Pacarina gripped Lawrence, and the cold touch of her fingertips was the last thing he felt as the guards dragged him away.

Chapter 17

"We're going to save her, but we can't simply march back up that rock and say 'Give her up or die.'" Chester wrenched a handful of lettuce from the head in front of him. "Believe me, I'd like to, but they have this annoying little thing called 'overwhelming force.'"

"Chester, I'm going to save my wife!"

"Yes, of course you are, but this isn't the way." Chester gestured with a fistful of lettuce. "Law, this isn't how it's supposed to be. I'm supposed to be the excited, irrational, erratic one, and you're supposed to be the level-headed one thinking up a plan for me to execute. I'm comfortable there. Can't we go back to it?"

Lawrence's teeth ached from clenching. "I can't bear to think of Pacarina in that filthy villain's house."

"Then don't think about it. Think about the best way to get her *out* of that filthy villain's house."

Lawrence bowed his head. He eased his teeth apart and let his baked breath flow over the table. It felt good to breathe new air, to feel the stomach muscles relax slightly. He uncurled his fists and laid his fingers on the table, straightening each aching joint on the wood.

Chester was right. He must think. He must plan. Lawrence rested his head in his hands. An adventure had become a nightmare faster than ink dries.

Footsteps clumped in the hallway.

"Helloo?" said an unmistakably Irish voice. "Is there anyboody as speaks English here?"

Chester was at the door in a moment. "Thank God! A voice of sanity in a land forlorn."

He let in a tall, red-haired soldier, a short, bewhiskered soldier, and a third man with the same soldierly bearing but a somewhat shadowier face. The third man stopped in the doorway and stared at Chester and Lawrence.

"Twins!"

"Yes," Chester said. "We've been that way for quite a number of years now."

The man sat at the table and folded his arms without another word.

The room was an excellent example of Roman architecture, although Lawrence noticed a few small points that had changed over the centuries. This was the first time that he had forced himself into enough presence of mind to really notice his surroundings. The night before, he and Chester had been dropped like dead cows in front of a library and left by their guard, who said something about that being the place they left the 'last ones.' The head librarian came out, cut their bonds, and gave them food and beds.

Any other morning, Lawrence's conversation with the librarian would have been fascinating. He was a Christian bishop and one of the leading historians of Vallis Deorum, with a long account of how the colony originated and grew. Yes, any other morning it would have been fascinating, but this morning Lawrence only listened to find some Roman weakness he could exploit to rescue Pacarina. There were plenty of weaknesses, but only the type that made Pacarina's danger more horrible.

"Aye, but it's a fine mess ye look-alikes have gotten us intae," the Irishman said. "Which o' ye thought oop the brilliant plan o' marchin' in here and playin' hangman fer our colonel?"

"We came to help your colonel," Chester said. "The gents back home figured that you fellows were making rowboats out of icebergs or playing tag with the Eskimos. You need to get your witnesses back to the queen before it's too late."

The little man tapped the table. "Too late for vhat?"

"Too late to save your colonel's friend. That's one of the reasons Lord Bronner sent us down here, to let Colonel No-name know that there's an ultimatum."

The Frenchman's mustache twitched. "His name is Colonel No*body*."

"No-body, No-thing, No-spine. I don't care what you call your drunken colonel, but I wish he were No-live right now, because trying to help him has gotten the best girl on earth into the hands of a Roman pig named Little Caesar."

"How dare you call my colonel a drunk?" The Frenchman bounded from his seat.

The Irishman grabbed his comrade by the neck-scruff and pulled him back into his chair.

"What aboot this ultimatum, young sir?"

Chester shrugged.

"Banastre Bronner has been using every gambling debt and love secret he knows about to get the queen's advisers ramming her about justice and the need to establish a precedent of firmness." Chester shook his head. "If you fellows don't get back to England with your witnesses by that date—" he laid a copy of the queen's order on the table, "—your lieutenant-colonel is going to dance the gallows jig."

The Irishman grasped the paper. "But that's too soon. We've hardly enough time fer the voyage."

"Hence our presence," Chester said. "Now all we need to do is break your no-name colonel out of his mine (presuming he's sober), get my brother's wife out of the palace, hail a convenient whaler, and sail home with your witnesses."

"But, we haven't found the sailors yet."

"Oh, splendid, then we'll add them to the list." Chester shredded a leaf of lettuce with his front teeth. "I say, what *have* you fellows been doing here?"

"Quiet, Chester," Lawrence said. "I think we had better officially meet our new friends."

"Patrick O'Malley," the Irishman said. "This here is Jack Frog—"

"Jacques Lefebvre," the Frenchman said.

"—and Matthew Preston." O'Malley pointed to the third man, who had thick jaws, a squarish face, and dark circles beneath his eyes. "We're Squad One—a part o' it, anyways—what used tae be the best squad in the best regiment in the whole Inglish army in Siberia. The squad left wi' Colonel Nobody, and since then we've been the on'y men as stayed true tae him."

"I'm sorry," Lawrence said, "but I can't say that I see the reason for such personal attachment after last night's exhibition."

O'Malley's eyebrows pinched together.

"We heard aboot that this mornin'. I thought aboot squeezin' some throats in the palace, but it wouldn't have helped the colonel any. Little Caesar, he's discovered that Jack can make some mighty tasty dishes, and Jack has 'em thinkin' that Matthew and I are his helpers, so that's why we haven't been executed. We're supposed to be oot noow finding some special ingredients, but I doon't plan on going back."

"Vhat you saw last night vas not our true colonel," Jacques said. "Colonel Nobody does not drink zhe fruit of zhe vine, but zhat *boeuf* of a Caesar forced it down his zhroat."

"Arrah!" O'Malley said. "How dare ye call him the same thing as ye call me? Call him a pig, if ye want, call him a Frinchman—well, maybe that's a bit too far—but doon't call him a boof."

Chester tapped his elbows on the table. "Much as I'm amused by your international bantering, I think we're forgetting the point of this tête-à-tête. Last night may have been your colonel's first time three sheets to the wind, but I saw his face. There was an awful lot more than a few too many wineskins happening there."

O'Malley looked at Jacques. Jacques looked at O'Malley. O'Malley coughed.

"I'm afraid he's been having a rayther hard time o' it these past months. He hasn't looked what I'd call well since the lieutenant-colonel was captured in Loondon."

Chester nodded. "What did Shakespeare say, Law? 'How soon my sorrow hath destroyed my face'?"

Matthew Preston's chair clattered behind him. "Twins! Poetry!" His eyes glared red inside dark circles. "Will it never end?"

Lawrence sat, stunned, while the angry steps faded down the hall.

O'Malley shook his head. "Colonel Nobody isn't the only one as has been taking things hard."

"I vill explain," Jacques said. "Zhis is a subject too sensitive for an Irishman to say rightly. Listen, young sirs, and I vill try to straighten zhe tangles. You haf no doubt read of how it vas zhat Colonel Nobody resisted zhe queen's officers, to save zhe Lady Liana's honor?"

Lawrence nodded.

"Vell, it vas during zhat last battle zhat Mark vas vounded. You see, Matthew is a tvin—he vas a tvin, I mean."

"That's 'twin,'" O'Malley said. "With a double-u."

"Zhey vere zhe closest brohzers I haf ever seen. Ve called zhem zhe 'rhymers,' because zhey alvays rhymed each ohzer's vords. Poetry, you see."

"We also called them the 'apostles,'" O'Malley said. "Them being named Matthew and Mark, and all."

Jacques tapped his forehead. "Mark vas vounded in zhe head during zhe fighting, but zhere vas only a little trickle of blood, so ve did not zhink it vas serious. But he did not act right. He complained zhat his head vas aching, and he did strange zhings. Ve zhought he vas joking, but he vould not stop. He vandered zhe ship-decks at night. He muttered."

"He was probably experiencing internal bleeding," Lawrence said. "A blow to the head is very serious."

O'Malley stared at the table. Jacques fiddled with a lettuce leaf.

"Zhe end vas on a Sunday. Ve had just finished prayers vhen Mark seemed to go mad. He zhought ve vere trying to hurt Colonel Nobody. He found a knife and attacked Matthew, so Matthew knocked him down before anyone could be hurt. Poor Mark hit his head upon zhe deck, and zhat began zhe end. He died in zhe arms of Matthew five hours later."

Chester looked at Lawrence as if to say that this was a rum lot.

"I'm awfully sorry," Chester said. He shook his head. "When I signed on for this scheme I didn't know we'd have to play wet-nurses. I suppose that explains our departed friend's red eyes, but what about your colonel? What are his other sorrows?"

"The colonel doesn't like being talked aboot," O'Malley said. "He's the only man famous because no one knoows anythin' aboot him."

Another day, Lawrence would have commiserated more wholeheartedly with these soldiers' sorrows, but the thought of Pacarina in Little Caesar's hands didn't leave much room for anything else. He forced himself to focus on the soldiers. Knowledge is power, and to survive this strange world he would need every ounce of power he could muster.

"I appreciate your reticence regarding your colonel's private affairs, but I don't think it's unreasonable to request a complete understanding of the present situation. I know you didn't ask us to come, and I'm genuinely sorry for the trouble our presence has already caused, but since we're here, we need to work together."

O'Malley raked his bright red hair and glanced at Jacques. "Ye're not getting a word out o' us aboot the colonel's past, but ye shouldn't be offended by that. We doon't knoow it, not much of it. Why, even Lieutenant-Colonel Burke doon't knoow who he really is. But we can talk aboot his present, can't we, Jack?"

"It is simple. Zhe colonel vas shot in the arm by General Tremont in zhe same fight zhat Mark Preston vas vounded. Ve had no doctor, so ve gave him to zhe man who knew most about vounds, and zhat vas Matthew. Matthew tried very hard, but he is no doctor, and he did somezhing vrong. Zhe colonel's arm never truly healed, and he cannot use it for varfare. So zhe colonel is learning zhat he cannot fight, and every time he does, Matthew remembers zhat it is his fault."

Chester whistled. "I sure found us a jolly lot of chaps to help out."

The door opened and Bishop Aulus's face poked in. "I have bad news."

Chapter 18

"Bad news?" Chester said, after Lawrence interpreted Bishop Aulus's words. "He's come to the right place. We're about as cheerful as a Quaker mourning party."

Bishop Aulus motioned for silence. His eyes squinted slightly, maybe from concentration, maybe from poor eyesight, maybe from fear.

"There is a crowd in the street," he said. "They are becoming violent. Joktan has closed the doors."

"What do they want?" Lawrence asked.

"You. I believe the priests have stirred them."

"Why would they do that?"

Bishop Aulus pushed past Matthew's fallen chair and spread the five fingers of his right hand on the table.

"Vallis Deorum has five classes. The government and its soldiers, priests, Christians, the natives, which most call Dogs, and everyone else. The government and soldiers want power and pleasure. The priests want power. Sometimes they share the power, sometimes they fight for it. We Christians want to honor God and worship Him in peace, which threatens both government and priests, because we worship the one God above everything else."

"Who are these natives?" Lawrence asked.

Bishop Aulus shrugged. "In centuries past, men have come over the mountains and been captured. The Dogs are their descendants, lower than slaves, fodder for the games, soldiers, and mines."

"Sounds like a ripe lot for a *coup de grâce*," Chester said.

"You mean a *coup d'état*," Lawrence said.

"Please!" Bishop Aulus held up his hand. "We do not have much time. Any Outsider threatens the priests' teaching. They can't harm you openly because of Little Caesar, but a mob has no face. They would also like to destroy my library, because knowledge shakes their hold on the people."

The hollow clatter of fists on wood fractured the library's silence. Joktan, the dwarfish son of Bishop Aulus, shuffled into the room.

"They beat on the door," he said.

Chester jumped up. "I move that we adjourn this meeting. Ask the bishop if he has any back exits."

"The crowd surrounds us," Joktan answered Lawrence.

Chester grinned. "Then we'll have to make a fight of it. 'Pacarina' is the war cry of the day, boys. Where do they keep their swords?"

Bishop Aulus's eyebrows jumped as Lawrence asked.

"Only the soldiers are allowed swords," he said.

"Only the soldiers, he says?" Chester clenched his right fist and rubbed his left thumb over the plane between his first and second knuckles. "Then the crowd isn't as dangerous as I expected. I hope you don't think bare knuckle sports are too ungentlemanly, Law."

Bishop Aulus shook his head before Lawrence could translate. Chester's gestures were fluent.

"The crowd is sure to have swords," Bishop Aulus said. "The criminals hide them beneath their cloaks."

"That's a brilliant arrangement," Chester said. "Keep them from the good fellows so the bad ones can sneak them." He inspected his fist. "This doesn't hold up very well against sharpened steel."

The room in which they had been eating was in the private living area at the back of the library. The only library staff who actually lived here were Bishop Aulus and Joktan, and they were also the only people in the building, as today had been declared a holiday in preparation for the festival. This festival was a greater event than a coronation.

Lawrence looked out the window at the narrow back-street below. A crowd of ruffianly-looking fellows milled near the doors or stood with craned necks watching the windows. They shouted as Lawrence's head appeared.

"Joktan is right," Lawrence said, returning to the table. "That way is blocked."

"Ask the bishop if they have any tunnels out of this place," Chester said.

Bishop Aulus shook his head.

Chester tore one of the curtains from the wall and tied knots in it at ten-inch intervals. "Looks like our deliverance will have to be from above. Pray— and climb."

Chester looped the end of a second curtain and tied it to the first. Jacques and O'Malley sprang to his aid and helped pull the knots tight. Lawrence sighed. He had a rough idea of what was about to happen.

Bishop Aulus was working his knuckles as if he was hand-washing. "What about the books?" he said. "I don't fear death, for I will go to heaven, but our books contain centuries of knowledge. They are irreplaceable."

"He has a point," Lawrence added to his translation.

"Yes, and a very hazy perspective of God's sovereignty." Chester draped the knotted curtains over his shoulder like a coil of rope. "A couple rooms full of dusty scrolls don't inspire me to much heroism, but this fellow *has* been good to us. We'll save his books yet."

A trap door led to the roof.

The breeze on the roof-top chilled Lawrence until *cutis anserina*—what Chester called 'goosebumps'—prickled all over his flesh. The tail to Chester's wolf-hat blew out horizontally. The banging on the doors below sounded like a court full of epileptic judges with gavels strapped to their hands. The crowd's tumult sounded more familiar, like market-day in London, except that London marketeers didn't usually yell about wanting to kill Outsiders.

Lawrence straddled the peak and grasped the ridge that capped the slanting tiles on either side. Logic said that feet should feel the same size whether they were sunk in mud or hugging a sheet of rock sixty feet above the earth. Logic lies sometimes. His feet felt about as wide as pencils and his balance had deserted the cause.

The marketplace in front of the library made an impassable gap. The other three directions showed promise, with a jumble of differently-shaped roofs crisscrossed by narrow swaths that marked alleyways and larger slashes that marked main streets. There were only a few buildings to the east before the open space in front of the palace rock, so the only good options were north and west.

Something about the roofs didn't look right.

"They don't really match the archeological models," Lawrence said. "There seem to have been some mistakes in the constructions of these roofs."

"Did you expect them to freeze their style for seventeen centuries?" Chester said. He shook his head. "All I can say is that if this is how their lifestyle was back then, our British schoolboys are victims of a conspiracy. These perverts are as much a model for civilization as a family of crocodiles. Less."

Chester dropped full-length on the tiles and slid down until his head poked over the roof's edge. He waved one arm at the crowd.

"Quit skinning your knuckles and look up here," Chester called.

The knocking transformed into a thunder of rage.

"If you understood English I'd give you a good talking to. As it is, I want you to all follow me for a merry little traipse across the roofs."

Each end of the roof was guarded by a stone statue. Chester ran to the one facing north, on the side of the house they had breakfasted in, and looped one end of the rope around the statue's legs.

"Go back down and keep the doors shut," Chester called to Bishop Aulus. His words were faint after struggling through the wind. "Lord willing, these cowards will chase us and leave your moldy scrolls in peace for a few more centuries."

Chester took three steps back from the roof-edge, crouched, and charged. He cleared the void with a foot and a half to spare and more coming, but the rope tautened, jerking his feet from under him and slamming him stomach first onto the peak. His wolf-hat flew off on impact and draped his knees.

"What's the hat all aboot?" O'Malley asked.

Lawrence shook his head.

Chester rubbed his stomach. "I need to practice that a bit more," he said. He tied the rope to the statue on his building and signaled them to cross.

Jacques and O'Malley were on the roof, but the third man was gone.

"Where's your friend?" Lawrence asked.

Jacques gasped. "Matthew did not come up! Ve must go back for him."

"It's too late," Lawrence said. "Cross."

"But we cannot desert our comrade. He may need our help!"

"So does your colonel. If our plan works, your friend is safer staying here than we are in leaving. Move."

Jacques and O'Malley crossed the rope in two moments. Lawrence crawled to the edge. The alley was full of men waving their fists at the sky. The priests had stirred the pot into an impressive boil. Joktan hid behind the statue, ready to untie the rope as soon as Lawrence crossed. He struggled manfully to stay stable on his uneven legs. It must be a hard life for him in a culture so devoted to bodily perfection as the Romans'.

Lawrence fingered the first knot in the curtain. His brain said that a rope which held O'Malley's massive frame wouldn't break under his own weight. His heart said that he would be a raving lunatic to extend one inch of himself over that chasm.

"Come on, Law!" Chester said. "We have a city to outrun."

The heart is usually wrong. Lawrence gripped the curtain and crawled out until his knees were the closest body parts touching the roof. He wreathed his legs around the rope and hung like a sloth. The wind swung him back and forth. The blue sky above flashed memories of other ropes and other heights, back on the *Miriam*, when that regrettable burst of jealousy sent him climbing skyward to impress Pacarina. But this time he was braving heights to stay free to rescue Pacarina. He shinnied the last three feet and reached the safety of stone tiles and friendly hands.

"Come on!" Chester said.

The tiles clicked under their boots as they raced across the roof. Shouts below followed them. The building they were crossing now looked like an *insula*, basically the Roman version of tenement housing.

The roof sliced off into another alley with a waiting crowd below.

"What's your plan?" Chester asked.

Plan? Lawrence had hoped Chester had one of those. He rasped his brain for stories of escape throughout history. The roof on the other side of the alley was close enough to jump to, but so was the roof on their left, which was at a lower level than the *insula*'s. Lawrence looked again. A kind of mist, or haze, hung over the building.

"Steam!" Lawrence said. "A bath house!"

"Zhat is good," Jacques said. He sniffed. "Zhe Irishman needs a vash."

"Me!" O'Malley said. "Says the Frog who drops a clove o' garlic in every dish he makes."

Chester patted their shoulders. "I'd love to hear more about the garlic sometime, but when the Professor has that look in his eyes it means there's more than bumblebees working in his brain. What's the plan, Law?"

The details were snapping into place. It would be rather unpleasant for the fellows at the bottom of the plan, but Lawrence had little sympathy for the nation that held his wife captive.

"We need to slide down to the roof of that bath house and get inside. I see a trap door."

Chester frowned. "But our friends below are likely to join the bathing party."

"Not if they see us jump to *that* roof." Lawrence pointed at the roof in front of them. He grabbed the rope. "Jacques, O'Malley, start dropping some of these tiles on the crowd. You don't have to hit them, but keep them dodging. They'll have less time to watch us. Chester, help me unknot these curtains."

"Don't ye worry, Mr. Stoning number one," O'Malley said. "If I miss a target that big, call me a Frinchman."

The knots had been pulled tight by the weight on the rope, but danger lends impetus to the fingers, and Lawrence and Chester soon had a wide canopy of two extremely wrinkled curtains.

"I have it!" Chester said. "You're going to fill this with steam and make it into a hot air balloon so we can float away."

Lawrence refrained from comment. Chester never was strong in his sciences. He explained the first part of the plan and sent Chester leaping over the alley to implement it. The crowd roared.

"I got that one," O'Malley said.

"You *boeuf*, zhat vas my tile!" Jacques said.

"Throw the curtains!"

Chester caught one end, fastened it to the tiles, and somersaulted back over the canopy.

"This is excellent practice," Chester said. "Did I tell you that I'm experimenting with a type of exercise focusing on efficiency in movement?"

Lawrence shook his head. Occasionally, Chester's enthusiasm could be delightful. Not necessarily infectious, but delightful. But this wasn't the best time to say so.

The plan was almost too simple to work. The mob below had seen one man jump the gap and hopefully presumed that the others were using the strange canopy to cross. The canopy had blocked their view of Chester's return, so if the plan worked, they would think all four had crossed onto the new roof.

Chester sidled to the roof edge and peeked over. "It worked! They're surrounding the other building."

"Thank God," Lawrence said. "Now for part two. I hope they haven't changed the way the baths work since the first century."

Chester led the way through the trap door. Lawrence stayed just far enough away to keep his nose out of Chester's wolf-hat. The ceiling was low—the room would be called an attic in London. The air was warm and vaporous like the jungle. The staircase at the end of the room had no door, but the steam blocked anything below from sight.

"There's far more steam here than I expected," Lawrence said. "I wonder if they've harnessed hot springs to take the place of wood-heated water. That would fit well with my theory of under-surface volcanic activity."

Chester tapped a door in the right wall. "Do we enter?"

Water splashed faintly. Lawrence swabbed his forehead with his handkerchief. Behind him, Jacques and O'Malley muttered about being boiled alive.

"This is where I want my pistols back," Chester said. "Pick the war-cry of your choice—we're going in."

The room was about eight feet square and empty. The steam was only in whiskers here, and the atmosphere was cooler. The two side walls were lined with benches, while a closed door in the far wall led beyond. Chester stepped through the steam and pressed his back against this door. He nodded. The splashing and talking were much louder now, obviously coming from the next room.

Lawrence searched the room for the reason he had come—and didn't find it. The benches were bare.

"Are we looking fer something?" O'Malley asked.

"Clothes."

O'Malley cocked his head and pointed at his trousers.

"They're not the right ones," Lawrence said.

Lawrence swept his hands over and under the benches in search of any hidden repository. *Ah!* A row of large cubbyholes like the bookshelves at the library stood in the farthest right corner, but the slots were enclosed by wooden flaps. Lawrence opened one and pulled out a tightly-wrapped toga.

"Splendid," Chester said. "This will be just like the bedsheets I wore in the old days when I played Saracens and Templars."

Lawrence raised his eyebrows. "You wore bed sheets?"

Chester winked. "You'd have seen stranger sights than that if you'd spent your early days outside with me instead of getting calluses on your nose from book-reading."

Togas weren't particularly handsome or practical, but they had plenty of fabric, and that right now was a providential trait.

Chester tucked the wolf-hat under his toga and raised his thumb. "All ready. What about the fellows splashing around in there? It seems rather hard on the chaps for us to pinch their clothes."

"You're right, we should pay in some fashion." Lawrence scratched his chin. To save his life he felt justified in borrowing some clothes. Still, he was a Christian, not a robber.

"Vhat about zhis?" Jacques said. He held a red gem in his palm. "It seems to be very valuable to zhe people here, for vhen I von it last night zhe man vas very sorry to part vihz it."

"I didn't know the 42nd gambled," Chester said.

"Ve do not!" Jacques's mustache twitched. "I von it fairly in a contest. I cooked best."

Chester snapped his fingers. "Do either of you have a knife?"

O'Malley slipped one out of one of the boots he had taken off. Chester motioned him to keep it.

"Take a whack at Jacques's mustache," he said. "These Romans don't grow fur on their faces."

"Vhat!"

The shorn undernose-hairs made a tiny swish on the floor and Jacques's indignant eyebrows nearly lost themselves in his hair.

Lawrence slipped the gem into the empty cubbyhole. "There, the clothes are paid for. Here's a sack. Stuff your clothes into it and let's get out of this foppish place. I have a wife to save."

Chapter 19

ach jolt stabbed a box corner just below Nobody's right shoulder-blade. Even the Romans' famous roads weren't bump free when you were stuffed into the bottom of a springless cart. The sack around his head blocked all light and too much air, making him labor to suck enough oxygen through the crevices to keep his lungs pumping.

One of the guards in the cart yelled and the box gave a final jab as the cart halted. Nobody wriggled off the corner and lay quietly, waiting for whatever was in store. There was no way to resist. Hands plucked him from the cart bottom and tore the sack off his face.

"Welcome to the Imperial mines," a familiar voice said. Bristle Hair doffed his helmet. "I hope you work better than you fight. Either way, you'll wish yourself in Tartarus."

Nobody faced a rock wall thousands of feet high. There wasn't a path good enough for a goat, and only a few places level enough for a few shrubs to cling to. It must be the outer edge of Vallis Deorum. The road behind led into a semicircle of trees which radiated on either side until the limbs melded with the rock wall, in some places so closely that the rock swallowed tree limbs.

A huge round pit, or quarry, was sunk in the center of the semicircle, with more unscalable walls at least sixty feet high. A detachment of legionaries was positioned here on the surface, while more helmets and breastplates below showed a strong armed force among the huts at the pit's bottom. It was like two worlds within sight of each other, but with no communication between.

The soldiers swung something out of the cart and it thudded next to Nobody's feet. It was Ennia, with a torn tunic and a purple bruise on her cheek where Little Caesar struck her. She stared up at him.

"See that hole?" Bristle Hair pointed to a hole in the base of the cliff large enough to admit several men. "That's the mouth of Hades."

A tight-lipped Roman in a dirty tunic followed by two slaves emerged from the hole and scowled at Bristle Hair.

"I ask for a hundred new slaves and you bring me a boy and a slave girl. What does Little Caesar think we do here? Does he think we just pick gems up and drop them into sacks?"

"Little Caesar doesn't think." Bristle Hair tested the cords around Nobody's wrists with a yank and shoved him toward the other Roman. "Use your time well with this one, because he has to die at the festival."

The mine manager eyed Nobody. "Are those clothes a new style?"

"He's an Outsider. Was living high until yesterday."

"What did he do? Murder? Theft? Steal a girl?"

"Worse. He offended Little Caesar." Bristle Hair crammed his head back into his helmet. "He's yours now. You can do what you like to him, just make sure that there's enough left to die at the festival. Little Caesar is looking forward to it personally."

At a nod from the manager the two slaves looped their arms through Nobody's and dragged him toward the cave. The manager brought Ennia. The slaves' hair was white, but whether this was from age or other causes, Nobody did not know. Their grips certainly didn't feel old.

Steps chiseled in the stone led from the cave entrance into the mountain's throat. Torches dotted the walls, but they were so far apart that the arcs of light wouldn't meet, leaving a swath of absolute darkness in the middle of each pair.

A key scraped in a lock and one of the slaves held Nobody's head down and shoved him through a low doorway. The door closed behind him, and the manager tapped its massive beams.

"There's no escape from this place, boy. The next time you touch surface grass you'll be on your way to the last bit of torture to finish you off at the festival."

The tunnel curved sharply to the left for so long that it finally pointed back towards the city, if this was where Nobody thought it was. The only place he had seen trees to match the ones at the mine entrance was the patch at the valley's north corner.

The tunnel discharged them out into the pit, which was mostly covered with grass and held about as many huts as would a small English village. At least, Nobody thought it did, but he had never actually seen a small English village.

The open spaces between the huts held a few lolling soldiers and a handful of dirty-faced women in rags who were polishing breastplates and helmets.

The manager sliced Nobody's bonds and ripped a piece of skin off his right palm with the same cut.

"So clumsy," the manager said. He grinned.

Nobody clamped his fingertips against the wound and said nothing. Words only goaded this kind of man.

"So, what should we do with you?" the manager said. He slowly stroked his chin, savoring each swipe as if he were in love with his beard stubble. "I think I will match your work and see what an Outsider is capable of."

The manager pushed Nobody into one of the tunnels that opened into the pit's walls. The sharp tap of iron on stone echoed in the darkness and mixed with the crackling of fires somewhere ahead. Occasional shafts in the ceiling let in faint light beams and almost enough air to make the stagnant atmosphere breathable. Iron grates blocked any access to the shafts.

As the manager and Nobody approached the first workers, a man holding a whip stood up.

"Where's the best slave?" the manager asked.

"Fire-setting at the end."

Nobody didn't know what 'fire-setting' was, but the air was hot enough for there to be roaring fires just beneath the surface. Slaves in loincloths hammered at the walls, sweat plowing the dirt on their backs. All had high-ridged scars from the whip, and many crouched, or limped, as if they had suffered other types of punishment as well.

The man with the whip, who seemed to be a low-level taskmaster, led the manager and Nobody to the end of the tunnel where three men knelt over a pile of wood. As Nobody approached, two of the men stood up and manned a large bellows, while the third slave applied a torch to the wood and stepped back. Curls of smoke soon rose, but the bellows sent these swirling into a gallery on the right, where they disappeared up a ventilation shaft.

"What's taking so long?" the manager said.

The slave who had lit the fire flinched, then hung his head and said nothing. He was young, somewhere in the middle of twenty and thirty, with a broad chest and muscles that rippled when he moved.

"This Outsider is going to work with you," the manager said. "Just you and he. I've decided to let you compete with each other. Whoever mines more rock by dark wins, and the loser will be punished according to my own imagination. But—" he stabbed his index finger into the slave's chest, "—if you work any slower than your usual speed then you *both* will be punished."

The slave raised his head. "But master, I am the fastest man you have. No untrained man can fairly compete."

The slave's tone was respectful and his sentence structure showed education. Nobody wondered vaguely what his story was, but his own fate was what most interested him.

Bare feet padded on stone and two women appeared from the direction of the pit with a water bucket in each hand. Their arms were thin and webbed with veins.

"Hello, pretties," the manager said. "Come to quench the fire's passion?" He pinched the first one's cheek. "Why, you're cold. Come warm by the fire."

The poor woman dropped her buckets, remembering, even in her terror, to not spill the water, and the manager pushed her close to the fire. He kept one hand firmly on her back, staying away from the heat himself, but keeping her so close that the flames singed her legs. She whimpered.

Nobody's stomach bubbled. He tried to shake his lethargy and knock the manager down, but the young slave blocked his chest with an iron arm and held him back.

The manager finally let go of the woman and let her stumble against the wall. He waved his hand at the fire.

"Douse it, then get to work. He with the least rock mined by dark will be sorry."

The manager and overseer walked away.

The women and the young man each grabbed a bucket. The young man nodded at Nobody. The slice on Nobody's right palm burned as he lifted the fourth bucket and, copying their actions, swung it back and launched the water at the rock. Clouds of steam blinded him and sent the whole party reeling against the wall as the cold water hissed over the heated stone. The other two male slaves dashed back to the bellows and slowly cleared the air.

"How do you survive this life?" Nobody asked.

The young man grunted. "Few do." He handed Nobody a massive hammer and pointed to the cooling rock, which had cracked in several places from the contrast in temperatures.

"You take the right side, I take the left. I don't know what an Outsider's muscles are made of, but I think it would be harder for you to beat me than for me to break this rock with my head."

Nobody gripped the hammer in his left hand and swung sideways. A stab of pain through his hand told him that he held the hammer too firmly, but the rock wasn't even scarred.

"You left-handed?" the young man asked.

Nobody gritted his teeth. "I am now."

He swung again. For a few minutes their hammer strokes fell in time, but weight and the novelty of the muscles he was using soon slowed Nobody's swings until they came once for every two or three of the other's.

The two bellows slaves and the women left. The young man worked in silence, his muscles rippling with each stroke, his breath deep and even.

Nobody thought about asking his name, but frankly, he didn't care. He swung, and swung, and swung, until his hand was almost too numb to hold the handle and his shoulder felt as mushy as snow on a warm Siberian day. His breath sounded strange, until he realized that he was actually sobbing.

147

He had thought his life in Siberia was hard, where each day was a struggle to survive and probably either a trek in freezing temperatures or an all-day ride through slush. But there, he was free. There, he fought hilt by hilt with his best friend and led men to victory. Here? He willed enough strength into his tendons for another blow.

What hurt worst? Was it being changed from a warrior to a one-armed weakling? No, he could be cheerful with only one arm working if Liana was at his side and Edmund was making ridiculous jokes from the other side of the room. Their absence was the void.

"What god do you believe in?"

"Eh?" The hammer slipped through Nobody's numb fingers and rattled on the floor.

The young man wiped his forehead. "I'm sorry for you, but you have no hope of winning. You had best ready yourself for the coming punishment. Do you have a god you'll go to for consolation?"

"I believe in the only true God, the God of the Bible. Christ."

The young man's head turned toward him. "They still believe in Christ in the Outside?"

"Yes."

The slave knelt and drew something in the dust with his finger. It looked like an oval—no, it had a tail. A fish?

"Perhaps you no longer use the symbol," the young man said. "It is a sign for Christians, to identify themselves to each other. I also believe in the God of the Bible."

God. Nobody stared at the penny-sized hole he had banged in the rock. God truly was present everywhere in the universe. Even in this ancient settlement, cut off from the rest of the world for close to two millennia, His people had kept the faith. Nobody slumped to his knees. For a man willing to claim faith in Christ in front of a Roman Caesar, he had spent little time praying these last months.

"May we pray together, brother?" Nobody asked.

"Of course. And, be prepared—you will need all of God's help to withstand what you must face when darkness falls."

Chapter 20

"I do not like zhis."

"Be quiet, Jack Frog. Ye don't even have tae lug yer own fopperies."

Lawrence scanned the street on both sides to make sure that no real Romans were within earshot. He had tried to keep the argumentative soldiers quiet, but they still managed to disagree while grunting, so he gave up.

The street which led to the bottom of the palace rock was almost completely empty, probably for fear of the mob which had just rushed through and was still howling several streets over, trying to find the four figures in togas walking sedately toward the palace.

"How dare you call my boots 'fopperies'!" Jacques said. "Zhey are half as heavy as yours, and of course you carry zhem, because our new young friends obviously observed zhat your intellect is best suited by a servile position."

O'Malley nearly dropped the sack he was carrying, which contained all the boots and other outward non-Roman attire that wasn't easily hidden beneath the togas.

"Ye insult me intelligence?" O'Malley said. "That's hard, comin' from an addle-brained Frinchman. That's right, me boots *are* heavier than yers, and so is me brain."

"Zhen ve are agreed. I know of few zhings more solid and less impermeable zhan zhe tangled veb at zhe center of your skull."

"I say," Chester said, "I thought you fellows in Siberia were fighting with rifles, not words. You're worse than Lawrence and me in the old days, and that's saying."

Lawrence stepped to the front as they approached the guards at the first gate. His plan wasn't as developed as he would like, but options and time were limited. The worst element was that it required a lie. Was it right to lie to an enemy? In wartime, in the Bible, Rahab was honored for lying to protect Joshua's spies, and Joshua himself was a spy who probably lied. On the other hand, this wasn't war—but yes, it was war, war to protect Pacarina. Lawrence believed that deception was justified in order to rescue his wife.

"What do you want?" the first guard asked.

"Obviously, we want to go up to the palace." Lawrence tried his best Roman wave. "Open the gates, man."

"Who are you?" the guard asked.

"Do you really expect me to list my lineage every time I take a stroll in the city? Come, open the gate before I report you to Little Caesar."

Lawrence tried to pretend that his nerves weren't shriveling with uncertainty. The guard's hand was on his spear, and he wasn't opening the gate.

"I've never seen you before," the guard said.

"Do you expect Little Caesar to wait for your approval before he selects new favorites?" Lawrence tried to sneer. "These are my friends, and that is my slave, and we want to go to my apartments in the palace, and I am getting most impatient."

"That's your slave?" the guard said. "Impossible. He's wearing a toga, and slaves aren't allowed togas. But he *is* carrying your baggage." The guard drew his sword. "I'm taking you to my officer."

"It failed, Chester," Lawrence said in English.

Chester somehow managed to untangle a leg from his toga and kicked the soldier in the stomach. O'Malley swung his sack and sent the second guard sprawling against the gate. Helmets sprang to life all the way up the path and raspy voices shouted the alarm.

"This is where we retreat," Chester said.

Lawrence hesitated. The palace was so close, and just behind those honeycomb walls was Pacarina. Chester gripped his shoulder.

"Law, even I'm not crazy enough to try it now. We'll be back, I promise."

Lawrence shook his fists at the soldiers and ran after Chester. How could he forget that slaves weren't allowed to wear togas? With all of the architectural changes that had been made since the first century A.D., it would have been helpful for that one little point of privilege to have changed as well.

The mob was now somewhere in front of them, and the soldiers were behind them. That didn't leave many places to go.

"Do you know of anywhere safe?" Chester asked Jacques and O'Malley.

"The only safe place as I knoow of is a blacksmith's house outside o' the city," O'Malley said. "But we'd have tae go through the mob tae git there."

To their right stood a vast *insula*. To their left stood a number of shops, attended by shopkeepers who were the only humans in sight. Everyone else must have either joined the mob or hidden from it. Lawrence tried to walk as if he had neither cares, thoughts, or a detachment of Roman soldiers on his mind. One of the shopkeepers waved at them.

"Wool, sirs, beautiful wool, sirs, can spin into anything the heart desires, sirs."

Lawrence shook his head. "The only thing I desire right now is a captive."

"Then get one," the shopkeeper said. "Visit the Dogs' hovels." He pointed to an alley framed by a rounded arch.

Dogs' hovels? That didn't make sense, but the alley did lead somewhere away from this open street. Few seconds remained before the soldiers would come past the corner.

"Thank you," Lawrence said.

He forced his legs to stroll until they were well inside the alley, then sprinted. The alley was completely enclosed above and had no lighting, which made the piles of garbage a danger. It would fit well in London.

"What is this place?" Chester asked.

"I have no idea. Something to do with dogs."

153

The tunnel spat them into a jumbled mess of buildings that leaned in every direction like drunken noblemen leaving a party. They were built from a little stone, a little wood, a little straw, and a little of everything else.

"This would be the poor quarter," Chester said.

The people working were far darker than the Romans, with thicker lips and tired, worn-out faces. The men stopped their work and stared at the intruders, while the women slipped into the houses. Footsteps echoed in the tunnel behind and metal clashed on metal. The soldiers were following.

"We'll have to take a calculated risk," Lawrence said.

He bowed to the closest native, a man with a white scar slanting from the top of his right cheekbone to the tip of his chin.

"Do you hate the soldiers?" Lawrence asked.

The native's cheek twitched, but he made no sound.

"I'll take the risk that you do," Lawrence said. "So do we. The soldiers coming through that tunnel are looking for us, and if they find us, we'll probably die. Can you hide us?"

The native looked from face to face. "It is a trap."

"No, it's not a trap, we're about to be arrested by the Praetorian Guard and you will be responsible for helping them."

The native's hands clenched, but that was all.

"Law!" Chester said. "What's wrong?"

"He thinks we're trying to trap him."

Chester threw the folds of his toga aside and showed his English clothes beneath.

"Does that look ancient, you staring Eskimo-Roman? Do we look like we fit with these Vanity Fair ruffians? Law, tell him we're from the Outside, where his ancestors came from."

The native struck his fists together. "We will help you. Come."

They glided behind a hut just as a shout announced the arrival of the Romans. The whole place was a kind of buried city within a city, surrounded by walls, and with huts scattered thickly 'with neither rhyme nor reason,' as Shakespeare said. Their guide paused next to a low building thatched with straw. A strange moaning, or whining, came from inside.

"Kennel," the native said.

As the door opened, dark bodies leaped up and the room erupted in a flurry of fangs, bristling hair, and throaty barks. These weren't terriers or fox hounds. Lawrence had only read of war dogs before, but he had no doubt that he was now looking them in the teeth.

The native snapped his fingers and the whole kennel slunk back into the corners.

"The Romans will not be quick to search here," the native said.

Jacques stood on the threshold with the skirts of his toga drawn halfway to his knee. "Surely, you do not expect me to enter *zhis*?"

"What did ye expect, poodles?" O'Malley shoved Jacques inside.

The open room at the front where the dogs were gathered filled about half of the building. Beyond the open room was a network of small rooms which could be opened or closed as desired, and where all the brushes, combs, buckets, and clippers necessary for grooming were stored. This was where the native stopped.

"Will the dogs behave?" Lawrence asked.

"Yes, they have just been fed. It was their last meal before the games."

The only sounds after the native left were the dogs' heavy breathing and Jacques's ejaculations when he stepped in something squishy. The air was ripe with the smell of canine deposits.

Lawrence pinched his nose. "I recommend that we disperse throughout these rooms in case the Romans do search here."

The footsteps of the other three slowly faded away and Lawrence was alone in the maze. He put his ear to the wall and listened. Faintly, very faintly, there was a murmur of voices, and at least once he heard the clink of armor. After seeing two of their comrades kicked and bashed with a weighted sack, the soldiers were unlikely to give up the chase easily.

Minutes passed. No one came. Heavy paws sporadically clomped the packed earth in the main room, but none of the dogs wandered into the smaller rooms. What did the native mean about them having their last meal 'before the games'? That was still some time away. Lawrence didn't want to think about how a room full of hungry war dogs would act.

"Psst."

Something in the shadows moved. A dark mass passed the doorway into Lawrence's room. Lawrence crouched and peeked around the corner into the corridor. Two figures met.

"You are one of zhe tvins?" Jacques asked.

"That's right," Chester said.

"Are you zhe smart one or zhe strong one?"

Chester growled. "I didn't know they were mutually exclusive. I'm Chester."

"Good. I found an excellent place to hide, but I am annoyed, for zhere is somezhing in zhe ceiling above my head. It scuffles and vhispers, and I vant your help to find out vhat it is."

"Probably rats," Chester said.

Lawrence squatted on his heels and inched after them. He might need some practice stalking for when he got into the palace, and if he could follow Chester without him knowing it then he could do more than many. Jacques and Chester walked slowly with their heads cocked at the roof.

Squish.

A steamy smell permeated Lawrence's nostrils. He tried not to think about the wet *squish* that now accompanied each footstep.

"Ah!" Chester said. "A trap door. Must be rats with style."

Something overhead creaked.

"Hello, ratties, you having a shindy up there? Ho!"

The dark mass that could only be Chester crumpled under a falling body. Lawrence jumped forward with his arms stretched wide and collided with a man in a short tunic, which left at least two feet of hairy arm exposed. Part of this arm looped around Lawrence's throat and slammed him against the wall. The stench of dog refuse mingled with the tangy smell of the man's last meal, which wafted over Lawrence as he struggled against the choke-hold.

The stranger's hands were collapsing Lawrence's chest, inch by inch, giving his lungs less space to expand with each breath. Lawrence's shoulder-blades ground into the wall. He wrenched at the stranger's arms with as much effect as if they were skin-clad steel rods. He stomped the darkness where the man's toes should be, and that made the man quiver, but the arms kept pressing.

"Vive la republique!"

Jacques slammed into the stranger and spun him off of Lawrence, but Lawrence's crushed chest had scarcely swelled for the first breath when a blow in the darkness dropped a body in the dirt and the arms returned.

Lawrence gasped. "Chester!"

The stranger's fingers formed a triangle around the bottom of Lawrence's sternum. Lawrence's eyes bulged. *Help, God!* Was this truly how he would die, in this inky passageway surrounded by bones and fetid smells? Was this how he would rescue Pacarina? Gasping to death in a kennel?

The arms yanked away from Lawrence's chest and a body slammed into the opposite wall. Lawrence bent double, trying to force air back into his aching chest, while men struggled two feet from his face. Someone yowled in pain, then there was silence.

"Stay still, do you hear?" Chester said. "Law, are you floating around somewhere?"

"Down here," Lawrence croaked.

"Well come up, then, it's not nap-time yet. I've got my knife on this bruiser's throat. He gave me a good crack on the skull when he jumped from his little attic thingy, otherwise I'd have taken care of him sooner. Shall I kill him?"

"Zhat is right!" Jacques said. "Kill zhe rogue! And when I get my hands on zhat *boeuf* of a sleeping Irishman I vill vring his neck like a duck!"

"Quiet," Lawrence said. He heard voices, and they didn't belong to anyone inside the kennel.

"Check this place," said someone outside the front door.

Armor clinked, and a hobnailed sandal dug into wood. The door cracked open.

Wough! Wough!

The kennel pulsed with the barks—more like roars—of the war dogs. The door banged shut and a gruff voice loosed a string of Latin words of which Lawrence guessed the nature, but which his tutor had never taught him. It took two minutes for the dogs to quiet into a universal grumble, punctuated occasionally by a rebel's howl.

The officer returned.

"Why are you dawdling outside? Have you checked the building?"

"It's full of war dogs, sir. The man who survived that could bind Cerberus with his own tail."

"Very well. I don't know where the imposters have gone to but I hope these Dogs roast them in oil. Come, back to the palace."

Lawrence realized that he had been repressing his breath and loosed it in a long sigh. The others did the same.

"I say, kill zhe villain," Jacques said.

"Patience, Jacques, you sound like a Frenchman waiting for a patty of goose liver." Chester's boot unexpectedly collided with Lawrence's shin. "Ah, there you are, Law. Chatter this fellow up and see if he deserves a knife in the gullet."

"His gullet isn't what you would want to cut, Chester," Lawrence said.

"Lawrence. Talk to him."

Lawrence considered the best way to construct his sentence. "Why are you hiding here?" he asked.

"I was hiding from the Romans." The man's voice was much more pleasant than his arms. "If you are doing the same, we may be friends, not enemies."

Lawrence briefly explained their situation.

"That's good," the man said. "My name is Varius Rufus. I am no friend of Little Caesar's, but I am happy to be your friend. I may be able to help you. Let's talk."

Chapter 21

There was no way to tell when darkness fell in the gloomy mines of Vallis Deorum. Nobody's first warning was the *flub-flub* of footsteps coming down the long gallery toward him.

His companion, whose name was Otho, stopped hammering and listened. Nobody had stopped hammering long ago.

"If you are destined to die at the festival," Otho said, "perhaps you should sell your life dearly now, before the pain."

"I would like to, but I'm not going to throw away any chance of life I have. I came to this valley for the sake of an imprisoned friend, and until my veins are empty, I intend to search for what I came for."

"God be with you."

Otho turned back to the rock as the manager swaggered into the torchlight.

"Well, well, who is our winner?" The manager stuck his nose close to the rock. "Did you think you were here to spit on the mountain, Outsider? You've gone nowhere. Did you think I wanted you to massage the rock?"

Nobody folded his aching arms. "Just get it done with, Roman."

The manager backhanded Nobody in the face and sent him staggering against the rock. The force of the blow against his teeth tore two holes on the inside of his cheek.

"Insolent dog! Take him."

A pair of slaves hustled Nobody down the gallery into the fresh air of the pit, where several hundred slaves, mostly men, were gathered around huge loaves of bread. The sun still sneaked a few beams over the mountain. The slaves ripped off Nobody's shirt and tied his legs and arms to a post in the center of the pit.

"Watch and learn!" the manager said. "We will see the color of an Outsider's blood."

The slaves swarmed into a close circle around Nobody. A taskmaster approached with a long wooden rod which he bent into the shape of a bow, then allowed to snap back into place. It didn't show the least sign of having been bent. The taskmaster took his position next to Nobody like a batter at cricket and waited.

"How many?" the taskmaster said.

The manager stepped to where he could see Nobody's face. "I want him dead, but Little Caesar already claimed the pleasure. So sad. I don't like his face."

I return the opinion, Nobody thought. In the old days, Dilworth had told stories about turkey shoots in America's western states. Shooters would take turns firing at the bird, until one man killed it, and he won the meat. In this match, Little Caesar and the mine manager were the shooters and Nobody was the meat.

"One!"

What felt like a hot knife blade seared a line across Nobody's lower back. He ground his cheek into the post and tried to stop the pain-tears from soaking his cheeks.

"Two! Three! Four!"

Nobody gnawed the post, no matter the splinters, and screamed to God for strength. *Banastre Bronner. His fault. Banastre. No, don't think of Banastre. Liana. Think of Liana. Dimples. Hazel eyes.* He stared. Two tear-filled hazel eyes loomed through the pain-mist. *Am I going insane?* No, it was Ennia watching from the crowd of slaves.

Nobody arched his back for the next blow, but it didn't come. His muscles trembled uncontrollably. The beating was over.

"You!" the manager yelled. "Bring me a bucket of spice."

Nobody blinked through the water in his eyes and glimpsed a slave in a tunic drop a bucket at the manager's feet. There was something peculiar about that slave. He wore the same clothes as the others, except for the slaves only clad in loincloths, but he didn't fit his clothing. That jaw wasn't Roman. Nobody tried to focus on his features, but the pain scouring his skull blurred his vision.

"Mustn't leave your wounds unattended, must we?" The manager stepped behind Nobody with the bucket. "What is it that those pesky leeches say? This will hurt."

A handful of what felt like fine glass bit Nobody's raw back. He screamed. His wounds were being salted—no, there wasn't salt here—but some spice like salt was digging every inch of his back with red hot claws. He slumped against the post. He could do no more.

A knife sawed at the rope and the cords snapped, one by one, until nothing held him to the post and he collapsed in the dirt. Nothing must touch his back. Nothing.

"Chain him in the mine for the night," the manager said, his voice coming as over a great gulf. "Tomorrow, we will see if he doesn't work as hard as I tell him to."

Nobody crumpled in the mine and hugged the cool rock to his chest and cheek. Metal bands circled his ankles and connected to chains buried in the wall. There was no escape from the soot-black darkness.

Nobody's back throbbed with each breath and stung in between. He licked his cracked lips. He needed water. His ears buzzed. He thought of blue rivers with white froth on the edges where the water swept against the bank, and the ocean plunges on Rahattan Island when he would dive from the dock into the largest bath in the world. But that was salt water. Nobody groaned. Even his dreams stung.

Water-dreams faded into the image of Liana's face, dimpled, calm, happy. Of course, that face wasn't always happy and peaceful. He thought of that horrible night on Rahattan when he told her that he didn't love her, and the look in her eyes on *The Hound* as she reached for his knife. In the old days, Edmund used to read from Sir Walter Scott's novels about the Crusaders dreaming in burning Holy Land sands about their sweethearts. Then, it seemed foolish. Now, Nobody understood.

His had been a short but varied career. Soldier, merchant, accused pirate, and outlaw. Death, destruction, despair, betrayal, anguish—these were all familiar faces, but he had never felt as he felt now.

Alexander Somerset, the *Times* reporter, told stories about the Cornwall tin mines. Sometimes the miners would break into reservoirs of water which rushed through the galleries, smashing men against the walls and ceilings and sweeping all in its path. If a miner was working near the shaft which led to the next level he might be able to climb the ladder in time to escape. Nobody was one of the miners at the gallery's end watching the water pour in and gripping the ladder rungs, unable to move, arms leaden, legs trembling, sucked to the ground by exhaustion.

A throb brought Nobody back from Cornwall to his own stone gallery. Alone, helpless, humiliated. The enemy had won.

No.

Nobody clawed the rock with his fingernails. He had never conceded defeat, and he would not now. Alone? He wasn't alone. Friends may be imprisoned, separated, betrayed, but God is always with His children. Helpless? He was the servant of the Creator of the universe, the greatest Helper who ever exited. Humiliated? No more than Christ, the Son of God, who was nailed to a tree and mocked by the same breed of men who now tormented Nobody.

Nobody clasped his hands and rested his forehead on them. *God, help me. I can't fight this battle alone. I've reached my end. I don't have the strength to continue. Only You can triumph over my enemies. Harden my arms to war, steel my heart to the battle, rest my mind in Your strength. You're my only hope.*

Chapter 22

"You call this food?" Chester shoved his plate away. "When I was two years old I made mud cakes that tasted better than that. Unfortunately, I was wearing my best clothes when I did it, and Mother didn't appreciate my culinary endeavors."

The natives had fetched Lawrence and his companions from the kennel after the soldiers left and were now feeding them in one of the huts, which had a small table made of beaten earth in the center and an exhausted fire in the corner. Chester was right about the food. The main and only course—a thick bread that weighed six ounces more than it should—was so coarse that it scratched Lawrence's tongue as he tried to chew.

"This is absurd," Chester said. "If I wanted to eat rocks I'd join a young ladies' voice class and swish marbles in my mouth all day. I'm going to give them some tips on cooking."

"Vait!" Jacques jumped up and moved between Chester and the fire. "I am Jacques Lefebvre, master chef, and camp-cook beyond compare. If anyone is to fix zhis horrible meal, I am zhe man to do so."

Chester pushed past Jacques. "I've no doubt you're good with sauces—all you Frenchies are—but the only sauce to be had in this place is your personality. If you must have a hand in the business, then follow my directions."

Lawrence studied Varius Rufus more closely now that they were in the light and found himself liking the young man. His arms were exceptionally hairy, as Lawrence had already noticed, his mouth curled cheerfully, and his hair was bright red. That was probably why one of his names was Rufus, meaning 'red-haired' in Latin. According to Jacques and O'Malley, he was the son of a friendly blacksmith who lived outside the city.

Varius sipped water from a clay cup.

"Why didn't your brother kill me?" he asked. "I would have done so. I tried to kill you, when I thought that you were an enemy."

Lawrence translated the question to Chester. Chester looked away quickly.

"What does he say?" Varius said.

Lawrence hesitated. "My brother hasn't always been as cautious as he was with you. That's why he is now." Lawrence leaned forward. "Look, Varius, we need to talk. While we sit here my wife is in the palace, and anything could be happening to her. You said you could help us. How?"

Varius raised a finger. "*Might* help you. If I am able. It depends on many things. You see, not all of we Romans are content under Little Caesar's tyranny. Most, true, are satisfied by the games, and the baths, and such, but many of we Christians are not."

"And what does that look like?"

Varius drew back his toga and showed a short sword hanging by his side.

"Resistance. We fight back. Our numbers are few, but we have more power than Little Caesar realizes, and we are committed to each other. Small raids, supposed accidents, men missing from their homes when soldiers come to arrest them—we have our ways."

"But are small things like those really going to impact a government as established as Little Caesar's?"

Varius leaned forward. "The small things, no, but every staircase has lower steps. We're approaching the top now. The day for only small things has ended." He waved around the hut. "That's why I am here."

A howl came from the fire.

"Watch your hair," Chester said.

Jacques slapped his head frantically with a rag while smoke curled up from his hair. The last spark was hardly dead before he was shaking his finger in Chester's face.

"You bump me! Zhe indignity! Zhe—zhe—insult—zhe—you are vorse than O'Malley!"

O'Malley, sitting with Lawrence and Varius at the table, laughed, clasped his hands behind his head, and waited for more.

Lawrence turned back to his conversation. "What do you mean by saying that the small things have ended?"

"This is our situation; although powerful in our ways, there are few of us true Romans who will oppose the government, and many soldiers to stop us. Most of the people will watch the struggle like any fight in the arena. But—" Varius's voice lowered to a whisper. "Where are there hundreds of men who also dislike their condition, and, if led properly, could overthrow Little Caesar?"

"You're starting a slave revolt?"

"The Dog will turn and bite the hand of his master. I'm here to arrange plans between our side and the Dogs."

The Dogs, yes, the natives. Lawrence considered the point. The words 'slave revolt' made him think of the Haitian Revolution not long ago, where the blacks of Haiti rose against their masters and killed and tortured thousands. If a revolt was to lose control like that, its organizers would be guilty of foul misdoing. Spartacus fit the situation better, since he revolted against the Romans, but that also wasn't an encouraging prospect. Approximately six thousand of his men were crucified along the Appian Way.

"How will you prevent the natives from going wild after they gain power?" Lawrence asked. "It would take a very intelligent mind."

Varius frowned. "Right now we are more concentrated on making them *want* that power and helping them succeed. Little Caesar has spies everywhere, even among the Dogs, and betrayal now means a long and lingering death."

"Are you the leader?" Lawrence asked.

Varius rubbed his hidden sword-hilt.

"Our leader is very cautious about revealing himself. He knows so much about our plans which no one else does that his capture might be fatal."

A louder exclamation than usual from Chester interrupted the conversation.

"I don't care if I don't know its name! If you want to classify it in a Latin *genus*, ask the Professor. I'm interested in eating the thing, and I want it in that pot."

"It is zhe vrong texture. Zhe taste vill absolutely spoil vhat you are already ruining."

Chester and Jacques were arguing over a long green vegetable which Lawrence had never seen before. Jacques held it behind his back while Chester pointed at the simmering pot.

"Arrah, young fellow," O'Malley said, "that's right. Stand yer ground wi' the Frog. I always find it helpful to squeeze the back o' his neck when he gets roiled like this."

Lawrence shook his head in response to Varius's puzzled glance. "Don't worry about them. Now, you said you might be able to help us. When will this revolt take place?"

"It must be during the games."

"So, the first day of the festival?"

"No, not the first day. We're still planning, and we need every day we have to put all things in place."

Lawrence dug his fingernails into the table. Pacarina was to marry Little Caesar on the second day of the festival. The revolt might be too late.

"Don't you think that with our help the revolt could happen sooner?" Lawrence asked.

"No. What we wanted was the other Outsider, the one who they say has commanded men in battle. With his skill we may have a better chance, but he's in the mines."

"Yes, he's also on our rescue list," Lawrence said. "Can't anyone escape from the mines?"

Varius wiped a hairy arm over his forehead. "Have you seen the mines? No, I didn't think so. See them first, then ask if any can escape."

"I say," Chester said, "what are you two chattering about?"

Lawrence explained that Varius was organizing a revolt.

Chester flicked his wolf-hat's nose, which passed for a tip of the hat. "Excellent. Find out if they can sneak my pistols out of the palace, will you? I'd love to introduce these stuck-up Romans to gunpowder."

"Varius," Lawrence said, "I need to meet your leader. I think we can help each other. These two men are soldiers, and my brother also has experience in warfare, though he's never commanded a revolt before. Will you take us to your leader?"

Varius tapped the table with his thumbs and index fingers. "Few of us know who our leader is. He has his own reasons for being secretive. Not all of his family even know what he does. If I take you to his home, you would have to be very cautious about speaking of the revolt."

"I'm the only one who speaks your language, and I promise to be cautious."

"Then I will take you." Varius rose. "First, I must finish my plans with the Dogs. We'll leave the city this evening."

O'Malley raised his hand. "I doon't knoow where this hairy fellow is goin', Mr. Stoning number one, but I'll remind ye that we're not all here. We still have our comrade Matthew holed oop somewheres back at the library, and Squad One niver deserts each other."

Lawrence didn't remember much in the glowering man he had met at the library to inspire loyalty, but of course, he had much on his mind. Colonel Nobody must have trusted him greatly to bring him to Greenland. Lawrence didn't yet share that confidence, so he wasn't sorry that there was an excellent excuse to not rejoin him at the moment.

"The priests will have men watching the library," Lawrence said. "He should be safe, as they don't know that not everyone left by the roof, so his best plan will be to stay hidden at the library until our plans are mature."

Chapter 23

"Clear the tunnel!" a taskmaster shouted.

The clinking of hammers stopped and dozens of bare feet padded away from the wall where four slaves were preparing to douse a fire. Nobody gladly dropped his hammer and joined the stream of slaves. His left arm ached from the work, but he hardly noticed it compared to his back.

"You have a strong will." Otho stepped next to Nobody in the line. "How is your back this morning?"

"I used to have a strong will, but all that is left now is a strong God. My back feels like the back of a man who was flogged yesterday."

"Be grateful for the spices. I don't know if they use them on us because they hurt, or because they heal, but they do both."

The slave next in line stumbled on some rubble and loosed a wracking cough. The coughs continued until an overseer yelled at him and sliced his legs with a whip. The slave gulped back the crusty hacks, but his shoulders shivered with the effort. Otho shook his head.

"Tomorrow's sun will be the last he sees."

"How long do they usually survive?"

"Not long." Otho ducked as they passed the overseer, then looked up again. "The overseers are unwise. They work too many of us to death. The city sends its malefactors here, and some of the Dogs, and they breed as many slave children as they can, but they always need more labor."

"How long have you been here?" Nobody asked.

"A year and a half."

"Why haven't you died?"

Otho pointed to a pile of rock and they both sat down, Nobody leaning forward so that his back wouldn't touch the rock. His kidneys were beginning to hurt from so much compression, but anything was better than the claws of pain when any pressure was applied to his back.

"There are two reasons I'm not dead," Otho said. "Although the overseers are unwise, they are not entirely stupid, and they know that I am their strongest slave. That is the first reason. The second is that I have hope."

"What do you hope in?"

"I hope in Christ, and I hope for a coming change."

Otho's fingers clenched and unclenched around a chip of rock. They looked strong enough to squeeze sweat from the rock.

"What," Nobody said, "do you mean by 'a coming change'?" He leaned closer. "Do you expect to be rescued?"

The chip clattered on the ground.

"Hush."

Otho slowly swiveled his head in both directions. There were no overseers within listening range, and all of the nearby slaves were taking advantage of the break to stretch out on the floor. Several were already snoring.

"Outsider, do you trust me?"

Nobody also lowered his voice to a whisper. "No. I don't say that to offend. I think that you appreciate honesty as much as me. I trust you partly, but I haven't known you long enough to trust you fully."

"Then why should I trust you?"

"You shouldn't trust me fully. I might be a spy—I have been one in the Outside. Still, few spies are dedicated enough to bear a flogging just to gain the trust of a man who is already a slave and under his masters' complete control."

Otho sucked a knuckle.

"I believe that you're an Outsider, for I've never heard anyone speak our language the way you do. Very well. I will trust you enough to tell you that I do hope for rescue. There are forces of which the government knows nothing, and one day soon I pray that the time will ripen like wheat on the stalk and we will gain our freedom."

"I hope so, but unless that 'one day soon' is within the next three days I won't see it. Do you think it could be that soon?"

"I've received word that a new persecution of Christians will begin with the festival, so if the day doesn't come very soon, there won't be anyone left alive to bring it to pass."

Nobody frowned. How had he received word? Had he spoken to Ennia? She and Nobody were the only recent arrivals at the mine, and it was unlikely that the overseers would share information like that with Otho. Or, could there be a secret means of communication with the upper world?

"Otho, are you saying that the Christians are going to rise?"

"Some of them. In the Scriptures, James warned us of being double-minded, and with good reason. Many of the Christians are double-minded. They want freedom, but they aren't willing to fight for it."

"Apathetic?"

"No, they think it's wrong." Otho shook his head. "Bishop Aulus is the most powerful Christian, and he truly is a good man. He is sincere, but he's wrong. He thinks that it is sinful for Christians to fight."

"What?" Nobody said. "Never? Not even to protect themselves?"

Whips cracked.

"On your feet!" an overseer shouted. "Back to work, you rubbish-sweepings."

Nobody's stomach gurgled as he decompressed his kidneys. Otho picked up his crowbar and angled it on his shoulder.

"If they let you out of the mine tonight, come to my hut. I'm a good judge of men, Outsider, and I like you. We have much to talk about if you're to survive the festival."

There was little light left when the slaves were released from the mines that evening. No one said anything to Nobody about staying in the mine for another night, so he dropped his hammer in the pile where the other slaves dropped their tools and walked toward the huts.

"You! Boy!"

Nobody spun around. One of the overseers was pointing at him with his whip.

"You're assigned to cleanup duty. Report over there." The overseer cracked his whip at a lonely hut about thirty yards from the farthest rock wall.

Nobody tried to keep his eyes open as he stumbled toward the hut. Lack of sleep, combined with mental exhaustion and some of the hardest work he had ever done was dragging at his legs, arms, and eyelids.

Two soldiers lolled near the hut with bored faces and drooping armor that was hardly tied together enough to hang over their shoulders. They straightened as Nobody approached.

"Here now, you can't go in there, it's being cleaned," the nearest soldier said. He was short, fat, and beady-eyed.

"I was told to help clean it," Nobody said.

He no longer wondered what 'it' was that he was supposed to clean. The odor coming from the latrine was almost thick enough to see.

The second soldier, a tall, lean man, cracked his fingers one by one.

"Oh, well, then," he said, "we'll have to check to make sure you're not a—but wait, he is. That is, he's either a man or a boy—certainly not female."

The soldier made no sense. Nobody tried to concentrate his thoughts to analyze the soldier's response, but it didn't mesh with any of the slots in his brain.

"He's not wearing a cloak," the fat soldier said. "Maybe it's not a problem?"

"But he's a man," the thin soldier said. "I'm going to go ask one of the overseers. You keep him here."

176

Nobody stood next to a pile of cloaks and tried to keep his knees from buckling until the thin soldier returned.

"He's supposed to go in," the thin soldier said.

"So, we can't check them anymore?" the fat soldier said.

"No, we still do, but this one's special. The head man doesn't like him, so he's making him work the mines *and* here." The soldier nodded at the door. "Go clean, boy."

Nobody covered his mouth and nose with his hand as the first stench-wave engulfed him. Skinny figures worked in the dim light shoveling sludge from a long stone trench into wooden buckets. A surprised murmur of female voices greeted him.

"What do you do here?" a woman asked. She held her shovel mid-way to the bucket and stared at him.

"I'm supposed to help you," Nobody said.

"A man?"

"Yes, a man. Why is everyone so surprised that I'm not a woman?"

The woman dropped her shovelful into the bucket.

"The men aren't allowed to work here because all their strength must be spent in the mines. We women aren't strong enough for the hardest mine-work, so one of our jobs is to keep this clean."

"And men don't ever work in here?" Nobody said.

"They used to wear our clothes sometimes and sneak here in the morning, because this work is much easier, but the guards found out. That's why we only wear tunics, without cloaks."

All the women were grouped around Nobody now, and he realized that they all wore the same kind of short-sleeved tunic extending to the knees. When he saw women in the open they usually wore a cloak as well, so that explained the pile of cloaks outside.

"My lord," a voice said. Ennia slipped from the circle and knelt by his feet.

"Er—hello. Good to see you too." Nobody coughed. He didn't know what to say. "I'm very sorry about all this—you being here, and everything. Well—I appreciate your trying to stand up for me to Little Caesar."

Nobody grabbed a shovel and took an empty place next to the trench. The buckets they were shoveling the sludge into were about two feet broad, built of thick wooden slats banded by iron, and they weighed at least thirty pounds when empty. How heavy would they be when they were full and Nobody had to pick one up?

The mine manager must be enjoying his power over an Outsider and making the most of the few days left before the festival. This was easy work compared to the mines, but hard work after a day in the mines. Jacques would shrivel if he could whiff this place.

The two women at the end of the trench farthest from the door finished first. They inserted a six-foot pole under the bucket's rope-handle and lifted it to their shoulders, thus carrying the bucket between them like the drawings always show the Israelite spies bringing grapes back from the land of Canaan.

Two by two, the women finished their sections, shouldered their buckets, and exited through a gap in the back wall. There were no houses between the latrine and the pit wall, but once the women stepped away from the gap Nobody couldn't see where they went.

"You are tired."

Nobody started. He realized that he had been wondering where the women were going with his eyes shut and had nearly stumbled into the trench. He stepped back and scooped another shovelful.

"I heard them say that you are to die in the festival," Ennia said. She was the last woman left.

Nobody grunted. "If I survive that long."

"I remember last festival." Ennia wiped her arm across her sweat-soaked forehead. "I remember the cheers when the two best gladiators fought each other, and how funny it was when the trained dogs ran in pairs, and jumped over each other's backs, and did tricks."

"Why are you here, Ennia?"

Her hair hid her face. She didn't say anything at first, but just kept shoveling as if she hadn't heard the question. Then she stopped and looked at Nobody.

"It is not uncommon when a slave girl falls from favor to be sent to the mines. The government doesn't like the people to think about the mines, so they prefer to have children born here and grow up to be mine-slaves than have to take many from the city. Slaves are not as expendable as you might think. We kill many of our children before or after they are born, just like freedmen, so there are not as many of us."

Nobody dropped his shovel. He didn't know what to say.

"Do you Outsiders sell slaves?" Ennia asked.

"What? Er—some do. My country—well, the country your histories call Brittania—abolished slavery a few years ago."

"Have you seen a slave market?"

Nobody shook his head.

Ennia shuddered. "Never do. I will kill myself before I am sold again. When my first master died I was sold in the market. We were exposed like shorn lambs on a platform and auctioned by a fat man with dyed hair who talked about us like cows. Many buyers were there. Some of us went to the mines, to breed slave children, but the palace bought me."

Nobody scraped the shovel along the trench bottom and imagined having the 42nd for one day, just one day, in this valley of horror. Little Caesar would stop laughing when he saw his Praetorians run like rabbits before English lead and English steel. Instead, Nobody had only three men from Squad One, and he didn't know if they were alive, dead, or destined for the same fate as himself.

"Why does everyone kill their children?" Nobody asked. "I thought the Romans were civilized."

Ennia shrugged. "We've always done it. It was done before our ancestors even came to this place. We don't like to trouble with many children, and the government doesn't like it either. Our valley is small—if we all had many children it couldn't support us."

"Then you leave the valley."

"But the curse!" Ennia's eyebrows jumped into her bangs.

"The curse is self-imposed, a silly lie, a child's bugaboo—I don't know how to say that in Latin. It's murder."

Ennia shrugged again. "Come." She slipped the last rod beneath the bucket's rope-handle.

"Aha!" a sour voice said from the doorway.

The dim light showed the thin soldier's shadowy outline. He closed the door behind him.

"You dawdle at your work today, pretties." The soldier dropped his breastplate next to the door and shoved Nobody out of the way. "How now, slave girl, what's this? Your eyes look red." He grabbed Ennia's chin and made her look up at him. "Yesterday you told me you could never cry again."

Nobody's fingers itched for a sword. He patted his hip where it should hang, but something felt wrong. He looked down. He had used his left hand, not his right. He must be getting more accustomed to his left hand.

"I think you lied," the soldier said. "I think you can still cry, and I know how to make you."

The soldier yanked Ennia's hair until her eyes watered.

"I knew I could." The soldier giggled. "Now, I'll make it all better. Give me a kiss."

That broke the dam. Nobody would stop this Roman even if it meant instant death and no possibility of finding the sailors. It was what Edmund would do and what Liana would want Nobody to do.

"Roman," Nobody said. "She doesn't want to kiss you. It reminds her too much of the sludge she has to shovel."

The soldier let her go and spun around. He grabbed his sword-hilt. Nobody launched his right leg high in the air and landed a crushing kick in the soldier's midriff. He bent over double. The memory of training young Thomas Bronner flashed into Nobody's mind—'We use our bodies, our opponents' bodies . . . everything and everyone.'

Nobody planted his right foot and put all his strength into a left kick. The soldier sprawled motionless on the floor.

Ennia hugged the wall, trembling.

"They will kill us," she whispered. "They will torture us to death."

Nobody shook his head. There must be some way to hide the body. Where? And even if they hid it the soldier would still be missing, and they would be blamed. Unless . . . unless the body was found but the death appeared natural. How? There must be a way. Years of spying upon and killing Cossacks had taught him that there was always a way.

"Do accidents ever happen here?" Nobody said.

Ennia chewed strings of her hair.

"Ennia!"

She started. "The other women said that sometimes, when it's dark, a man will stumble into the trench and break his leg."

"This time he'll break more than a leg. Help me pick him up."

The body's weight fought Nobody's aching muscles, but he thanked God that it wasn't the fat soldier. They propped the body against the wall and held it there, limp, while Nobody finished the last details of his plan. A skin bag hung from the soldier's belt. Nobody took the stopper from the neck and sniffed. Wine.

A splash on the face, a dribble down the tunic, and the fellow smelled like he had walked out of a drinking party. The next step wasn't to Nobody's taste, but it had to be done, and quickly.

"Let go," Nobody said.

Ennia stepped away. Nobody propped the soldier for one more second against the wall, aimed him right, and let him fall headfirst into the trench. The body's thud reminded Nobody of past battlefields—only then, he hadn't fought with his feet.

"Quick," Nobody said. "Lift."

He and Ennia lifted the sludge-bucket and staggered through the back exit. If the Lord was gracious, no one would see them leave and would assume that the latrine was empty when the thin soldier entered. Then his death would be blamed as a drunken man's misstep. That was the plan, anyway.

They scurried as fast as they could to the wall-face, where Ennia pointed to the opening of a cave, or tunnel. Women's voices echoed inside. The tunnel ended in a ledge above a torrent of foam-flecked water which dropped into the mountain's stomach. The other slave-women helped tip the last bucket and unload the slime, which sank through the clean white water and disappeared.

The women collected their cloaks from in front of the latrine and dispersed. There were no guards to question them, and no sign of discovery of the body inside. The plan had worked. That was Nobody's first plan that had worked in a very, very long time.

All the other male slaves had finished their scanty meal and were either sleeping or talking in tiny groups around the huts. It was a clear night, with thousands of brilliant stars and a beautiful sliver of moon shining down, but Nobody spared few glances for the heavens. He was too concentrated on putting each bone-tired foot in front of the other.

A hand grabbed his arm.

"I have waited for you," Otho whispered. "Come, my hut is here."

Nobody leaned his back against the wall inside and slid down until he lay on the earth with his head cushioned on his arm. The blisters on his feet cried for freedom, but he ignored their protests and left his boots on. He was too tired to take them off.

"I have a surprise for you," Otho said.

Nobody squinted. It was too dark to see much, but a white gash in the lower half of Otho's face suggested a smile.

The door opened and a figure stood framed in the starlight. Nobody blinked. The man wore trousers and a shirt. No tunic. No toga. Those clothes were English.

"Who are you?" Nobody said.

"He speaks English!" the man said in salty sea tones. "My, but you're a sound for poor ears."

Five men entered, one by one, and sat down on the floor of the hut.

"Answer me one question," Nobody said. "Are you sailors from the *Miriam*?"

"That we are."

Chapter 24

Matthew Preston eased his grip on the wooden leg he had wrenched off a chair. The library was utterly quiet, and the crowd which had been beating on the doors ten minutes ago seemed to have evaporated. He wiped cold sweat off his forehead and studied the room he had run to after leaving his comrades and those twins.

It looked like all the other rooms in the library, full of this outdated Roman junk. If his brother Mark was here they two would have enjoyed writing a few ditties about this place. But Mark wasn't here.

Footsteps snapped Matthew's thoughts back to earth. He stepped behind the door and lifted the chair leg, ready to bring it down on an attacker's skull.

"*Salve*," someone said.

Matthew didn't know what the word meant, but it didn't sound threatening. It sounded like the word of a man with fears of his own, and that probably meant that it was Bishop Aulus or that dwarf. But maybe not.

A head slowly advanced through the doorway, not where Matthew expected, but lower, about four feet from the ground. Matthew dropped the chair leg and folded his arms. It was the dwarf. As squat as a wharf. Matthew scowled at himself. He had to stop rhyming, he had to forget, or he'd go mad.

The dwarf saw him and touched his chest in a gesture of peace. Matthew nodded. Bishop Aulus followed, and the three of them were alone in the room.

Matthew shrugged his shoulders and made signs asking where his comrades were. Bishop Aulus signed that they had crossed the roofs. So, they had gone, had they? They had left him here alone with these Romans. But that's what they should have done. Jacques and O'Malley had first duty to Colonel Nobody, and it was their job to try and help him any way they could. And the twins had no reason to wait for him, either.

Matthew kicked the chair leg across the room and stalked out of his corner. He wouldn't think about twins.

"How do I get out of here?" Matthew asked, explaining the words with signs.

Bishop Aulus and the dwarf jabbered together for a few minutes, then the dwarf motioned for Matthew to follow. Matthew shrugged and picked up the chair leg.

The dwarf shook his head violently.

"What, you want me defenseless?" Matthew flung the leg into a corner. "Fine. I might as well be taken prisoner. I've let you savages capture my colonel, and I'm no better than him to be free when he's in chains."

But they seemed to be friendly enough, and fed him well throughout the day.

That night, the two Romans led Matthew to a nearby house, probably a Christian's, and stuffed him into a four-wheeled wagon. They tried to completely bury him under tanned hides, but he kept an eyehole from which he could watch the dwarf. A blind soldier is a soon-dead soldier. The wagon was drawn by a single musk ox, with incredibly shaggy hair and wickedly sharp horns. Sharp as thorns. *Stop rhyming.*

The wagon jolted through the quieting streets without interruption until it reached the gates, where a guard whistled for it to stop. Matthew parted the fur around his eyehole and scanned the situation. The dwarf stood, head hunched low, before a pair of sneering Romans.

Matthew set his jaw. The hides piled on top of him were too heavy to move, so if the Romans decided to do anything to the cart he couldn't do a thing. Powerless. He should be used to that by now.

One guard shoved the dwarf against the musk ox while the other spat on him. They let their arms hang low and stamped, mimicking his deformity. Matthew chewed hide. If only he could get out of this smelly cart and sell his life dearly—but that wouldn't help Colonel Nobody. No, he couldn't die now. Mark wouldn't want him to.

Someone shouted and an officer moved into the circle that Matthew could see. The guards fell back and the dwarf raised his head. His face was blank—either he was pretending that his mind was as weak as his body, or he was crushing his emotions in. The officer waved them through the gates.

According to what Bishop Aulus had signed to him back at the library, they were going to a safe house in the country, which was probably the house of that blacksmith, Balbus. If Jacques and O'Malley managed to get out of the city they might go there as well.

The jolting became rhythmic and Matthew closed his eyes, knowing that the sleep he had avoided last night would come back to claim his allegiance.

If only he couldn't sleep.

Then he wouldn't dream.

Chapter 25

"He isn't here yet," Varius said.

Lawrence stood in front of a lonely house plopped in a pasture. There were only a handful of sheep grazing nearby, though the sheepfolds were large enough to accommodate a far larger flock. The city walls were in sight, but only because the valley was so flat, as they were several miles away.

"I will let you meet my family, then I will take you to our leader," Varius said.

A big-muscled man greeted them from the head of the table.

"Who have you brought, Varius?" the man asked. "Ah! I recognize the big and little ones, though they wear our clothes now. Who are the others?"

Varius conducted the introductions. The host, his father, was named Balbus, and apparently he had already met Jacques and O'Malley. His wife was a gracious-looking matron with gray hair that reached her middle-back. A baby on a bed in the corner was sleeping so soundly that he looked dead, with his little mouth drooped open, and his shriveled arms spread eagle on the blanket.

Beside the baby sat a pretty young woman, maybe eighteen years old, wearing a tunic. The baby couldn't belong to Balbus and his wife, so he must belong to this young woman. But she wasn't wearing a *stola*, the long dress that signified a married woman. Had Roman fashions changed?

Lawrence pointed at the baby and looked at Varius.

"My father rescued him from the baby pit," Varius said.

Ah, then Varius's sister wasn't married. Suitors probably wouldn't be long in coming if they could see that face, though she wasn't as pretty as Pacarina. Her beauty was more peaceful, almost shy, compared to Pacarina's vitality. Lawrence eyed Chester, who was bending over the baby and taxing his diaphragm with some surprising gurgles. The young woman looked good next to him.

Balbus raised a hand, as if in blessing.

"If you are Christians, as my son says, then I welcome you as brothers, but I also pity you. This is a bad time for any Christian in Vallis Deorum."

"I think it is time to defend ourselves," Varius said. "God told the Israelites to destroy the pagan nations of Canaan."

"Hush!" Balbus's gaze roamed the room. "It's foolish to talk like that."

"Are you afraid of soldiers hearing? Father, it doesn't matter what they hear. The proclamation was clear. The persecutions are beginning again, and they won't wait for excuses to take our lands, our women, and our lives."

Varius clenched his fists.

"You know what happened when the tall and short Outsiders were last here, and you know what will happen in the market when the time for choosing slaves comes." He pointed at his sister.

Balbus rubbed his hands on his tunic, first his palms, then the backs of his hands, again and again. His arm-muscles quivered.

"Bishop Aulus believes resistance is wrong."

"I love Bishop Aulus, but he's not my God. Christ said to buy a sword. David was a man of war *and* a man after God's heart. Samson's last righteous act was to kill three-thousand Philistines."

Balbus sliced the air with his hand. "That's enough. We've talked about this before."

The fire faded from Varius's face. "Yes, Father." He turned to Lawrence. "Would you like to see our farm?"

The forge attached to the house obviously brought Balbus some extra money, as he had a number of storehouses in addition to the empty sheepfolds. It was to one of these storehouses that Varius led Lawrence.

"Are you sure your leader is here?" Lawrence said. This situation was rather odd.

"He's supposed to be." Varius opened the door. "Wait here and I will bring him to you."

The storehouse had no windows. It did have the sour smell of wheat in which fats have gone rancid. And there was another smell like human sweat. Lawrence sniffed again. It wasn't his sweat, but the room smelled like someone was sweating in it right now. Someone else.

An arm circled Lawrence's neck and compressed his windpipe. Hands stuffed dirty wool into his mouth. Sunlight flashed on him for a moment as he was dragged out the door and into another shed. That door closed, and a knife's point replaced the arm against his throat.

"Yell and you die," a voice whispered.

The breaths of two men blasted his face. The knife pressed below his Adam's apple at the base of his neck in the depression above his clavicle. The pressure sparked the reflex to gag, but Lawrence fought the urge. Gagging would impale him.

"We want to know who leads the fighting Christians," the voice said.

Lawrence tried to speak without moving his neck-muscles. "I—don't—know."

"Yes, you do. If you're here you must be a fighting Christian."

"Faulty logic," Lawrence said. "You're here. Are you—fighting Christians?"

"Tell us anything you know about your leader. Where does he live? Does he have family? How old is he?"

"I'm not feeling—conversational," Lawrence said.

A hand like a claw gripped his chest and slammed him against a wall.

"Do you know the sound a sheep makes when its throat is cut?" the voice said.

"No. I'm not a farmer."

"It's the sound you'll make if you don't tell us everything now."

Tremors coursed Lawrence's spine. He wasn't courageous. He didn't like to think about last stands. He shivered when he read about the tortures of the Waldensians, or the customs of the Romans he was now among. But he wouldn't betray another Christian.

"Cut away," Lawrence said.

"We won't hurt you if you speak. Just tell us anything. Does he have a family? Is he married? Tell us!"

"No."

"Good man."

Lawrence shuddered. Had his brain turned? He thought he had heard his captor say 'good man.' What was happening?

Sunlight streamed through the opening door and Varius entered.

"You're a true man," Varius said.

Lawrence blinked. The knife was gone from his throat and two men he had never seen before smiled gravely at him.

"What—"

"I needed to know that I could trust you," Varius said. "I'm sorry for the inconvenience. I've only survived this long by extreme caution. You see, I'm the leader of the fighting Christians, and these are two brothers in the Lord."

Lawrence rubbed his throat. He understood why Varius was so cautious, but it would have been nice if he had thought up a different way to prove Lawrence's trustworthiness. Lawrence was used to taking tests with the sharp end of a pen, not a knife.

"Your wife is well."

"What?" Lawrence froze. "What do you mean?"

"Your wife is captive in the palace, but she's still well. I tell you that to show that I have access to knowledge which most don't have."

"You mean that you have spies," Lawrence said. "But telling me that my wife is well doesn't prove anything. I'm sure that rumors have spread about her being held in the palace. You can say she's well, but she may actually be dead."

Varius smiled. "True. Tell me, did anyone in the city see you when you were taken to the palace?"

"No, it was dark. Only our guards saw us."

"Well, I will tell you that your wife is wearing a blue dress with a bright yellow piece of fabric around her shoulders, and that she is darker-skinned than you, very pretty, and has black hair."

Lawrence grabbed Varius's arm. "You've seen Pacarina?"

"Not with these two eyes, but I've seen her all the same. Now, you need to know more about us. First, I'm not my father's eldest son. My older brother was the leader of the fighting Christians, but he was sent to the mines because he fought against the soldiers who took my older sister as a slave to the palace."

"Your sister?" Lawrence pointed to the house.

"Not that one. They took my other sister a year and a half past and we have not heard of her since then. I took my brother's place as our leader, but our power is not as great as it may sound. We have eyes and ears who work for us, but few of them are willing to spill blood for freedom."

"Wait a moment," Lawrence said. "You've forgotten my wife. If you have people inside the palace, then you can get her out."

"I can't. It's not hard to buy eyes for the price of enough wine to make them water, but I can't buy hands willing to risk Little Caesar's torture chambers. Men willing to risk them can only be brothers, true Christians, and none of these are in the palace."

Lawrence extended his arm.

"Varius, I will help you destroy your tyrant. I will help you with my every thought, my every breath, and every ounce of what little physical strength I possess. I will rescue my wife, and nothing in the world except the glory of God is of more importance to me. What do you want me to do?"

Varius grasped his arm.

"We need your help to fight the Praetorian Guard. We aren't trained to fight, but six trained warriors from the Outside could give us the leadership and confidence we need."

"The man you need most is the one whom Little Caesar just sentenced to death at the festival," Lawrence said. "The three men who came with him were all soldiers, but they weren't officers in their army, and my brother and I have very limited army experience. The man you want is who they call 'Colonel Nobody.'"

Varius stroked his chin, which showed just a hint of bristles poking through the smooth skin. He wasn't so young that this was his first beard, so he must shave. Most of the Romans did so, which was why Jacques's whiskers had looked so foreign.

"The Dogs have agreed to rise on the festival's second day," Varius said. "That is when the marriage ceremony will be held. If we can free my brother and your 'Nobody' from the mines, they will help us organize our forces and know the best way to strike."

"Then that's our plan," Lawrence said.

"Yes, our plan." Varius bit his knuckles. "But, Outsider—I fear."

The knife that had tickled Lawrence's throat lay on a pile of hides. Varius gripped the hilt and held it blade down, like a seal.

"The first day of the festival is the slave auction, when slaves are traded and Little Caesar picks the best of the people as slaves."

Fury flashed over Varius's face and he smashed the knife into the wall.

"The *pig* will choose my sister. What do I do?"

Lawrence pointed up. "Petition God for her safety. And tell my brother."

Varius left the knife in the wall and wiped his forehead. He was regaining his composure. There must have been an incredible amount of emotion fermenting inside to bubble into that outbreak. He sucked a breath.

"Look."

Varius moved the hides off the pile, one by one, until he reached the floor. He brushed a layer of dirt away, revealing a trap door, which he opened. A gray cloak covered whatever was inside. Varius whisked the cloak away and showed a pile of Roman short swords, each beautifully polished, lying in alternating rows on the bottom of the compartment.

"These would bring fire to my home and death to my family if the government found them. My father is conflicted," Varius said, "but there's nothing conflicted about his metalwork. I don't know if he'll join the fighting Christians or Bishop Aulus, but his swords will arm my men."

Varius dropped the door. "You hold my life in your hands, Outsider. I trust you to keep the faith."

Lawrence nodded. "I will. Now take me back inside. It feels years since I've played with a baby."

"Tonight we play. Tomorrow we plan. The next day we act—and maybe die."

Chapter 26

The wall was a welcome support to Nobody's back as he sat on the floor of Otho's hut and studied the five men he had risked his life to find. He couldn't see much of them through the darkness, but if they were just normal sailors, there probably wasn't much to see. The men themselves weren't special. What they could attest to in court before Queen Victoria was.

"Were you men aboard the *Miriam* when she traded with Rahattan Island in the South Seas?" Nobody asked.

The sailors gasped.

"How did you know that?" the one who had answered before asked. "Who are you?"

"Nobody."

"Who?"

Nobody licked his dry lips and tried to ignore the smell of human refuse that lingered in his nostrils and on the roof of his mouth. This next question would settle his destiny, humanly speaking.

"Were you on board the *Miriam* when Colonel Nobody requested that she return to port so that he could search her?"

"Er—yes, I remember that. Oh, so then you must be Colonel Nobody—but what are you doing here?"

Nobody let his head fall back against the wall and closed his eyes. God was good. The weary months of travel and searching, the days of frustration and agony, that night of horrors—God had used it all to direct him to these five sailors. True, as Edmund would say, they were still all prisoners in an Ancient Roman mine in a lost valley on an ice-ridden island at the end of the world. But the God who created the universe could rescue a few of His creatures from a little valley.

"I don't think you're Colonel Nobody," the sailor said. "Last time I saw Colonel Nobody he didn't fall asleep when people asked him questions."

Nobody opened his eyes.

"Look, fellow. I've just sailed hundreds of miles, frozen in an Eskimo umiak, had wine poured down my throat 'til I vomited, been scourged, worked nearly to death in a mine, and am currently sentenced to death at an Ancient Roman festival. Why? Because I was looking for you. I'm slightly tired."

"Look here," one of the other sailors said, "why do you come after us? Did somebody hire you to assassinate us?"

Something about that voice, a little high, and a little weak, reminded Nobody of something. Some feeling of disaster. Why? Disasters weren't uncommon in his life, but he couldn't place which one he was specifically thinking of.

"I doubt he'd do all that just to slit our throats," the spokesman said. "Besides, Mr. Trumble, I might prefer a trip to Davy Jones's locker over this pigsty of a life."

Mr. Trumble. The *Miriam*'s second mate, who promised Tremont that he would swear in court that Nobody was a pirate. Nobody glanced at the spokesman's silhouette. One ear was missing. Yes, it was Bill, the one-eared man who had nearly brought the 42nd to blows on the voyage from Siberia to Rahattan, and who probably killed old Mathers, the *Miriam*'s captain.

New fear squeezed Nobody's innards. He had spent all his thought-energy on finding the sailors and getting them back to England, but he had never considered what they might say when there. What if these men followed Banastre Bronner's story and called Nobody a pirate?

Otho, who had been listening, but of course couldn't understand anything, muttered about fresh air and retreated from the hut. Nervous tension bound up Nobody's need for sleep and held it captive somewhere behind his eyelids. Right now, the most important thing was the sailors sitting around him and their attitude towards him.

"Tell me what happened that day off Rahattan."

"You hove us to," Bill said. "What, did you lose your memory with your name?"

"Did I use force? Did you turn around because Captain Mathers was happy to oblige me, or did you turn because I had you outmanned?"

Bill snorted. "You and your one boat crew? As if we couldn't have thrown you to the sharks if we wanted. Of course Mathers turned around with free will."

Nobody squinted through the darkness. He wanted to see their eyes.

"That wasn't what you said when you were with Banastre Bronner."

For five seconds the only sound was the snores of sleepers in surrounding huts.

"Memory is a funny thing," Bill said at last.

"What will you remember if I get you out of this place and ask your testimony before the queen?"

"You get us out of this slime-pit and we'll remember the truth."

Nobody leaned back against the wall. Edmund was saved. Well, saved if Nobody could get out of Vallis Deorum. Nobody's soul had an excellent chance of leaving shortly, but he was rather interested in his body going with it.

Otho came back in with something in each hand. He set one of the things down carefully in the dirt and plunked the other beside it.

"Hold this." Otho handed Nobody half a tunic.

Otho knelt behind the cover of the rag, slipped a hammer from beneath the dried grass that formed his bed, and began pounding. The blows were light and far-spaced, so that they mirrored the snores. *Crack.* Either metal or rock broke, and Otho stopped hammering.

"Hold it close," Otho said.

He made sure that the rag was between him and the door and held something against the object on the ground. It flamed. He had apparently taken an ember from the cooking fire and lighted a cast-off piece of torch wick. Two halves of a rock lay next to the hammer, their insides coated with metal. Otho unrolled a tiny scroll from a hollow in the largest piece and read the contents.

"Tomorrow is the day," he said.

Chapter 27

Pacarina pressed her cheek against the window's bars and watched the tiny patch of city that had been her only connection to the outside world for these long days. Really, it was the inside world. The Outside was somewhere beyond the mountains that her window did not show. But her world, Lawrence, was in the inside outside.

Thump. Thump.

Pacarina spun away from the window. It wasn't yet time for the slave to bring a meal, and she had never had any other visitors. She covered her heart with her palm and felt her fingers tingle with each pulse.

"Come in."

A slim figure in a gaudy dress slipped inside.

Pacarina breathed again. It was only the slave girl assigned to her. Over the girl's arms was draped a gorgeous violet dress with delicate red embroidery circling the wrists, elbows, and waist. The pattern looked like rows of tiny wheat stalks, first one standing straight, then one upside down, in a repeating pattern. Roses would have looked better. Ah, but these Romans had probably never seen roses.

"Caesar," the slave girl said. She said much more, but that was the only word that Pacarina understood.

The dress must be a gift from Caesar.

Pacarina turned back to the window. It wasn't much of a window, really, only as wide as the hand-mirror sitting on her nightstand in England, and with even that space further blocked by an iron cross forced into the rock. The rock was three or four feet thick, and the opening for the window sloped down such that it was probably invisible from the outside.

A hand touched Pacarina's shoulder. She leaped away, pressed her back against the wall, and reached up her left sleeve. Oh. It was only the slave girl, who looked almost as scared, crouched in the center of the room and watching Pacarina as if she were a tiger about to pounce.

"I'm sorry," Pacarina said. "My nerves are usually better, but this waiting has unsettled me."

The girl smiled as if she understood the words and held the dress out again. Pacarina shook her head.

"I don't care if you bring me the most beautiful dress in the world. I won't wear any gift from your sweaty Caesar." Pacarina held both ends of her capelet against her neck. "My husband gave me this dress, and I'll wear no dress for the pleasure of any man but him."

The girl cocked her head like a terrier. It wouldn't be kind to send her away with the dress, because she would be blamed for Pacarina's refusal, so Pacarina took it and laid it on the bed. She wouldn't wear it, but at least the only person who would be blamed for her not wearing it would be herself. That was her least fear in this horrible place, but she tried not to think that way. God would protect her, and Lawrence would come.

Pacarina turned back to the girl and gasped. The dress wasn't the only thing she had been carrying. There, hanging from the girl's fingers, was the most beautiful and most expensive necklace that Pacarina had ever seen. Rubies, diamonds, sapphires, and strange gemstones hung in gold settings from an exquisite chain made of tiny gold links woven together.

The girl pointed at Pacarina's neck, raised two fingers, and pointed at the bed.

"You mean that I'll be expected to marry Caesar in two days?" Pacarina said. "I don't care what they expect. I'm already married to one of the best men in the world, and no human can separate us except by death."

Pacarina's throat tightened. What if that was how they intended to separate them? What if they were going to kill Lawrence? What if—

Pacarina grabbed the necklace, crunched it into a ball, and flung it at the wall. "That's what I think of your Caesar."

The slave girl trembled. Of course she would. What must it be like to live at the whims of a fat Roman pig who divorced his wives every time he wanted a new one, and probably threw the old ones to the lions. Or were there lions in Greenland? Probably not. No roses, no lions, and no decency.

Pacarina had to discover what had happened to Lawrence. She had spent hours watching that little patch of city, hoping she would see him, but her tiny room was so high in the palace that even if he had walked into that one street he would just be another of the moving dots.

Oh, why hadn't she learned more back in those days at the Stoning estate when Lawrence had tried to teach her Latin? It just hadn't seemed important, and she loved to hear Lawrence's steady voice translating the old books to her as she embroidered carnations, or sewed, or drew. What were the words they had labored over? *Marita.* That meant wife, she knew, because Lawrence would call her that. But what was husband?

"*Maritus,*" Pacarina said. "Where is my *maritus*?"

The girl's painted eyelashes jumped. "*Maritus*?" She smiled and nodded. "Caesar."

"No, not him," Pacarina said. She shook her head. "I want my *maritus*, not Caesar. Where is Lawrence?" She ran to the window and pointed down. "There, out there, he might be out there, or he might be in the palace."

She held her hand a little above her head, just at Lawrence's height, then patted her stomach, trying to show that he was lean. If the girl could interpret her motions then there was no chance that she could think Pacarina was talking about Caesar.

The girl did seem to understand. She pointed outside and raised her thumb. That must mean that he was in the city, and alive.

Pacarina dabbed with her left sleeve at the tears that she hadn't been able to stop. Something brushed her skin—the knife she had hidden in her sleeve slipped loose and clattered on the stone at her feet. The slave jumped away as if it were a snake.

"Yes, I have a knife." Pacarina scooped it up and clasped the leather sheath, her thumbs on the hilt's pointy end. "If you knew my husband's brother you wouldn't be surprised that I have a knife, or that I know how to use it."

The girl traced a finger across her neck and pointed to Pacarina. Pacarina shuddered.

"No, I'm not going to kill myself. That's against God's law. But what your Caesar wants to do is also against God's law, and if he tries to marry me, I'm going to kill him. Please, don't tell anyone what I have."

The girl couldn't understand the words, but she must understand Pacarina's eyes. These Romans might be called 'ancient' because their society had hardly changed for so many centuries, but the slave girl was a woman, just like Pacarina, and must have the same emotions. Yes, there was pain and fear in the slave girl's eyes too, and the room wasn't cold enough to explain why her fingers trembled. They were sisters in bondage, but this poor girl had no husband to hope for rescue from.

Chapter 28

"It's about time that things became exciting," Chester said.

Yes, things were certainly exciting, which would be nice if Lawrence enjoyed excitement. At the moment he wanted to be at his desk in England working on an essay with Pacarina at his side and Chester's horrible harmonica-playing somewhere in the background giving him something to grumble about. Lawrence's critique of Gibbon's *Decline and Fall of the Roman Empire* had earned him some recognition, but this experience would make him an expert on Roman culture.

Regrettably, this experience wasn't over yet.

The trees blocked nearly all of the moonlight, which was a good thing, because it would have glinted on Varius's armor. The clink of the metal plates sounded extraordinarily loud to Lawrence—but so did his heartbeats.

"This is an odd-looking picnic party," Chester said. "An Ancient Roman pretending to be a soldier, two English gentlemen looking very out of place in waistcoats, and the girl. Remind me why she's along?"

"We don't know how unhealthy their brother is," Lawrence said. "Remember, they haven't heard from him for a year and a half. Their contact drops these rocks with messages, and they've heard that a man about Otho's size has been seen below, but that's all."

"That doesn't explain the girl."

"If you were in bad shape, who would you rather have tend to you—Pacarina, or me?"

Chester laughed. "I call you Professor, not Doctor."

"Precisely. And I'm sure this girl can do a much better job tending to her brother than any of us can. Which is why she's here."

Chester shrugged. He really was a sight, striding through these woods around the mine entrance with a borrowed leather belt slung from right shoulder to left hip and three knives strapped to the band. Varius's sister had wrapped her light-blue dress in a black cloak which blended excellently with the shadows beneath the trees. She hadn't said a word since they left Balbus's house. That balanced Chester nicely.

Jacques had been indignant that the girl was allowed to come and he was not, but O'Malley had managed to calm him. This plan called for stealth up to a certain point, and the fewer bodies to make a mistake the better. Besides, it removed the danger of the Frenchman and Irishman arguing within earshot of a Roman sentry.

The man who had argued hardest of all to come was Matthew Preston, whom Bishop Aulus's dwarfish son had smuggled out of the city. Joktan seemed like a very nice fellow. He had asked many questions and been quite interesting. But when Matthew found out that a party was going to rescue Colonel Nobody, he eclipsed the dwarf with his passionate insistence to go along. Lawrence wouldn't agree. He didn't trust Matthew, and this expedition was dangerous enough without risking instability among its members.

"Wait here," Varius said. "I'm going ahead to count the campfires. If anyone sees me they'll think I'm a sentry. If my information is right, most of the soldiers were withdrawn this afternoon to help with the festival tomorrow. If my information isn't right—" he dragged his index finger across his neck.

Chester sat down with his back to a tree and examined his pistols. Varius had somehow managed to get these sneaked out of the palace. The Romans didn't know enough to value them highly yet, but tonight was going to introduce them to the power of hot lead.

"You don't *really* mind having her along, do you?" Lawrence asked.

Chester looked up. "Her? Oh, you mean the girl." He peeked past Lawrence's leg at where the girl was leaning against a tree. "No particular objections, why?"

"I think she'd do very well for you."

The darkness masked Chester's face, but his snort told Lawrence exactly what he looked like. Wide smile, sarcastic eyes, rolled up forehead, and wrinkled nose.

"You're hilarious, Law. Absolutely hilarious. I thought it was bad enough when the love-thingy chewed on you and you married Pacarina and forgot my existence, but ever since you remembered that you had a brother you've been trying to find me a mate."

Chester exaggerated, as usual, but Lawrence couldn't deny that he had been making a list of possibilities. Chester needed a softening influence in his life. It might be the only way to stop travesties like that wolf-hat.

"Don't simply pass her off, Chester," Lawrence said. "I had an excellent conversation with her father and her last night, and she showed an impressive amount of character and intelligence."

Chester shook his head. "Too quiet."

"That's a good thing. It's called balance, and it's a quality you're a little lacking in. Look at Pacarina and me—our personalities aren't exactly similar."

"No, that's true," Chester said. "Opposites work well in your case, and it's a good thing, because I don't think the world is ready for a female Lawrence. But seriously, Law, I don't think I could stand a quiet wife. I need somebody excited about life, somebody to share my dreams and adventures."

Lawrence threw up his hands. "Then why didn't you marry Pacarina?"

"She had far too much sense to marry me."

Lawrence deflated. How do you argue with someone like Chester?

"Chester, are you saying that you've added lack of sense to your list of necessary qualities in a wife?"

"No, but I mean—Pacarina was obviously perfect for you. Besides, why isn't this girl already married? I thought the Romans tied the knot when they were twelve or thirteen."

"The customs have changed here over the centuries, primarily because smaller families are popular."

A hand touched Lawrence's shoulder. He nearly jumped, and found himself staring up at Varius's sister, who had a finger on her lips.

"Please, tell your brother that he speaks too loudly. The sentries may hear."

"Er, right." Lawrence tried to smile. Thankfully, the darkness hid his blush. "Too loudly. Right. I'll tell him."

She shook her head. "What is so important to talk about now?"

Lawrence coughed. "Er—it's rather—complicated. Brotherly love, and all that. Planning for the future."

Varius saved him further embarrassment by slipping into their little glade at this moment. He said the camp was nearly deserted and the few soldiers remaining were enjoying the fruits of the vine more than was consistent with their professional duties. That was the beauty of fighting against pagans. There was always some lack of self-restraint, some weakness, that could be exploited, and wine was the second-most common.

Now, should they sneak around the camp or bluff through it? Sneaking was more appealing, but that's what the enemy would expect. A solid bluff in a country as unaccustomed to surprise as this one might just work. Then again, it might result in a *gladius* to the heart.

"Are you ready?" Varius asked.

Lawrence shook his head. "Not really. Let's go."

Varius's sister remained in the glade and the others moved forward, watching even more carefully for sticks that might crack underfoot or rotten branches they might brush against. There were probably still roaming sentries in the woods, and at any rate, they were getting close enough to the edge of the tree-belt to be heard by someone in the camp.

The night air made Lawrence wish for a thicker waistcoat. It was colder than England, though not as bad as could be expected. There must be some volcanic energy warming the ground. The steam vents made this almost certain, and the crops shouldn't grow so well in a normal Greenlandic environment. In different circumstances Lawrence would have gone hunting for volcanic rock to prove his theory. Instead, he was hunting for man.

Crack.

Lawrence stopped, his right foot mid-air. The other two became statues. None of them had stepped on a stick. Someone else was out there.

Footsteps approached.

Chester took control. One pointing finger sent Varius scurrying behind a shrub, while Chester cupped his hands, knelt beside a tree, and motioned for Lawrence to climb. Lawrence gulped. This wasn't in the plan. But a planner's merit isn't proved by the strength of his plan, but by the ease with which he adapts it. Lawrence climbed.

The owner of the footsteps was heavy and not trying to be quiet. It was someone who had every right to be in these woods, and the only person possessing that right would be a Roman sentry. Lawrence's tree had no lower branches, so all he could do was hug the trunk with his legs and arms, dig his fingernails into the bark, and pray that the friction would hold him up.

Crunch. CruNCH. CRUNCH.

Lawrence peeked under his arm. A Roman soldier stood directly below him. His helmet nearly brushed Lawrence's boot. His sword-belt hung in shadow, but Lawrence knew exactly what it contained. Should he drop on the sentry? He was in the perfect position—simply let go and they'd both tumble into a heap. But the Roman would probably shout and that would mean discovery or postponement of the rescue, both of which were equally bad.

Chester was up his own tree with a knife in each hand. He shook his head at Lawrence. Good, he didn't want Lawrence to drop. The sentry began walking again, his path heading straight by Chester's tree. As long as he didn't look up they were safe.

Squawk.

The Roman's head tilted back and he stared up—directly at Chester. One kick sent him sprawling wordlessly, his armor rattling like a tinker's pack. Chester was at his side in a moment and finished the job with his knives.

Lawrence inched back to earth with a decidedly unsettled stomach. He knew the deed had to be done, he knew it was justifiable before God, because they were essentially at war with the Romans, and he knew that men just like this one were holding his wife captive. Intellectually it all made sense, but

213

his intellect couldn't stop that dark splotch on the ground from curdling his bowels.

They waited for any sign that the armor's rattling had been heard, but the camp was quiet.

"Trust me to pick a tree with a bird up it," Chester said. "Come on, let's go rescue this soldier without a name."

They paused at the edge of the trees and examined the campfires.

"What do you think of the odds, Law?" Chester whispered.

"Eleven point six to one."

"Eh?"

"Ten fires averaging three men per fire equals thirty, plus an extra five to account for any odds and ends. That's thirty-five, divided by the three of us. That makes eleven point six to one."

Chester shook his head. "Only you could spoil the fun of fighting overwhelming odds with decimal points."

"You're not thinking of attacking, are you, Chester?"

"I'm thinking of nothing else, but that's why you're supposed to do the thinking in these arrangements. What's your plan?"

To the left of the fires was a great black circle where this fabled pit must be. That was one of only two paths to their goal, but with unscalable cliffs, part of a Roman legion camped on its edge, and no knowing what at its base, it wasn't a promising entrance. The other option was a tunnel which opened in the base of the hills on the other side of the camp. This was how the Romans brought up ore and sent down prisoners, according to Varius's information. This was how they must enter.

"Time runs short," Varius said.

Lawrence motioned to hand out the sheepskins. If there was any brilliance to the plan, this was it. Three men couldn't walk unchallenged through a Roman camp, but three sheep hugging the cliff might slip by.

"I wish these walking mutton-bags were a bit larger," Chester said.

He tried to don the skin over his wolf-hat, but that didn't work, so he had to stuff the pelt in his knife-belt and try again.

Lawrence smiled. "You're an excellent example of Matthew seven, verse fifteen."

"Eh?"

"A wolf in sheep's clothing."

The inside of the sheepskin was tight, smelly, and dark. The back legs were slit open to allow the boots to pass through, and the front legs were treated similarly for the hands, so that Lawrence was walking like an upside down U. By the third hobble his hands were coated with mud and grass stalks and the stuffy sensation in his fingertips warned of serious caking under the fingernails. Adventuring isn't clean.

"This is ruining my taste for mutton," Chester said, his voice muffled by the two layers of skin between his lips and Lawrence's ears. "Let's move before I start baaing."

No wonder sheep don't usually travel in straight lines. Then again, their eyes matched the holes in their head for eyes, while Lawrence's didn't. The tight skin scraped his trousers against his thighs at each step and aches began dotting his back. Graze on a few stalks here and there, make a zigzag or ten—who would know the difference? Lord willing, no one was watching.

They were halfway now. Lawrence peeked under the sheep's left eyebrow. The fires were too close. Edge right, closer to the hills, farther from—

"Halt!"

Everything in Lawrence wanted to freeze in place but he forced himself to put his right arm down, then his left, then a leg, slow, methodical, no change.

"Don't stop!" Lawrence whispered.

Sheep understand dogs, not words. Halting at a sentry's command would be a sure sign that something was wrong with these midnight strollers.

"What is it?" asked another voice in Latin.

A *gladius* scraped in its sheath.

"There is something moving, there, by the hill."

215

"Hmm? There's no—oh, over there. It's sheep, you fool. Never seen a fleece before? If there were any demons down from the hills tonight they'd join the deviltry in the city, not skulk around camp. Come along, I have a flask begging to be emptied."

Their footsteps faded away.

Lawrence wanted to wipe his forehead, but it would take five minutes of tugging to get to it, so he postponed the luxury. They crossed the rest of the distance without incident and huddled by the tunnel's opening. Even more than in the woods, silence was essential.

They left the sheepskins piled behind a rock and inched towards the opening. From here until the end of the tunnel there was no real plan, because Lawrence didn't know what was inside. That's why Chester led the way.

Chester peered past the corner, jerked his hand into the 'stop' position, and backed slowly away. He lifted one finger. One sentry. He patted his pockets, stuck his fingers into his waistcoat, and dug his hands in his trousers. He signaled Lawrence and rubbed his fingers together. What? He wanted to borrow money *now*? Lawrence shook his head in wonder and handed him a penny.

Clink.

Chester had tossed the coin into the cave entrance. Someone inside breathed sharply and hobnails clacked toward the opening. Chester slipped a knife from his chest-belt.

The sentry's armor would cover all the vital areas on his torso, and a knife in the leg would only bring a bellow of rage and a rush of angry legionaries. The only vulnerable place that would immediately silence him was the face. The footsteps reached the corner. Chester drew back his knife. Lawrence closed his eyes.

Thud.

No scream. No shout. Only the rattle of the man's armor on the rock. Chester's aim was true.

The moonlight lit the tunnel for the first several steps but after that it was ink-dark. Lawrence kept his hand on Chester's shoulder and Varius gripped his. No one could see them coming, but they also couldn't see anyone they were coming to. Silence weighted the air.

Earth would rotate Greenland back into sunlight in a few hours and the grand slave auction would begin. Vallis Deorum was too small to hide something if Little Caesar truly wanted it found, and once his soldiers told him about Varius's sister, he would certainly want her found. This plan had to work.

"*Quo vadis?*"

The unexpected challenge nearly wrenched a gasp from Lawrence.

Varius instantly stepped forward, his armor clanking, and began explaining to the voice. Lawrence had planned for this contingency, which was why Varius was wearing the armor. It was old and rusty, but might deceive someone squinting in a dark tunnel.

"No entrance at night," the voice said. "The door is locked."

Door? There wasn't supposed to be any door in the tunnel.

"Do you think Little Caesar cares whether you've locked your measly door?" Varius said. His voice was brash like a soldier's. "We have to take these Outsiders down. Don't blame me for Little Caesar's whims."

Metal struck on stone. Chester wrapped himself in a cloak to hide his knife-belt and pistols while Lawrence bent his aching back and hung his head, trying to look like a disheartened slave. A spark flashed into the flare of a torch.

The guard wore the same hobnailed sandals, leather belt, and breastplate that all the others did, but the one different point was the huge key hanging from a strap over his shoulder. Behind him loomed a massive door with planks resting in grooves to block it from opening.

"Why are there so many Outsiders?" the guard said. "And why does everything have to be at night? They brought in five Outsiders a few weeks ago."

"These can join them," Varius said. "Are you going to open the door or keep us chattering until Little Caesar orders our tongues torn out?"

The guard laughed.

"You think he cares about a couple Outsiders right now? He's got the pick of the country tomorrow *and* a new wife the day after, and I hear she's a beauty. I've got three bets running that he'll keep her for at least two months before he divorces her. What do you think? Have you seen her?"

Lawrence scraped his canine teeth together.

Varius growled. "No, I haven't seen her, and I want some sleep before a full day of controlling crowds. Are you going to let us in or not?"

"You can go in if you have orders, but you're not coming back out until I get orders straight from the manager. That's how it works here. You have orders?"

Varius handed him a scroll. Chester's cloak crinkled slightly, and Lawrence knew that his hand was on one of his knives. If this guard could read they would have to kill him. The scroll was Balbus's listing of last year's new-born lambs.

For three long moments the guard held the scroll between his fists and studied the words. Then he rolled it up, flicked it with a dirt-crusted fingernail, and handed it back.

"Hello in there, you awake?" The guard pounded on the door.

"What's the password?" a voice said from the other side.

"By the beard of Bacchus."

On this side the guard hoisted the planks out of the grooves one by one, three thick timbers banded by metal, and turned the key in the lock. There was more grunting from the other side, more timbers thumping the ground, and another key scraping in a lock. The door creaked open.

The first guard gave them his torch.

"If I were you I'd wait until morning to hand the prisoners over to the manager. He's a beast when he's well-fed and slept. Wake him up in the middle of the night and he might have your head flogged off."

Another danger passed, Lawrence thought. The tunnel finally dumped them in the bottom of the pit at the foot of the cliffs. There were no campfires. The cold air was charged with the smell of misery.

"Now what?" Chester asked through Lawrence.

"We need to find Otho and your Outsider," Varius said.

Chester grunted. "He does like to state the obvious. The point is, how do we find them? We could knock door to door at these slave hut places, but I don't think that would have quite the result we're looking for."

"I wrote for them to meet us as close to the entrance as possible," Varius said. "If they received my message they should be here."

"Which is probably why there's a fellow crouching behind that boulder." Chester leveled his pistol. "Come out of there before I scratch your ribs with a bullet."

Chester's English commands probably didn't have much to do with it, but the man did rise and step into the moonlight. His sleeveless tunic did nothing to disguise his tense muscles and broad chest. If this was Otho, his sister wouldn't have much healing to do.

It was Otho. The brothers clasped each other and whispered much louder than Lawrence liked to hear. He was sympathetic to reunion scenes, but he was most interested in his own reunion scene with Pacarina, and that wasn't going to happen until they got out of this place.

"Where is Colonel Nobody?" Lawrence asked.

Otho released his brother and snapped his features back to an intense calm.

"He's chained in one of the mines. The manager is taking advantage of the poor boy's last night in his power."

Lawrence clenched his fists. He'd had enough of everything Roman.

"Take me to him," he said.

"We have another problem," Otho said. "The Outsider wants to also rescue five other Outsiders who were brought here."

Lawrence blinked. This was supposed to be the precise extraction of two individuals, not an open invitation to everyone in the proximity. This colonel was rather presumptuous.

"Very well," Lawrence said, "you and your brother figure out how to get these five extras out and my brother and I will find Colonel Nobody."

Chapter 29

"Doesn't this bring back memories, Law?" Chester said.

Lawrence held his arms into the darkness ahead in case there was an unexpected turn in the tunnel. The tap of his boots on the rock, the slight difference in atmospheric pressure caused by the surrounding miles of solid strata, the cold sweat on his forehead, and the utter darkness—yes, they all brought back memories. At least this time he wasn't being chased by a tribe of blood-hungry natives. That was an interesting thought. Were the uncivilized South American tribesmen actually any worse than these 'civilized' Romans?

"Law? Are you there?"

"Oh, sorry, Chester. I was thinking about this Roman society. I think we in the Outside have succumbed to a millennium and a half of gloss. We teach our schoolchildren Latin, and Roman mythology, and make them read the foundations of Roman philosophy like Plato, Socrates, and Aristotle. Even when I wrote my critique of Gibbon's *Decline and Fall* I was only combating his false perspective on Christianity, not arguing with the premise that the Roman empire was a good thing."

Chester grunted. "Could you summarize that lecture for we yeomen?"

"The Romans were—and are—a perverted society which should only be taught as a lesson of what *not* to do."

"Point taken. I hope I live long enough to see the papers trashing your epic book about the problems of Roman civilization. But in order to do that—live that long, I mean—I recommend silence."

Chester pointed to a glow far down the mine, drew a knife with each hand, and silently slipped ahead of Lawrence. The firelight wasn't directly ahead, but somewhere around the corner, so that they were only looking at the glow's fingertips. As they approached the corner the light bled on hammer-scars on all of the walls.

Voices muttered in Latin. Burning wood crackled, and there was a strange rat-a-tat of metal on metal. Lawrence and Chester reached the corner.

Chester inched his head past the corner while Lawrence dropped to his knees, pressed his cheek against the rock, and did the same. The sight was not a pretty one.

The gallery was much wider than the tunnel behind them, probably because there had been an extra-large deposit of ore here. A metal grate leaned against the left wall and to this grate was bound an Englishman. His head was turned away, but he must be the fabled Colonel Nobody.

He was tied face-first, so that his shirtless back was exposed to the air, and there were strange shadows darkening his skin. Lawrence looked closer. His cheek nearly slipped from the rock. Those weren't shadows. Those were the scars of a recent flogging which webbed Nobody's back like thick spider-threads and were crossed by new, unhealed stripes.

"You did it on purpose," a voice said.

Lawrence inched farther out. A huge bucket of liquid bubbled over a fire at the base of the right wall. Two Roman soldiers stood next to this with their sword ends actually in the fire, while a man in a fur-lined cloak tapped together the arms of a pair of red-hot pincers.

"I gave you every chance," the man in the fur cloak said. "You come to my mine to work. Well, I says, you may work. I let you race my best man, my best man! And what do you do? You fail. So of course, though it pains my heart, you must be punished. Then, I say, I will give him another chance. Even though he has already gotten to work in the mine all day, I will send him to clean up the waste with the women. What kindness!"

"All right, beast," Colonel Nobody said. His voice was weak. "So you're a jolly gift-giving grandfather. I don't care if you call yourself the Sultan of Turkey. Do what you intend to do without wasting all our oxygen."

Lawrence put a mental notch in his brain to translate this to Chester when he had a chance. This colonel combined boldness and repartee, two of Chester's favorite qualities.

"You have a sharp tongue, Outsider." The mine manager stepped closer. "Where was I? Ah, yes, I let you clean up our waste, but still you are not grateful. So what do I do? I send you back to work here, expecting honest labor, and you try to destroy my mine."

The manager was close now, his lips next to Nobody's ear. "You tried to mine through a pillar. Do you know the penalty for that? Death."

"Then it's unfortunate for you that Little Caesar already claimed that privilege."

"True." The manager turned his back on Nobody. He tapped the pincer arms together. "It is a shame. Not that your death will be clean or quick in the arena, but I like to think that I have a special touch for such things." He whirled. "But you need not gloat, for there's much that I can do to a man before he dies."

"Then close your mouth and do it," Colonel Nobody said. "You can't do anything more to me than God allows."

"Ha!" The manager threw his arms out toward the two guards. "You hear? This one still believes in his god. I told you he was a strange one." He turned back to Colonel Nobody. "Slaves who come to the mines forget their silly gods. They believe in me, pain, and death, all three of which come true."

"I'm tired of you, Roman," Colonel Nobody said. "I prefer my villains honest and brief. You know you told me to hammer that pillar. You know you did it because your twisted brain likes having excuses for enjoying pain. Enjoy away, and leave the echoes of this place in peace."

"They will echo your screams."

The manager's tone had changed.

Lawrence touched Chester's knee. It was time.

"Greetings from London." Chester stepped into the light. "Nice mine you have here. Say hello to Death for me."

He drew back his arm and flung a knife at the manager, but the man dodged to the left and the knife only sliced a chunk of fur from his cloak.

"Disgusting," Chester said. "Can I use pistols yet?"

Lawrence shook his head. "Too loud."

"Oh, well. Swords out, Law."

Chester reached for his back where his *gladius* was hidden while Lawrence drew his from beneath his coat and clasped the cold handle with both hands. He didn't care if it was a one-handed sword.

"Kill them!" the manager screamed.

The two guards advanced from the fire, their swords extended and red-hot. They must have been about to help with the torture, for there was no mistaking that evil red glow along the last quarter of the blade.

Chester was still reaching for his sword.

"Rather—tight," he grunted. "If I'd known I would have to wear a sword back here I'd have had this waistcoat made a little larger."

The guards were coming.

"What do I do?" Lawrence waved his *gladius* at them but he knew he couldn't win. He had better chances with a sharp-pointed pencil.

"Do you know the *passata sotto*?" Colonel Nobody said.

"The what?"

"Then dodge, duck, and knock out their legs. You must use their blades against them."

The guard on the left reached him first and lunged. Lawrence struck in that direction with his sword and side-stepped right. Sparks flew from the hot steel.

"Down!" Colonel Nobody shouted.

Lawrence dropped his sword, crouched, and charged the guard's legs. The heavy Roman collapsed onto Lawrence's body. Lawrence tried to roll away but he was trapped, his head and legs exposed to the second guard. He closed his eyes and prepared for the blow.

"A Stoning!"

Chester had his sword out and now the real fight began.

Steel against steel, wit against wit. The shuffling of the combatants' feet sounded like someone flipping pages at top speed, while their breath came in short bursts punctuated by quick sucks. The guard on Lawrence rolled off and joined the fray. Lawrence crawled toward his sword but by the time he reached it there was no need.

There were two shrieks, then silence. The two guards lay lifeless on the stone floor, their red-hot blades used against them.

"Good show," Colonel Nobody said. "You don't fight like a soldier, but you also don't quite fight like a civilian. What are you?"

Chester wiped his sword on one of the dead Romans' tunics.

"I like to think of myself as a warrior-civilian. Now, what do we do about that swine?"

The mine manager trembled in the corner. The coat pulled tightly around his shoulders lacked a chunk of fur on the right shoulder where Chester's knife had sliced.

"Shed no needless blood," Colonel Nobody said. "Take him prisoner."

Lawrence grabbed a torch from one of the wall-brackets so that he could see to untie Colonel Nobody's bonds. He tugged at the knots, but they were extremely constricted. Chester tapped him on the shoulder and motioned to guard the manager.

"We're not trying to save the wrapping paper, Law."

A few clean slices bypassed the knots and let the ropes fall. Colonel Nobody staggered away from the grate.

"I don't know who you are, but I thank you."

Colonel Nobody spread his arms out and reached for his toes to stretch his muscles.

Chester shrugged. "Happy to oblige. Actually, we came to Greenland specifically to find you and get you back to England. Queen Victoria has set a date for you to present your evidence by, otherwise your second-in-command is going to be tried for treason."

Colonel Nobody stopped with his fingers ten inches from his toes. His head shot up.

"When?"

Chester held out his copy of the proclamation. Colonel Nobody snatched it.

"No! How can that be enough time to return?" Colonel Nobody's hands clenched into fists. "I will not fail Edmund. You, I don't know your name—help me into this armor."

"Right-ho. I'm Chester, by the way. That's Lawrence."

Chester hesitated for a moment with the shirt in his hands, looking at the colonel's scarred back, but Colonel Nobody waved him on. The skin on the colonel's face screwed in agony as the fabric touched his raw flesh. Chester lifted the armor onto him as gently as possible and loosely buckled the straps on his shoulders and chest.

That's when it happened.

Watching this mysterious colonel had taken too much of Lawrence's attention. He saw movement in his peripheral vision and spun, but it was too late. The mine manager slipped out of his corner and dashed to the far side of the tub of liquid.

Colonel Nobody grabbed a sword with his left hand and Chester leveled both of his pistols, but all three stopped when they saw the manager's face. His cheeks creased away from his lips in a horrible smile while his hands rested on the bucket's lip.

"Boiling oil," he said.

The bucket stood on a base of iron legs. One hearty push would send a flood of boiling oil over the Englishmen's legs.

"Shall I shoot?" Chester asked.

"No! That will bring guards from outside," Lawrence said.

"But there have already been screams!"

Lawrence pointed at Colonel Nobody. "There were supposed to be."

"You meant to kill me." The manager cackled. "You thought you would escape *my* mine, but the only way to escape my mine is through the door of Hades."

"Chester—your knife," Lawrence whispered. He raised his voice so that the manager could hear. "You'll kill yourself as well if you dump that oil. Oil will find its level. Dump that and you'll be scalded into oblivion."

Chester's hand inched towards his knife-belt.

"Fool, you think I don't know that?" the manager said. "There is a ledge behind me from which I will watch your agony and smell the sweet odor of your roasting flesh."

What to say? Lawrence had to keep the villain talking. Chester's fingers were touching one of the knife's buckles now, but the manager could tip the bucket in a single second. The torch in Lawrence's hand did not heat the cold sweat in every pore.

"Er—roasting, you say? I thought you were intelligent. Roasting is accomplished by dry heat, not liquid. Scalding would be more correct."

"You silly fool, I will—"

Chester's arm whisked away from his chest and a knife flashed in the torchlight. The manager leaned against the bucket too late. The knife struck and his body thudded on the rock.

"Good show again," Colonel Nobody said. "I admire a man with the presence of mind to insult someone about to deluge him with boiling oil."

Lawrence laughed weakly.

"You had some choice words of your own for the villain when you were on that grate. I would have recommended a little more diplomacy."

Colonel Nobody stuck his sword into his new sword-belt.

"That was Edmund's job. I'm just a fighting colonel."

He started for the passageway.

"I think this next day is going to require much more fighting than diplomacy."

Chapter 30

"The question is, how do we get out?" one of the brothers said.

Which name belongs to which? Nobody wondered. One was Lawrence and one was Chester, but he couldn't remember who owned which face. The swordsman had introduced them. The other one seemed more mature. He hadn't been much good in the fight, but the way he kept the manager talking was brilliant. He seemed to be the older one—no, they must be twins.

"Your name was . . . ?" Nobody held out his hand.

"Chester."

Chester's hearty grip sent splinters of pain up Nobody's right arm. He disengaged as quickly as courtesy would allow.

Quite a detachment had formed at the mine's exit into the open air. Both of the English brothers and Otho and his brother crouched in the shadows. Indeed, it was a haven for brothers. Only Edmund was missing, Nobody's brother, not by birth, but certainly by blood.

"The guards at the entrance won't let us out tonight," Lawrence said. "But we need to get out."

Chester shrugged.

"We fight our way out. It's as easy as dropping a knife. I can use my pistols since we won't be worried about making noise, and the guards will be dead before they have time to think that we've bottled lightning and spat it at them."

"It's not that simple," Lawrence said. "We can kill the guards on our side of the door, but it needs to be unlocked from both sides. Fighting isn't an option—at least, not the way you described. We need a diversion."

"What does that mean?"

"I'm hoping Otho can tell us. Fire is always a good option. For this plan to work we need to start a disturbance, a revolt, even."

"You're joking." Chester's face wrinkled. "Are you saying that we spent all that sweat and brainpower *not* making a sound in this mine so that we could run down to the entrance and scream our lungs into pneumonia?"

Chester sounded like Edmund.

Lawrence and Otho discussed the best way to create a distraction. It was odd to not be an intimate party to such a discussion, but Nobody listened quietly. He had ideas of his own—he could never have become the 42nd's colonel if he didn't—but he was interested in this young Englishman. What would bring these two brothers so far just to help Nobody?

Something blocked the moonlight. Nobody scooped up his sword but the rasping of an English voice reassured him.

"You anchored in here, Colonel Nobody? This Roman Jack came aground aft of our hut and wanted to tow us somewhere, but we wasn't sure what to do, so we talked it over and decided that since he seemed to be friendly with you and you've given your davy to get us out of here we might as well see what he wanted."

It was impossible to mistake one of the sailor Bill's sentences. All five sailors squatted inside the mine's mouth and raised the group to a substantial number. In a place where it was supposedly impossible for one man to escape they now had to get out ten.

"All right, we have a plan," Lawrence said. "I need to know our exact resources. Colonel Nobody, are you able to fight?"

Nobody looked at his arm. "Not with a sword, but I can use a pistol."

Chester coughed. "I'm not sure that I like that idea. You see, I've had a great deal of practice with the pistol, and I'm rather a good shot. Every shot must count."

Nobody grunted. "Have you heard of the 42nd? It was the best regiment in the army. Frankly, it was the best in the history of our army. I didn't get to be colonel of the 42nd by simply being 'rather' a good shot."

Nobody held out his hand. Chester gave him a pistol, donned some incredibly odd headgear, and headed for the huts.

"Let's get this noise-making on the move," he called.

"Wait a moment, Chester." Lawrence signaled him to return. "The most important part of this plan starts on our knees."

Nobody bowed his head and waited for Lawrence to begin.

"Father," Lawrence prayed, "we ask Your protection and blessing on what we're about to do. We seek to glorify You, and we seek to rescue the innocent. Strengthen our arms to war, tighten our sinews like iron, give us clear heads, and bless our endeavor, we pray, if it be according to Your will. In Christ's name, Amen."

Lawrence gave each man an objective before they scattered. Nobody followed Otho toward a slave hut in the north corner of the pit.

"Would the slaves fight if we give them weapons?" Nobody asked.

Otho shook his head. "With as much work and little food as they get they hardly have the strength to sleep. As you've seen, I'm treated slightly better because I work so hard. As for you, I don't know how you're still moving. Maybe because you've been here only a few days?"

"Has it only been a few days?" Nobody sighed. "Frankly, I'm channeling what I call my 'fighting fury' into my limbs to keep moving. And if you knew how my back felt at the moment you would know why there's no chance of my falling asleep."

This was the perfect time for an escape. So many guards had been pulled from the pit to help in the city that it was easy to slither around the few that remained and make for the smoldering fires. Most of the remaining guards were snoring in the barracks, a long stone building tightly roofed against the weather. If this had been thatched with hay like the other huts, Nobody would have started his burning here, but it wasn't.

The plan was simple. Light as much dry hay as possible on fire, bring the entire slave population out in one screaming mass, and hope the soldiers above would descend to control the situation.

Nobody inched a small log out of one of the cooking fires which had died down and crept toward his goal. The log's end glowed orange. He held the burning end into the hut's thatch. Smoke whiskers curled momentarily before a section of hay flared into flame. At that instant half a dozen points of light dotted the night in all directions.

The sleepy sentries were the first to shout but their yells were engulfed by a cacophony of sounds as slaves poured from every hut, shouting, cursing, tripping over each other, and wandering in the ever-increasing arc of light with faces heavy with sleep so deep that even a fire couldn't quite clear the cobwebs.

Chester's pistol cracked. Dozens of swords scraped out of their sheaths. Nobody cocked his own pistol, peered around the hut's corner, and waited for a helmet to emerge from the throng of frightened slaves. His fat friend from the latrine bowled through a knot of slave children and ran toward the hut with a blanket in his arms. One trigger pull and he was on his face, lifeless, the blanket crumpled into a heap by his head.

Nobody threaded the blazing buildings and joined the rest of the group at the tunnel exit. Horns blared on the clifftop. Nobody dropped to a crouching position and laid his right ear on the rock. That vibration must mean that the door was opening.

"Into the rocks!" Nobody said.

They hid behind boulders on both sides of the tunnel's mouth and waited. Hobnails clacked on rock and metal clashed against metal as a stream of soldiers entered the pit and charged the huts. Three moments after the last Roman stumbled from the darkness Nobody led the way into it.

"The time for quiet has ended," Nobody said. "We run hard and fight harder from here to home."

The door was still open. Two shots and two thrusts finished the blinking guards and the path to freedom was clear. The memory of this pit would return in nightmares but the hideous reality was over and there was nothing that would draw Nobody's thoughts back to—

"Wait!" Nobody said.

The English brothers stared at him.

"There's a slave girl back there whom I must rescue."

"What?" Anger streaked Lawrence's face. "You're betrothed to Lady Liana. How dare you!"

"I didn't say I love this girl, I said I need to rescue her. She's here because she spoke in my defense and it's my duty to get her out. Can't you see that?"

"He's right," Chester said. "That's a gentleman's duty."

"But—" Lawrence was panicking. "You can't go back in there. I need your help to rescue my wife."

Nobody waved them on and ran back toward the pit. He didn't want to go back but it was his duty to save Ennia. Footsteps followed and the brothers drew abreast of him as he reached the exit.

"Leave," Nobody said. "This has nothing to do with you."

"Wrong," Lawrence said. "You're the ticket to the revolt necessary to rescue my wife."

There was no time to argue. If they wanted to throw away their lives they might as well do it down here as up there.

The whole pit floor was lit by the fires. It was a testament to the slaves' discouragement that no enterprising fellow had touched off a fire before. The soldiers were too busy fighting the flames to watch who was coming or going, and the slaves were too frightened to do anything besides mill like shepherdless sheep. Nobody pushed his weary body into the confusion's heart.

"Ennia!" Nobody called.

A body flung out of a hut's shadow and arms clung to Nobody's armor. He screamed as his borrowed tunic rubbed against his raw wounds.

Three soldiers turned, realized that something was wrong, and grabbed Ennia from Nobody. A hobnailed sandal kicked his right thigh and the sudden shock narrowed his vision into two tiny tunnels. He sank through the haze into someone's arms.

233

Chapter 31

Nobody blinked at the ceiling. It wasn't straw. It wasn't stone. It was thick wooden rafters crossed by wooden slats. A host of confused impressions and memories cavorted in his aching brain like water swishing in a crucible. He lifted his head and found Jacques sitting on a stool at the foot of the bed.

"You haf avoken at last, sir! It does my eyes good to see you again."

Nobody held his hand between his eyes and the light.

"Hello, Jacques. It's good to be seen. If you're here, I suppose this is Balbus's house. How long have I slept?"

"About zhree hours. I am afraid zhat I had to beat upon your feet for many moments before I could vake you, sir."

"Three hours?" Nobody groaned. "Three minutes, rather. What happened and what's happening?"

"According to zhe strange tvins who haf followed us here, you vere attacked by a soldier, whom zhey shot, and zhen zhey dragged you avay."

"What about Ennia? Did they rescue the slave girl?"

"Zhey said zhat she vas once again too secure of a captive to rescue. Zhe smart tvin talked about you, much about shock, and loss of blood, and more, like a dictionary of medicine."

Nobody sighed. He had done his best, but the Lord's plans once again differed from his own.

"You ask vhat is happening?" Jacques said. "Everyone is preparing for zhe day vihz great earnestness. I myself haf not felt so since ve left Rahattan Island, and zhat Irishman is ruining my nerves."

"I'm glad to know that at least a few things never change." Nobody forced his legs out of bed and followed with the rest of his body before he could sink back into sleep. "I hope you have something ready to eat. Mining builds the appetite."

Jacques grimaced. "I vill do my best, Colonel, but zhat English tvin who is infatuated vihz knives has stolen my cooking fire for vhat he calls a 'culinary experiment.' Bah!"

The main room in Balbus's house was bustling. Otho, his brother, and the more normal-looking twin—Lawrence was his name—were studying maps on the table. Chester squatted over the fire with O'Malley and Matthew, and the rest of the room was filled with sailors, two women, and a squealing baby. Balbus wasn't visible but his hammer clanged metal in the forge.

"Do you feel well enough to lead an army?" Otho asked. He didn't look like he had slept, but his eyes were focused and his whole face was tense, ready for action.

Nobody dropped into a chair and bent forward so that no part of his raw back touched. He had expected his head to clear as he woke up fully, but it hadn't. The pressure in his sinuses squeezed the backs of his eyeballs. His clogged nostrils and the pain in the back of his throat when he swallowed finished the story. He had to add a bad cold to the list of enemies he was battling.

"Do you feel well enough?" Otho said.

"Mmm?" Nobody forced his eyes to open. "Oh, you were talking to me. An army? Er—right. What kind of an army?"

"Dogs and Christians."

"How armed?"

"Irregularly. Swords, sickles, clubs, stones, makeshift weapons."

Balbus's hammer beats sent a throb every three seconds through Nobody's brain.

"Not exactly the 42nd," Nobody said.

Balbus's daughter handed Nobody a horn of water and brought a sort of cake made of bread and eggs from Chester. It was nice to know that strange as this valley was it did have chickens. The food hurt going down, but it helped clear Nobody's mind and make him feel slightly less like a sack of moldy potatoes.

"What are your plans?" Nobody asked.

"The Dogs have agreed to rise on the festival's second day, which is tomorrow. We think that the general swoop on Christians will happen tomorrow before the marriage ceremony. Little Caesar has been accumulating his power for years. By destroying the Christians he will destroy the last people that do not hold him as their absolute authority."

Nobody traced lines across the table-top with the pointy end of his horn. That gut-wrenching nervousness of planning a battle was creeping back, and with it came slivers of remembrance of the thrill of warfare. In most ways he hated war, but he was born for war.

"Why wait until tomorrow?" Nobody said. "Why let them attack? Surprise is a smaller force's best friend."

Otho nodded. "We want to use surprise, but not today. The soldiers will be concentrated today on the marketplace where the slave auction takes place. Tomorrow will bring in the entire valley for the beginning of the games, and more people means more confusion. With that confusion and the soldiers dispersed to look for Christians, we will have a better chance to attack them piecemeal."

"Divide and conquer," Nobody said. "I like it. What are the difficulties?"

Lawrence had been twisting the ends of his cravat into balls. Now he pulled it off entirely and strung it between his fingers.

"I'll tell you the difficulties," Lawrence said. "The difficulty is that the woman Little Caesar plans to marry tomorrow is *my* wife, and I'll have no pagan rituals uniting that pig with her, strategy or no strategy."

237

Nobody kneaded his temples. He felt like boring his thumb through and blowing off some of the steam inside.

Lawrence looked militant. "Colonel Nobody, Otho will not assure me that this revolt will take place in time to stop the ceremony."

Otho opened his mouth, but Varius was already out of his chair.

"Do you think we want the delay? *Today* is the slave market, and who do you think must go to that? You weren't here when the soldiers came for her, but *he* was." Varius pointed to Nobody. "You know that Little Caesar is going to pick my sister as one of the palace slave girls. Today. *Before* tomorrow."

The room and the forge were silent. Otho dropped his head on his knees. Varius's arms quivered. Varius's sister clung to her mother's shoulder, her cloak covering her face. Her cloak—covering her face. The image of a pile of cloaks in front of the latrine sparked in Nobody's mind.

Nobody stood up. "You say she'll be taken to the palace today?"

"Yes."

"Then I have an idea." Nobody looked again at the girl and her cloak. "I think the time has come for me to be a spy again."

"You've been a spy?" Lawrence said. "But—how old are you?"

Nobody squeezed the drinking horn's ridges. "Please—we're in the middle of Greenland in an Ancient Roman settlement. For a few days I would simply like to pretend than no one cares who I am, how old I am, or where I came from."

"Of course."

"Thank you. Now, this is my idea." Nobody turned to Otho and Varius. "Do you know of the tall mute in the palace? Yes? Do you think you could manage for him to be the one to conduct your sister to the palace?"

"Maybe." Otho looked up. "Why?"

"Your sister must wear her cloak. The mute must be the one to take her to the palace. Somehow, they need to be in a building together away from the public eye at least for a second, and that's when I'll dispose of the mute and wrap myself up like your sister."

Now Otho rose, and the only one sitting down was Lawrence. "What do you mean?"

"My man there—O'Malley—he'll play the part of the mute and I'll be the slave being taken to the palace. I'll cover my face with a veil. We'll get inside the walls, and then, if God wills, I'll figure out some way to get to Little Caesar. With him as my prisoner we may not even need a revolt."

"But the risk!" Otho said.

"Welcome to my life. I'm going to get out of this place and save my friend's life, and I think this plan has no more problems than your revolt plan."

Nobody switched to English and relayed the same information to his men and Chester.

"I'll do it," Lawrence said.

Nobody stared down at the Englishman. "You'll do what?"

"I'll do it." Now Lawrence was standing, and his face was calm. "It's my place. I'm going into that palace to rescue Pacarina."

"No, you're not. You don't have the skills. It's going to take a mind trained in war by chess move against bloody chess move to survive in that palace, and that mind is mine, not yours."

Half a dozen plates clattered on the floor after the sweep of Lawrence's arm.

"She's my wife!" Lawrence's face was red now. "It's my place to risk my life for her, not yours. It's not your fault that she's in there, it's mine, and it's my responsibility to get her out."

"Hold a moment!" Chester said. He dropped whatever he was holding into the fire and strode to the table. "Don't forget that she's my sister, by law, at least, and it was my idea to come after this Nobody fellow in the first place. I know what to do with knife, pistol, and sword, which seems to be more than you do, Colonel. I'm going in after her."

These brothers did everything together. They even got in the way together. But they didn't look alike, except for being twins. Chester had his pistols out as if Little Caesar was standing at the other end of the room, and his muscles bulged under his waistcoat. Lawrence stood beside him with his thumbs clenched into his fists—that would be a broken thumb at the first punch—and a body built for study. But his soul was shining through his eyes.

Matthew growled from his spot by the fire.

"Why do you need to prove yourself, twin? You've already got the girl. No need to impress her by a damsel in distress gig."

"That's the point," Lawrence said. "I've got her, and that makes it ten times more important that I protect her. You don't understand the strength of the bond between husband and wife. It makes the love you feel before marriage look like a candle compared to a burning cathedral."

The room was quiet.

Nobody sighed. "You're right, Lawrence. She's your wife, and it is your right to rescue her. But I'm going with you."

Lawrence grasped his hand. "You're a strange man, Colonel Nobody, but a good man. I respect you."

"As for you, Chester, you can't go. Having two of us doubles the danger. Three would at least quadruple it." Nobody sank back onto the edge of his chair. "If I'm to risk death with you, Lawrence, I'd like to know your last name."

"Oh, you don't know? Of course, I also don't know your name. I don't mean to pressure you, but circumstances considered, I think you could trust us enough to tell us who you really are."

Nobody watched Lawrence's face.

"My best friend beside my future wife doesn't even know. Trust is not a factor. What is your last name?"

Lawrence shrugged. "So be it. Our surname is Stoning."

"Stoning?" Nobody nodded slowly. "A good name. I knew a very good man by that name, once. It must be a common one."

"Not particularly," Lawrence said. "I've never heard it outside our family. My father only had one brother, and I don't think he had any children. I think he was some type of soldier. Isn't that right, Chester?"

Chester nodded. "I remember you saying that. I think Father said he was in some outlandish place—Africa, maybe? No, maybe Siberia."

Nobody stared at Chester. "Did you say Siberia?"

"I think that's what Father said. He told Lawrence, not me, but that's how I remember Lawrence putting it."

"What rank?"

Lawrence scratched his head. "I can't say that I remember. It wasn't very high, I don't think. There was something about a colonel, but I think that was my father's sister who married a colonel."

Jacques and O'Malley left the fire and flanked Lawrence's chair, looking down with wide eyes. Nobody rose.

"What rank?" Nobody repeated.

Chester wrinkled his forehead at Nobody. "I think he was a corporal."

A corporal! Nobody grasped Jacques and O'Malley by the shoulders.

"Corporal William Stoning. Men, these are old Stoning's nephews."

The ejaculation that burst from Jacques's mouth was nearly a squeal.

"You are zhe venerable ancient's nephews? You are of his bloodline? I recall every uncomplimen*tary* zhought I have zhunk of you! You may cook anyzhing you like, and vihz my blessing! It is *extra*ordinary!"

Lawrence stared at the bubbling Frenchman. "Then—where is my uncle?"

"Where most good men are," Nobody said. "Dead. He led Squad One, of which Jacques, O'Malley, and Matthew are members. He took a bullet to the head because of his loyalty for me, fighting Tremont and Bronner in the South Seas."

Nobody steadied himself against the table with both hands. His mind was rolling cartwheels. The 42nd was no more, as far as Nobody was concerned, but Squad One had never left him. Squad One were his sons—it sounded funny, but that was how he had always thought as an officer of his men.

These two men came from England just to help him. Each had unique skills, and each had a unique personality. The first quality was essential for Squad One. The second seemed to happen automatically, especially since poor Mark died and the twins were no longer the same body with two names. Here were two men with unique skills, and two empty slots in Squad One where Stoning and

Mark Preston had served. And, they had Stoning's blood. They were nephews of Colonel Hayes, because Stoning's sister—their aunt—married Colonel Hayes.

"Stonings," Nobody said, "will you join Squad One? There is no such thing in the army's official books, but it exists in our hearts and through our hands. What do you say?"

Chester thrust his hand out. "I'm in."

Lawrence hesitated, looking from Nobody, to Jacques, to O'Malley, to Chester, then back to Nobody.

"I'm not a fighter," Lawrence said. "If I was, my wife might be here beside me instead of up there. I wouldn't be of any use to a secret military society."

"You have a brain." Nobody held out his hand. "All I ask is your brain and Chester's brawn. Together, we'll rescue your wife."

Lawrence's hand locked with Nobody's. "It's yours."

Lawrence bent over the baby one last time. The little fellow was sleeping with his arms spread wide on the blanket, and as Lawrence stroked his hand with a finger a tiny smile sneaked onto the wrinkled lips.

"Pacarina would love to see you," Lawrence told the baby just loud enough for Nobody to hear. He snuggled the blanket higher up the infant's chest. "Pacarina *will* see you."

Chapter 32

The marketplace overflowed with soldiers, citizens, slaves, and Dogs. That was the order of preference here. Soldiers to control everyone, citizens to own everyone, slaves to do their masters' bidding, and Dogs to be worked or abused as desired. And scattered among the crowd through every class, body type, and age were the hated Christians who gathered to watch this slave auction with the curiosity of dread.

Lawrence stood two inches from Chester, but they couldn't talk. A few English words heard by the wrong person—basically, any person in the crowd crushed around them—would kill the plan in its babyhood. Chester's eyes were not quiet, though, and they showed as much disgust as Lawrence felt.

The sunlight had to struggle through a gray sky before it lit the wooden platform as tall as O'Malley and as large as a hut's roof which stood in the marketplace's center. To the right were three lines of wooden cages stuffed with slaves to be auctioned. On the platform stood a weasel-faced man in a dirty tunic.

"Lot number twelve," the auctioneer said. "Male, twenty-seven years, normal height, wide in the chest and strong as a war dog. Comes with a six-month guarantee."

The revolving platform slowly swung the front of the slave into Lawrence's view.

"How strong?" someone yelled.

The auctioneer prodded the slave's bare chest with a stick.

"Show your muscles."

The slave lifted his arms into L shapes and clenched his fists. Men in the crowd around Lawrence shouted that he should be a gladiator. Someone shouted a number and the bidding began.

Little Caesar's mute must be somewhere around here. A man his height would poke out of this sea of heads like a mast on the ocean, but there were no masts in sight. Unlike O'Malley, who should be skulking somewhere in this human undergrowth, the mute had no reason to conceal his height. If he was here, he could be seen.

"Too much flab," one of the bidders yelled.

"Nothing that a week of drawing water can't sweat out of him." The auctioneer pointed at the bidder. "Come feel for yourself."

The fleshy clap of a palm against loose skin penetrated the chattering crowd as a shriveled piece of gray-haired man worked his hands over the slave's ribs.

A small shed to the platform's left might work perfectly for the plan, but it kept swallowing and regurgitating purchasers going there to pay for their slaves. That wouldn't do. But where else could the clothes-switch take place? The gray-haired man bought the slave and the auctioneer beckoned for the next piece of merchandise, a woman.

Otho had been right about the soldiers being concentrated on the marketplace. Helmets dotted the crowd, some stationary, some plowing the crowd constantly as if looking for something. They were looking for many somethings, actually. An officer elbowing through this section didn't look twice at Lawrence, but he appraised Chester's muscles with his eyes before clapping a hand on the shoulder of a good-looking lad about twelve years old. Little Caesar had the pick of the entire country, slave or freedman.

The officer lifted on his toes and stretched his neck to see above the crowd.

"They'd better have brought her," he said to one of the soldiers at his side. "They'll be sorry if they didn't."

"But won't they be sorry if they did, too?" the soldier said.

The officer laughed and removed his helmet long enough to wipe his forehead. His hair bristled.

"You're right there, soldier. Ah! I think I see her brother."

Chester tapped Lawrence's shoulder and pointed to the man the officer was pointing at. It was Varius. The soldiers were after Balbus's daughter. Oh, where was the mute? O'Malley could never pass as this bristle-haired officer—none of them could. If he took the girl to the palace now then both parts of the plan would fail before they'd even begun.

Varius's face flamed red as the soldiers grabbed his sister and shoved her toward the line of slaves destined for the palace. Balbus stood at his son's side, head bowed. He made no sense. Either he was a weakling and had given up or there was an incredible struggle inside his head. He looked up briefly and that look mirrored the sky—gloomy, gray, and foreboding.

A square wooden box ten feet from Lawrence and Chester was a constant battleground for toughs who jumped up to see over the crowd and were promptly felled by others who wanted the same chance. The strongest might last for forty seconds, and get in a few catcalls and jeers at the slaves before another brute took the field. Lawrence pushed close to the box and nodded at Chester.

The current possessor of the box crumbled under the earnest application of Chester's fists and Lawrence jumped up to see what he could. The revolving platform currently had the auctioneer's and the woman's backs to Lawrence. The slaves for the palace stood in a line on the platform's right, some weeping, some grinning at the possibilities their new position presented. There was the mute! At the end of the line of palace slaves, almost in the shadow of the platform, stood the mute with his impassive face high above the crowd.

Chester was struggling with a beast of a man in a ragged tunic—only a few seconds more to look. Lawrence scanned the fringes of the crowd for any sign of Nobody. Joktan the dwarf was there. Ah, there on the other side of the marketplace was the familiar young face peeping out of a produce shed.

Chester grunted at Lawrence for staying on the box so long, but all he could do was rearrange his rumpled clothing and glare. It was refreshing to have Chester wordless for a few hours. His annoyance apparently transferred to his arms, because he did a magnificent job of breaking a path through the crowd and had Lawrence standing near the palace slaves within ten minutes.

247

A particularly interesting slave was on display at the moment and everyone in the crowd was bidding if they had money or gawking if they didn't. This was Lawrence's chance. He dropped on his palms and kneecaps and scurried between the lines of legs until he saw the mute's hairy knees. He breathed deep, assumed the calmest face he could manage, and stood up.

"So, are you taking my master's daughter to be a slave?" Lawrence tried to smile slyly. It felt a bit lopsided, but it was the best he could do. "I wish I could see her scrubbing floors in the palace."

The mute stared at him but said nothing. Of course not. He was a mute.

Lawrence shook his head. "You wouldn't think an old man would get so attached to her, but you tell me if he hasn't." Lawrence whisked a leather coin pouch from beneath his tunic and dangled it at his side. "Will you let my master say goodbye to his daughter?"

The mute's hand closed around the bag. He shrugged. Lawrence yanked Balbus's daughter's arm and dragged her toward the produce shed, trying to act the part of the revengeful slave delighting in his former tormentor's misery. The mute stalked behind them and the crowd parted for him like the Red Sea before the Israelites.

The produce shed's roof was coated with spectators but the building itself looked empty. This was where Lawrence had seen Nobody signaling. This was the second pivotal point. Lawrence unhooked the latch and pushed into the gloom within, still gripping the girl's arm in an unkindly vise. The mute followed.

The door slammed, wood cracked on bone, and the mute's body thudded to the floor. Candlelight filled the room.

"Wait here for your family," Nobody said to the girl. "They'll be here as soon as we leave. Now, your cloak."

Nobody pulled on a woman's tunic, wrapped himself in the girl's cloak, and dropped a veil over his face. As long as he walked right and didn't talk he was safe. O'Malley pulled on the mute's outer garments and between his height and his black-dyed hair he looked enough like the mute to possibly survive this venture.

"Quickly," Nobody said to Lawrence. "You're only *dressing* like a woman. You don't have to take as long."

Lawrence growled. This was the worst part of the entire plan. Nobody had decided that Lawrence's face might be too familiar to the palace guards, so Lawrence also had to go veiled, as if the mute was bringing two slave girls ahead of the rest.

As he pulled the light dress over his head he thought once more of the command in Deuteronomy: "neither shall a man put on a woman's garment." He had thought this through constantly since Nobody outlined the plan this morning and decided that as he was not dressing this way as a perversion of worship, and certainly not for pleasure, it was a valid exception.

Jacques drew wrinkles on O'Malley's face with a chunk of charcoal.

"It is horrible." Jacques gripped O'Malley's hand. "I am so sorry for you. I vill pray zhat you haf zhe strength to bear it. You are a *boeuf* of an Irishman, but even so I do not vish zhis fate upon you. Do you zhink you can do it?"

Lawrence drew aside his veil and cocked his eyebrow at Nobody.

"I didn't realize how close they were. Jacques really seems distraught about O'Malley's danger."

"Danger?" Nobody laughed. "Jacques is comforting him because he has to pretend to be a mute. He can't talk. To a Frenchman, that's a fate worse than death."

Nobody put his hand on the door latch and turned to the girl.

"I hope to see you again, but if not, know that we did our duty as men. O'Malley? Lawrence? Let's go."

Chapter 33

Nobody wiped at the trickle from his nose. He stood with Lawrence and O'Malley in a deserted hallway in Little Caesar's palace.

The floor was bare rock. The walls were covered with a complicated mythological fresco full of Jupiters, Saturns, Venuses, Dianas, and all the rest of the false gods and goddesses. The figures were hardly visible through Nobody's thick veil, and this was perfectly fine with him. According to Lawrence, most English schoolboys had to study all these pagan deities as part of an education. Well, if Nobody survived long enough to marry Liana and they had a child, the little he or she certainly wouldn't have to learn this bosh.

None of the three men could safely talk to anyone in the palace. The guards hadn't given them any problems so far because they thought that O'Malley was the mute, but now that they had penetrated the palace there was no way to inquire how to get anywhere. Nobody and Lawrence couldn't talk because slave girls don't sound like men. O'Malley couldn't talk because mutes aren't supposed to talk, and definitely not in English.

A little man rounded the corner at the end of the passageway and scurried toward them. Every inch of him looked busy.

"Ah, here you are at last. Have you seen Little Caesar?"

Nobody tensed. Mutes can't speak, but they can hear and should be able to nod. O'Malley didn't know Latin. There was half a chance he would answer what they needed and half a chance he wouldn't. He hesitated for a moment, then shook his head. That was the right half.

"Then, move!" the little man said. "You know he always wants to inspect new slaves."

The little man drove O'Malley and the two "slaves" into Little Caesar's personal section of the palace. A tickling in Nobody's nose spread to his throat. He was going to sneeze. He didn't know what a slave girl's sneeze sounded like, but it probably didn't sound like his, and any attention from the steward could quickly become suspicion. He closed his nasal passages and fought the sneeze with every muscle in his face. It passed, but not before his eyeballs threatened to pop out.

The little man poked a finger at a jewel-encrusted door, next to which stood a stony-faced guard.

"After he's done put these with the rest of the slave girls and find me. What a life. A festival *and* a marriage at the same time!"

His muttering faded down the hallway.

There was no escaping Little Caesar now. The guard's presence forced them inside, and it was with less than an easy spirit that Nobody glided behind O'Malley into the room beyond. He caught his right foot in the sheep-fleece carpet and nearly fell. It was just an entry-room with tapestries hanging from the walls, pictures ornamenting the ceiling, and life-sized statues carved from black rock.

"Who is it?" a voice called. It was Little Caesar.

The entry-room led into a far larger and more elaborate bedchamber, with the largest bed Nobody had ever seen in the center and a dizzying profusion of furniture, art, fabric, clothing, and fleeces. Little Caesar sipped wine in a high-backed chair next to the bed while a slave girl scrubbed his balding head. He never looked dignified, even when on his royal dais, and a crown of soap lather didn't contribute to his image now.

"Oh, here you are," Little Caesar said. "These from the new batch? Veils must be a new fashion. I don't like it."

Something about the girl washing the tyrant's head was familiar, but Nobody couldn't see enough of her through his veil to identify her. It couldn't be

Lawrence's wife. For one thing, Nobody hadn't ever seen his wife, so she wouldn't be familiar, and for another thing, a soon-to-be-queen wouldn't be sopping oil out of Little Caesar's hair.

"You don't look well today," Little Caesar said. He tried to point at O'Malley, but his hand was so shaky that his finger made circles. "You're too quiet." He laughed, hiccuped, and took another swig.

Nobody kept his right hand buried in the folds of his cloak. Little Caesar probably wouldn't even notice the missing hand. If he did, he would think the "slave girl" was hugging her limbs close with fear. Actually, Nobody grasped a knife. A pistol wouldn't be much good, as Little Caesar didn't know enough about pistols to be scared by one, and a shot would bring guards running. Nobody swallowed against the fighting fury rising into the soreness in his throat, fueled by each stripe on his back and each memory of the indignities he had seen and suffered in this place.

"Take off their veils," Little Caesar said.

This was the critical moment. O'Malley couldn't understand the words, and a nod or shake of the head wasn't going to satisfy Little Caesar. O'Malley nodded. Little Caesar cocked his head and blinked a pair of bleary eyes.

"What? Oh, you want me to do it. You always have the best ideas."

Little Caesar beckoned the "slaves" closer. Nobody stopped a foot away and waited, his hand almost outside his cloak, his lips in a grim smile.

"Are you very pretty?" Little Caesar said. He tore the veil away and stared up into Nobody's face.

"I've been called 'pirate,' 'scum,' and 'villain,' but never 'pretty.'" Nobody pressed his knife-point against Little Caesar's throat. "I've also been called 'deadly.'"

O'Malley covered the real slave girl's mouth before she could scream while Lawrence tossed off his veil and fumbled his own knife from beneath his dress.

"D-d-don't hurt m-m-me," Little Caesar stammered. Soap suds streaked his cheeks and piled like snow on his eyebrows.

"Keep your mouth shut," Nobody said. "Answer my questions and save the rest of your thoughts for your own warped brain. Now, where is his wife?" He nodded at Lawrence.

253

Little Caesar blinked at Lawrence.

"I d-d-don't know. My steward t-t-takes care of them."

Lawrence clenched his fists. "Where is my wife?"

"I don't know!" The rolls of fat on Little Caesar's neck quivered. "Ask my steward."

Nobody grunted. "That's not an option at the moment, so you'll have to wrack that dizzy brain of yours and give us an answer."

The slave girl made guttural sounds behind O'Malley's hand. A pair of hazel eyes stared into Nobody's face.

"Ennia!"

A gurgle from Little Caesar reclaimed Nobody's attention. In his surprise at seeing Ennia, Nobody had nearly skewered the tyrant's neck. Wasn't a bad idea, actually. He eased the knife away from the flabby flesh and looked back at Ennia.

"How did you get here?"

O'Malley released the girl and she breathed hard for a moment to regain her wind.

"He heard that you tried to save me. He was going to punish me by making me watch you die."

That was just like these Romans. They didn't understand chivalry or gentlemanly conduct. Try to rescue a girl and you're immediately assumed to be her lover.

"I know where the Outsider's wife is," Ennia said. "I will take you to her."

"Traitor!" Little Caesar's anger momentarily booted his fear. "I will have your skin flayed from your body and hung from my gate!"

Nobody emptied the bowl of dirty water and suds over Little Caesar's head.

"Concentrate on your own skin, pig," Nobody said. "Ennia, where is she?"

Ennia pointed up. "Her room is high in the palace, but I can guide you there."

"Is she safe?" Lawrence asked. "Has she been harmed?"

"She has not."

"Praise God!" Lawrence wiped his forehead. "I think we're in time, Colonel. But what if this girl leads us into a trap?"

"She won't. Guide us, Ennia."

Nobody dug his fingers through the rolls of fat on the back of Little Caesar's neck until he found two pressure points, which he used to drag the pig out of his seat and point him toward the door.

"I want my toga," Little Caesar said.

His tunic covered him from shoulder to knee but left his arms completely bare. These arms were fleshy and webbed with veins, as were his legs, and his paunch made a large bump in the thin tunic's front.

"No toga," Nobody said. "Now squeeze those lips into a fish's mouth and keep them that way until I ask you a question."

Lawrence was just finishing stuffing some rolled up fleeces under the bed-blankets.

"It will look like he's sleeping in case the guards enter," Lawrence said. "It might give us an extra three minutes."

"The guards won't come in," Ennia said. "Little Caesar is often here for long times. They will not dare to enter until he calls them."

Nobody's right arm was tiring from the strain of keeping the knife in the vicinity of Little Caesar's neck, so he gave him to O'Malley and joined Ennia.

"Will we face any guards?" Nobody asked.

"I will take us a back way," Ennia said. "It should be safe because most of the soldiers are in the city for the festival."

Ennia led deeper into the royal suite, through a door into the slave girls' apartments, and finally into the main network of hallways. She and Nobody led the way, followed by Little Caesar, who whimpered when his bare feet left the fleeces and touched cold rock. O'Malley walked one step behind with one hand on Little Caesar's neck and the other on a short sword he had found in one of the rooms, while Lawrence formed rearguard and carefully shut each door or pulled back each set of hangings behind them.

The passageways were much quieter than when Nobody had been a guest here. Everyone must be down at the slave auction or buried in the kitchens somewhere in the heart of the rock slaving over the next two weeks of luxurious feasting.

"Thank you for trying to save me."

"Mmm?" Nobody looked at Ennia. "Oh, any time."

A window in one of the passages showed the entire city spread out below, with its villas, temples, and slums, and the huge crowd in the center marketplace gathered around the platform. The current figure for sale was only a speck, but Nobody realized that he had more respect for the humanity of that speck than did the people standing next to him or her, squeezing muscles and legs to test strength and conditioning.

"I don't like that," Lawrence said. He pointed to the foot of the palace rock, where, if the sun had been able to shine through the glowering cloud cover, it would have glinted on the helmets of a detachment of soldiers.

Nobody moved aside so that Ennia could see. "Why are they coming back?" he asked her.

She shook her head. This sudden return of strength seemed to surprise her as much as it did them.

"We need to move faster," Nobody said. "How far are we from Pacarina?"

"Not far."

Ennia led them up a zigzag staircase without railings, which would give a nasty fall to anyone inexperienced with the stairs maneuvering at night. Little Caesar was panting after the first three steps and sounded like a Siberian blizzard by the time he reached the top.

"We are close," Ennia said.

Voices murmured ahead.

Nobody raised his hand. "So is someone else."

Ennia darted through a door in the right wall and held it open. The only light, once the door closed, came from a small hole in the outside wall, but it was enough to reveal a couch in the middle surrounded by a strange array of herbs, odd-shaped instruments, and knives. Something dark—maybe tar, or paint— splattered the floor.

The voices were outside the door.

"I want to see the play," a man said. "Two hours of the funniest lines and acting. I don't know how these writers do it, but you'll laugh so hard you'll lose your lunch."

"Plays aren't hard to write," another man said. "Raising a war dog is hard. I want some good blood and gore and death screams."

The voices faded as their owners continued down the stairs. Nobody relaxed his shoulders as the danger passed and looked around the room.

"Chester would have loved this." Lawrence held a pair of razor sharp knives to the light. "What are all these things for, anyway?"

"This is where the leeches kill babies," Ennia said.

The knives slipped through Lawrence's fingers and clattered on the floor. Nobody stared at the stain beneath his feet. It wasn't tar, and it wasn't paint. It was dried blood. His insides rippled.

"Is this why there are so few children in the palace?" Nobody asked.

Ennia pointed at Little Caesar. "He doesn't like children, and they're inconvenient, so we get rid of most of them."

Lawrence gripped Little Caesar's shoulders and bent him back so that he looked up into Lawrence's face, which showed more anger than Nobody knew it could contain.

"You miserable murderer." Lawrence shook the trembling Roman. "You should vomit at the thought of this room's horrors. Your fat should shrivel on your bones in disgust. If I weren't a Christian I would cut your throat and mingle your blood with the blood of I don't know how many innocents, but vengeance is God's, not mine, and I know that as sickly perverted as your mind is, I could be in the same place without God's saving grace."

Lawrence shoved Little Caesar back into O'Malley's arms and brushed a sleeve over his eyes.

"I would give all of my worldly possessions for one of the babies killed here."

Nobody moved to the loophole. It slanted out too far to see much, but it looked like the detachment of soldiers had already entered the palace. Why would they come back? Could they have found the mute? But Otho was sure he could smuggle him out of the shed. Perhaps they were an escort to bring Little Caesar down to the auction—but no, everyone seemed to expect Little Caesar to stay in his rooms for some time yet.

Nobody turned and found Ennia close beside him.

"We need to find Pacarina now," he said.

She took his hand. "This way."

The passageway terminated in one door framed by solid rock. Ennia knocked.

"Who is it?" a woman asked. She sounded nervous, but not panicked. It was a good voice.

Lawrence pushed forward and put his mouth to the crack between the door and the frame.

"Dear, it's me."

There was a little scream followed by the thud of a body hitting the door. Pacarina undid the latch and Lawrence sprang inside. Nobody folded his arms.

"He gets two minutes of reunion," Nobody said.

"Not tae question yer orders, sir," O'Malley said, "but shouldn't we be leavin' this death-palace as soon as can be?"

"As soon as can be after two minutes. I know what it means to lose the woman you love and then be reunited. Give them a few moments alone."

Nobody stepped a few feet away and leaned against the wall, his arms still folded, his right temple resting on the cold stone. Even a momentary lull sapped the battle-energy that kept the sinus pressure at bay, and sent his thoughts flying across the ocean to some pretty English room where Liana sat, reading, or sewing, or talking with Elyssa. It had been so long since they had seen each other. Even when they were both in London, Bronner's watching men kept them apart. Sometimes it's easier to be far away from the person you love than to be near and yet separated. And yet, being far is not easy.

"You look tired."

Nobody opened his eyes. "Yes, Ennia, I suppose I do. I suspect that most people who spend a day working in the mines, get flogged, and then only sleep for three hours do."

"Are you thinking of your wife?"

"Of the girl who will become my wife. Is the other Outsider finished reuniting with his wife?"

Ennia frowned. "I don't think so."

"Too bad. We're leaving now." Nobody grabbed Little Caesar's chin and forced him to look up. "I don't know if you're familiar with the concept of hostages, but you are one. You're going to figure out a way to get my friends and me out of this place. Understood?"

Little Caesar wiggled a tiny 'yes' through the chin-hold.

"Good. Now, try not to offend my giant. The neck that he's used to squeezing is much smaller than yours, so if you start wiggling he may not realize how tightly he's gripping."

Nobody saw just a glimpse of Pacarina before he turned to lead the way out, but she looked pretty. Dark hair, slightly brown skin—she certainly wasn't English—a small nose, and a cheerful-looking face. Pretty, but nothing special compared to the pair of dimples, hazel eyes, and headful of jet black hair waiting for him at home.

There was no sign of the two men they had nearly stumbled into. They reached the bottom of the staircase when Pacarina paused.

"My capelet!" Pacarina grabbed Lawrence's arm. "I've left the capelet you gave me."

Capelet? Wasn't that some kind of shawl? Lawrence wasn't the type of man to marry a woman willing to let a missing shawl interfere with a prison escape. It probably had some deep sentimental meaning, but the throbs in Nobody's head occupied too much space to think it through deeply.

Pacarina shrugged. "Oh well."

"I will get it," Ennia said.

She was up the stairs before Nobody could stop her, so he turned and led onward. They had to get out of here quickly. Now, how could they sneak their hostage out? Perhaps Lawrence had a plan.

Nobody looked over his shoulder at Little Caesar as they hurried through the passages.

"Last year a girl was brought here as a slave. Her father's name was Balbus, and she was a Christian. What happened to her?"

Little Caesar shivered in O'Malley's grip. "Ch-Christian? She t-tried to convert me. She d-died."

Click. Clack.

That was the sound of hobnails on rock. It was followed by the clanking swish of segmented armor.

It took one second to think about hiding, another to realize that it was too late to hide, and a third to be seen.

The soldiers already had their swords drawn. They didn't seem surprised—just ready. There wasn't enough room in the narrow passage for Nobody to try much kicking, and the knife in his hand wouldn't block a *gladius*. Should he kill Little Caesar? No, killing hostages wasn't Christian.

Nobody simply stood still and let the soldiers bind him. Lawrence made a few waves with his sword before his capture, and O'Malley managed to knock two of the Praetorians' heads together, but he was too tangled with Little Caesar's fat to realize his full potential. They were captives—again.

An officer removed his helmet and revealed the familiar bristling hair.

"The gods have brought us together again," Bristle Hair said. His lips stretched in an evil smile.

"*God* has brought us together," Nobody said. "You disappoint me. I thought you Praetorians were predictable. What possessed you to come traipsing in here during the slave auction?"

"Little legs and big ears."

Bristle Hair snapped his fingers. The guards parted and Joktan the dwarf, Bishop Aulus's adopted son, stepped forward.

"Joktan!" Lawrence tried to twist away from his guards, but they held him fast. "What have they done to you?"

"Paid him." Bristle Hair sneered. "Paid him well. And often. This here is one of our best spies. We're so very grateful to your librarian bishop for saving his measly little limbs from the cold, else how would we know that you Christ-worshipers are planning a revolt?"

"But—" Lawrence's eyes were round as musket balls, "—how could you do it?"

Joktan spat. "You're not a dwarf. You don't know what it's like to be pitied and powerless. But money is power." He grinned.

Nobody closed his eyes. Liana and Edmund were very far away.

Chapter 34

The dungeon smelled of urine, blood, and vomit. It wasn't exactly a dungeon, though. It was an unlit cage in the bowels of the arena where gladiators were kept before games. Nobody had done many strange things in his life, but being a gladiator was neither a plan nor a wish. It was fitting. His plans and wishes had stopped working long ago.

Nobody stepped back from the bars and balanced on his left leg for another kick. He wished—forget wishes—he would have liked to have his heavy boots in the place of these light Roman shoes, but he would make the best of what he had. With his bad right arm and his untrained and overtaxed left, he wouldn't be much good with a sword, spear, trident, club, or any other of the weapons he was likely to be given. His legs were his best chance.

He was thankful for having his own section of the vast underground chamber. Apparently, Little Caesar didn't want some over-aggressive gladiator to deprive him of the pleasure of seeing Nobody die by killing him tonight, so he had been given his own separate cell, as had Lawrence and Chester. The main cage was stuffed with Christians from all over the city who had been swooped upon as they prepared for the next day and carted off to the arena before anyone knew what was happening.

Nobody tensed his calf and kicked, using the muscles around his left knee as the main impetus. His right heel rattled the bars. A blow like that in the pit of the stomach would fell most men, but the challenging part was getting close enough to strike without being skewered by the other man's sword.

A light bloomed in the darkness and steps approached. Nobody quickly scraped filth away from a small spot and sat down, the seat of his tunic instantly wet through by the soggy earth. Smaller meant less intimidating, and less intimidating meant better treatment from the guards.

"By Venus, it's your lucky day," a harsh voice said.

The lamplight showed one of the arena slaves, not an actual soldier, but with the same power below the amphitheater, and beside him a closely veiled figure. The key clicked in the lock, the hinges croaked a rusty complaint, and the second figure slipped inside.

"Don't make any trouble," the slave said. "I'm off to turn some of your coin into wine."

The figure knelt beside Nobody and a pair of soft hands touched his arm.

"Are you hurt, my lord?"

"Er—not more than usual. I'm sorry, but I don't see very well in the dark. Who are you, and why am I your lord?"

"I am Ennia."

"Ah. You have a knack for travel, girl. I'm thankful you went back for that shawl when you did, otherwise you would be a prisoner too. How did you get out of the palace?"

"A disguise."

"But how did you get in here?" Nobody asked.

"I gave the guard all the money I've hoarded across the years," she said.

"Why? Is there a plan for escape?"

Her cloak rustled, probably because she was shaking her head.

"My bribe brought me in, but it can't bring you out."

Nobody nodded. "That's too bad. Well, why did you come?"

The girl was silent. Somewhere in the recesses of the dungeon a man moaned. Otherwise, the only sound was Ennia's breathing.

"Ennia?" Nobody said. "I asked why you came here."

"I thought my lord understood."

"Well, if you're not here to help me escape, you probably have a message for me. Am I right?"

Her cloak rustled again. That must be another head shake.

Nobody growled. "Look, Ennia, I don't have the patience to play twenty questions right now. Be a good girl and tell me why you've come?"

"I love my lord."

Nobody blinked. The only girl he could get to give a straight, clear, unequivocal answer was Liana. What was Ennia trying to say? She loved her lord . . . the welts on Nobody's back tingled. She had just called *him* her lord. Was she saying—

"Ennia, are you trying to say that you love *me?*"

"Yes."

The man in the other dungeon stopped moaning. His moans were replaced by the bumping of Nobody's heart. Nobody swallowed.

"But Ennia, I told you that I'm already betrothed to a girl. I love her. I'm going to marry her if I ever get out of here."

"But you are going to die!" Ennia's voice broke the constraints of the meek slave and her words tumbled out. "You are the only man who has ever been kind to me. I have been a slave all my life, mistreated, jeered, mocked, unloved. I never knew my mother. My father sold me as a slave. I have never had a kind master. You are different. You are kind, you treat me like a person, you care."

Hot tears splashed Nobody's right hand. He flexed his fingers, trying to figure out what to say, how to respond to this completely unexpected torrent. He was accustomed to people saying that they hated him, but not that they loved him.

"Ennia—" he breathed deeply. "Ennia, I'm different because I'm a Christian. God has saved me from my sins, though I am still a sinner, and I seek to obey His commandments. We Christians honor women because the Bible teaches us to, but we do so for *all* women. I didn't treat you kindly because I loved you. I treated you kindly because you are a woman. The girl I love is named Liana."

"But you will never see this Liana again. Please, say that you love me before you die."

"But I don't," Nobody said. "Ennia, I usually don't like repeating myself, but I don't mind saying this many times. I love Liana."

"But she's not here, and I am. You can love me now. She'll never know."

Nobody slowly rose and put his hands on Ennia's head.

"Poor girl. You don't understand what love is. Few of you Romans—probably none of the ones you've ever served under—comprehend true love."

She bowed her head. Her hood had fallen down, and a ring of plaited hair formed a crown.

"True love," Nobody said. "What a phrase. True love is what Christ showed when He suffered humiliation, agony, and death to redeem us from our sins. True love is sacrificing anything and everything for another, protecting another, striving for another, being willing to do whatever is best for that other, being faithful, and loyal, and true. If my Liana didn't want to marry me, Roman love would tell me to pursue her anyway. True love would not. True love thinks of her, not me."

Nobody knelt beside Ennia and took her tear-dripped hands in his.

"Do you understand why I could never dream of being false to her? You appreciate me because I'm not like these Romans. I'm *not* like them, and *that* is why I will always stay true to Liana and never love another woman. Do you understand?"

The girl's face dropped into his hands. "You are a—good man."

"No. I serve a good God." Nobody raised her to her feet. "You must go now, and I must prepare for my battle tomorrow."

Ennia shook her head. Her chest heaved, and her hands gripped his as tightly as dried blood on a blade.

"There is no battle."

"What?"

"They will tie you to a stake."

Nobody staggered back. "And?"

Her head dropped to her chest. "And then they will release the war dogs."

Chapter 35

"Law, I told you we shouldn't have used those skins," Chester said.

Lawrence wiggled his fingers. The leather thongs felt embedded at least half an inch in his wrists and deeper above his elbows. The stake his back was bound to would be an excellent exercise for straightening one's posture, but that was probably not why the Romans had trussed him, Nobody, and Chester, in that order, in the center of an amphitheater seating most of the city.

"Well," Chester said, "at least we cleaned our skins out before we used them. I feel like haggis."

Lawrence studied the bloody sheepskin wrapped around his torso, waist, and legs. Sheep-blood smeared his clothes and face, and chunks of warm sheep-meat made squishy bulges all over his body. Blood nearly hid the snake-like birthmark below his elbow crook.

The amphitheater was much like the paintings of the Colosseum, except that there was no sand on the floor. Instead, the dirt was packed tightly, and heaps of dried grass lay around the arena waiting to be spread out and soak up the blood.

A troop of acrobats and dancers was finishing their act around the stakes, jumping leapfrog style, climbing poles and posturing horizontally, conducting imaginary sword fights on tightropes, and more. They showed extraordinary agility and an impressive understanding of mathematics and choreography. Sadly, these were simply the prologue to the festival to occupy early comers while the populace gathered. The games' real beginning was to be much less mathematically precise, and Lawrence was one of the leading stars.

"I feel absolutely empty," Chester said. "They've taken every knife. Every single knife! They even found the bodkin I strapped below my right shoulder."

Their stakes were positioned so that they faced Little Caesar, although they were in the middle of the arena so that everyone could enjoy the spectacle. In the booth below Little Caesar's great fleece-covered throne, guarded by four soldiers, sat Pacarina. She was too far to see her face clearly, but Lawrence only had to close his eyes to see every detail. Today's games would conclude with her marriage ceremony. But Lawrence wouldn't be here to watch.

The acrobats retired to a smattering of applause and the arena's buzz lessened as socialites moved to their seats and the crowds prepared for the real entertainment.

"How are your spirits?" Colonel Nobody asked.

Lawrence looked sideways at the young warrior.

"Lord Banastre Bronner said that I couldn't get a woman. He should have said that I couldn't *keep* a woman. Death would come much easier if I were joining my wife, not leaving her with that bloated pig."

Nobody's face was set. "Yes. Our deaths spell ruin for many—and death for one."

A trap door opened in the arena floor below the imperial booth. It gaped at them like a hungry mouth, silent, deadly, dark.

"I'm sorry it ends this way," Colonel Nobody said. "You two work together so excellently that I expected you to make a name. Have you always been that way?"

Lawrence forced a smile. "Have you always been a warrior?"

"Yes."

"Oh." Lawrence coughed. "Disregard that rhetorical question, then. No, we haven't always been like this. I would like to tell you the story, but I don't think we have time."

Chester sighed. "I wish I'd been able to teach you the new exercise I'm developing, Colonel. Now that you fight with your legs it would fit you perfectly."

A pack of dogs bounded out of the darkness and stood at the edge of the opening, blinking, their red tongues lolling over their gums and their tails pointed at the sky like quills. The crowd roared.

"Their teeth are filthy," Chester said. "The nerve! If I'm going to be ripped apart, it could at least be done hygienically."

Lawrence scanned the broad muzzles, the flaps of loose skin above the eyes, and the tough, massive frames.

"The Romans had a breed of war dogs known as Molossus, which was one of the best breeds until they met a new breed in Britannia, called Pugnaces Britanniae. Since the original settlers of this valley came from Britannia, I would guess that these dogs are a specially bred strain which combines the fiercest qualities of both breeds."

Chester grunted. "Sometimes I wish you didn't know so much history."

Three native handlers emerged behind the dogs and prodded them forward with angry yells. The pack loped toward the stakes. The lead dog stopped suddenly, lifted his nose, and gave a long howl. Lawrence clenched his teeth. The moment was come.

"'We are accounted as sheep for the slaughter,'" Lawrence quoted. "Romans 8:36." He stared at the approaching figures. "Wait—those dog-handlers aren't prisoners, but they are Dogs—natives, I mean. How much did Joktan know?"

"He knew what Bishop Aulus knew," Chester said.

"Did Bishop Aulus know that the natives were going to join us in the revolt?"

Chester's eyes widened. "I don't think he did."

The war dogs scented the sheep blood. Their eyes gleamed hungrily. Once, many years ago, one of Chester's fox terriers bit Lawrence's calf, and he still remembered the sharp puncture pain. That bite compared to the coming feast like a mosquito sucking blood compares to an eagle's skin-rending attack.

Another native ran out of the underground passage and yelled a command at the dogs, at the same time tossing a leg of mutton in the dirt. The dogs wheeled away from the stakes and became a yammering mass of bodies fighting for food. The natives ran toward the center stakes.

The crowd leaped up and roared, but there was nothing they could do. The natives reached Lawrence and his companions and sawed at their bonds with bone-knives. The cords snapped one by one until the terrible pressure was relieved, leaving Lawrence leaning dizzily against the pole. He rubbed the grooves in his wrists and stamped his feet to restore circulation. Chester had already borrowed a knife from the main dog-handler and was shaking it at the crowd.

"Are the Christians free?" Lawrence asked.

The dog-handler shook his head. "Too many soldiers down there. We Dogs have risen against the arena and the palace."

Soldiers leapt into the arena from the walls and ran out of the underground passage. The natives handed each of the Englishmen a sword.

"We have rescued you, now you must lead us to victory."

"My pleasure," Nobody said. He dropped the sword. "You fellows chop away and I'll use my feet. Are you ready?"

Lawrence fit his fingers to the four ridges on the sword's pommel and held the blade across his body like Chester. Far above the crowd's roar, the soldiers' shouts, and the dogs' growls, came the blast of a horn. The crowd hushed. Lawrence knew what that blast meant. At the top of the palace rock was an ancient signal horn which had only sounded once in all the centuries of Vallis Deorum. It meant utter danger, and it called the soldiers down from the mountain to fight the threat. The path for escape would be open.

The first wave of soldiers charged, about a dozen strong, their shoulder-plates bouncing at each step and the strips of metal-studded leather which hung from their belts swishing like skirts. The natives yelled at their dogs and pointed at the soldiers. The fight for the sheep's bone ceased and the whole pack charged the Roman line and broke it, men and beasts rolling in mortal combat. Lawrence, Nobody, and Chester dashed through the fray and charged the rest of the soldiers.

The entire amphitheater broke into pandemonium, with natives popping out everywhere and citizens and soldiers leaping into the arena or being thrown down head first. Little Caesar's box was empty—Pacarina was gone—then the world's chaos faded into the present chaos and Lawrence found himself amidst a whirl of swords, flapping leather, and groaning men.

Chester darted among his opponents, making each slash count, his face bright with the light of battle and the grin he always wore when he found a good fight. Nobody was strangest to watch as he leaped at his enemies on the tips of his toes, like a ballet dancer, and kicked, sometimes breaking ribs, sometimes cracking knees. He had robbed a body of its steel arm-guards and strapped them to his shins so that each kick landed like a club's blow.

"The 42nd!" Nobody shouted.

"A Stoning! A Stoning!" Chester returned.

Lawrence saved his breath for fighting. A thick soldier emerged from the dust and slashed at Lawrence, but Lawrence blocked the blow with his own sword. The force of the impact jittered through his fingers. The soldier drew his arm back to thrust. Lawrence tried to side-step, but tripped on a body and fell forward into the soldier's legs.

The Roman fell undermost and Lawrence scrambled away as fast as he could, but his sword was stuck. He opened his eyes. The soldier lay dead in the dirt with Lawrence's sword trapped beneath his back and a knife in his throat, just where the top of the armor ended and before the helmet began. Chester must have found a throwing knife. Lawrence swallowed, tried not to look at the blood, and yanked his sword out from under the body.

"Watch out!"

A foot whizzed past Lawrence's face and flattened a charging soldier. Colonel Nobody gave a grim smile as he whirled past.

Somehow amidst the whirl, and clash, and screams, and blood, Lawrence found himself next to the trap door from which the dogs had come. His companions were still surrounded by clumps of soldiers, while screaming natives armed mostly with scythes and clubs darted among the combatants and slashed at legs and faces. This was the ultimate entertainment—the inclusion of the audience in the blood sport.

Lawrence slid down the ramp into the darkness below. The Romans used to build their theaters and arenas with radiating passages called *vomitoria* which allowed large crowds to exit quickly into the street. Little Caesar might have used one of these, but more likely he had a private passage away from vulgar eyes. Lawrence needed to find that passage, and more importantly, Pacarina.

The din of battle penetrated the hot passages below. Bodies thumped on the roof, and the victor's shout of triumph mingled with his victim's death-rattle in a horrible cacophony. Lamps burning on the walls showed dozens of pillars supporting the roof, and lifts, worked by four-spoked capstans, which lifted animals and gladiators to ground-level.

Lawrence held his sword at the ready, but there didn't seem to be anyone down here. They must have all joined the fight above or run to the palace when the horn blared. He heard a voice. It wasn't angry, and it wasn't loud. It modulated in a speech—someone was giving an oration down here? No, it was a prayer.

The passage led directly into one of the lifts, which was positioned against a doorway on the right so that anyone or anything coming out of the doorway would instantly be in the lift. The doorway was blocked by an iron door made of crossed vertical and horizontal bars. The voice came from inside.

Nobody put his mouth to one of the square gaps in the door. "Hello!"

The voice stopped. Fabric rustled, but that was all.

"Christ is risen," Lawrence said.

"He is risen indeed!"

A cluster of faces crowded the passage.

"Who are you?" someone asked.

"I'm one of the Outsiders. How many Christians are in there?"

"Most of my flock is here," another said. It was Bishop Aulus. "There are many cells, all connected, containing several hundred of us."

Lawrence rattled the lock. It was solid iron, massive, and not going anywhere. Lawrence ran his hands across the walls, but there were no pegs for a key. It was probably flapping against a guard's belt in the middle of the battle.

"Can you release us?" Bishop Aulus asked.

Lawrence clenched his hands. Somewhere up above, Pacarina was being dragged away from him, but he couldn't leave these people trapped in their cells at the mercy of the soldiers. Besides, they had to join the fight. The Dogs had started it, but they couldn't win unaided. But how to get them out?

Chester would probably try to break the door down, but flesh and bone has little effect on iron. Lawrence needed some type of leverage. He knelt and examined the hinges. They were typical Roman architecture, pivots resting in holes in the rock. That wouldn't work. He shook his head.

"Are you sure there aren't any other ways out?"

"They are all locked," Bishop Aulus said.

Lawrence stuck his fingers through the bars and rattled the door in frustration. He needed leverage. *Leverage*. Wait! He looked up at the lift, which was capped by one massive beam. On the other side of the lift was the capstan that, turning, generated the force to raise the cage.

Lawrence grabbed a nearby sledge-hammer. He wasn't strong enough to bash in the door itself, and the lock would probably withstand a significant beating without breaking, but there was one spot which the Romans couldn't really make stronger, and it was the last place that most men would look. He swung the hammer with both hands over his head and felt the iron head rebound off the rock. If he could crack the face of the rock which held the top hinge-pivot, he might be able to get this door down.

Two minutes. One stroke every three seconds. Forty strokes. The rock showed a white blotch where the blows had chipped it, but it was still strong. Forty-one. A crack! Lawrence wiped his face and drank in the sight. The crack was only as long as his pinky was wide, but it was a crack.

Fifty. The tone of the metal on the rock had changed. The rock was absorbing more of the shock. Lawrence's pounding heart was stealing most of his oxygenated blood and his arms were tingly from the theft. Just a few more strokes.

At last he let the sledge-hammer drop and surveyed the network of cracks scarring the square foot of rock behind which the hinge was embedded. Lord willing, it was weak enough.

Lawrence found a length of chain, threaded it under and over four bars in the door, and tied it off as best he could. Flakes of something scraped off the chain's links. Lawrence lifted a handful to the light. It was dried blood. This chain had no doubt seen the torture and death of many a miserable wretch.

It took thirty seconds more to press a small log against the stone just above the doorway and hold it in place by looping the chain over the lift's top beam so that it maintained a steady pressure against the log.

Lawrence put his shoulder to one of the four spokes in the capstan. It swung easily for two feet, until the chain tautened, then the real work began. Lawrence clenched his arms into horizontal L shapes, with his elbows pressed tightly against his chest, and heaved. The capstan budged. He heaved again, driving his legs into the ground so that every inch was an inch gained, and straining until the sweat dripped from the tip of his nose.

"It's creaking," Bishop Aulus said.

Lawrence gasped for breath. "I think those are my joints."

"Is it possible zhat I hear vords in zhe English tongue?" That voice could only belong to Jacques. "I could never haf believed zhat such a barbaric language could be so beautiful."

"Aye, says the fellow as is called a barbarian by the first Roman as claps eyes on 'im."

Jacques and O'Malley must have just come out of the labyrinth of cells to the crowded passageway inside the door.

"O'Malley!" Lawrence called. The tendons in his legs and arms were trembling from the strain. "I don't think I'm strong enough."

"Move aside, ye fellows," O'Malley said. "This is a job fer an Irishman."

"And a Frenchman," Jacques said. "I cannot stay in zhis place any longer, it smells of—I do not vant to say—but it is even vorse zhan London."

"Aye, let the mosquito shove his Froggy back into it, too."

The soldiers pushed against the inside of the door and Lawrence felt a slight relief in the tension on the chain. He pushed harder, trying to keep the momentum, and flakes of rock fell from the passageway. The higher the lift went the more force tried to tear the top of the door outwards through the weakened stone.

A little higher—the creak of iron gave way to a mighty crash as the entire door burst its stony bounds and dangled at the lift's bottom. O'Malley and Jacques sprawled on the lift's floor and the other Christians began pouring out of the cell.

"Praise God!" Bishop Aulus said. He grasped Lawrence by the shoulders. "Brave man. You have saved our lives."

Lawrence borrowed a handkerchief from Jacques to wipe his face. It didn't require much bravery to push a capstan. It did require sacrifice, maybe an unbelievably hard one if Pacarina had been whisked away during this delay, but that was something the bishop didn't need to know.

"Grab as many weapons as you can from the walls," Lawrence said. "These two Outsiders will lead you. I have to find my wife."

"Weapons?" Bishop Aulus held up his thin arms. "We fight not with the weapons of this world."

Lawrence stared at him. He had forgotten that the bishop didn't support violence. This couldn't happen. Pacarina could be anywhere by now.

"Please, Bishop, listen carefully and quickly. God sent the Israelites into many nations bearing the sword, He called the warrior-king David a 'man after His own heart,' He established rules for warfare, Christ told Peter to buy a sword, and Christ Himself used a whip on the moneychangers in the temple. There is 'a time for war,' says Ecclesiastes, and that time is now. Fight for your family, your home, and your God."

Lawrence handed the bishop his sword and ran. Somewhere up above was his wife, and that somewhere was where he must go.

Chapter 36

A thick white snow-sky capped the mountains around Vallis Deorum, and the air was colder than Lawrence had yet felt in the daytime here. Specks of white floated toward the street—maybe flurries, maybe bits of wool captured by the wind in the arena and whisked over the walls.

Most of the crowd had already escaped the amphitheater, leaving only a few stragglers still dashing to shelter. The caterwauls of the natives mixed with the stern one-word commands of the soldiers, all underlain by clashing steel and death-screams.

One of the stragglers howled at the sight of Lawrence and nearly broke his neck leaping a merchant's cart and fleeing up an alley. What was so frightening? Lawrence looked down. His clothes were stained red with the sheep's blood, and streaks of blood clung to his arms and legs beneath his tunic. Lawrence shuddered. If the scholars at his club in London saw him they would probably faint and then forswear his society for all time.

The amphitheater was close enough to the palace rock to hear the clash of battle from both places. Judging by their shouts, the Praetorians at the palace were getting the best of the fight, and they must already have been reinforced, because there was no sign of life on the mountain-path leading out of Vallis Deorum. If Lawrence could gather the rest of his party they could climb that path without a soul to oppose them.

One of the *vomitoria*, the exit hallways from the arena, was smaller than the others and was flanked by two statues clothed in purple and holding scepters. The faces were obviously modeled after Little Caesar, though the bodies were tall and fit. At least they were clothed, unlike most of the statuary in this place. Lawrence ran inside, ready at any moment to encounter a guard, but the place was deserted. He ran through a clutter of luxury and art and came out into the open air of the emperor's box, looking down on the bloodbath below.

It looked like one of the enormous mock fights which Nero orchestrated, and indeed, there were still patches of hardened citizens in the stands watching the real battle below as if it was simply a planned part of the day's festivities. Lawrence scanned the crowd for Chester and Nobody, but the melee was too confused to pick them out. The seat where Pacarina had sat was on the level below, accessible by stairs, but it was empty. Lawrence turned and ran for the open street. He had to find his wife.

The way to the palace was to the right, but Little Caesar wasn't the type of man to run toward a fight. He would probably go to the nearest public building— he wouldn't trust a private house—and there should be some sign of his guards there to give Lawrence a clue. The street was lined mostly with shops hawking refreshments for arena-goers and a conveniently located morgue. Would Little Caesar hide in a morgue? No, it didn't fit his type.

Across from the morgue was another large building. A haze hung in the air. Smoke? No, steam—like the steam rising from the bathhouse near the library. That fit Little Caesar's type.

Just as the history books said, there were three entrances, one for men, one for women, and one for slaves. Which was which? The men's was probably the one with the most worn-down steps, so Lawrence pounded up these and entered.

Four soldiers stood in front of the inner door with drawn swords. Lawrence stopped in the doorway and remembered, too late, that he had given his sword to Bishop Aulus. He was unarmed. The soldiers stared at him and he stared back. The man on the far right dropped his sword.

"Ghost!" the soldier said.

Lawrence blinked. Of course, with all of this sheep blood smeared over him a superstitious Roman might well think he wasn't a living man. He opened his eyes as wide as he could and stepped closer. Another sword dropped. Another step, and another sword. But he was trapping these men against the door, and what he wanted was for them to get *away* from the door.

One man remained holding a sword. Another step, and Lawrence was close enough to reach one of the dropped blades.

"It's a lie," the fourth soldier said. "I don't believe in gods and I don't believe in ghosts." He swung at Lawrence's head.

Lawrence dropped, grabbed a sword, and rolled toward the wall. How did he pick the only atheist in the Praetorian Guard? God must have a sense of humor.

The soldiers rushed. The wall was coated with shelves for bathers to put their clothes in, and several togas and tunics were stuffed into these cubes. Lawrence threw a load of the fabric at his assailants and rolled out of the way again as their blades splintered the shelving above his head.

Lawrence had to get through that door to Pacarina. He knocked away one soldier's sword and sprang into the midst of them, felt their hands grasping him, squeezed harder and felt his blood-slimed tunic slip through their fingers. He was free. Another moment and he was on the other side of the door, his back to the wood, a shiver shaking him from spine to heel as the soldiers threw themselves against the door.

He couldn't hold the door long against four men, each of whom was stronger than him. The pressure eased as they drew back for another blow. To his right was a rack of towels and to his left was a statue of Jupiter. Lawrence snatched a towel, looped it around Jupiter's neck, and dragged down with all his strength. The statue tottered and fell across the door just as the soldiers rushed it again. The upper half of the door bent outward under the force, but the weight of the statue laying across its base held it in place.

"Lawrence!"

Lawrence turned. Only one voice was capable of thrilling his heart-strings. He had found Pacarina.

Little Caesar stood on the other side of the cold pool of water in which bathers would begin the bathing process. His arm gripped Pacarina's.

"Unhand my wife," Lawrence said.

Little Caesar drew back toward the door to the next room.

"She's to be *my* wife," he said.

"That's where you're wrong," Lawrence said. He closed the space between them rapidly, his sword pointed at Little Caesar's neck. "I assure you that I don't wantonly insult men, but I don't consider calling you a dirty Roman pig to be an insult, for that slick of oil on your forehead can certainly be classified as dirty, you are Roman, and you distinctly resemble the four-legged beast from which we derive bacon."

Lawrence glared down his blade. "And, your hand is on my wife."

Little Caesar yanked away from Pacarina like a naughty child caught playing marbles on Sunday.

"W-will you kill me unarmed?" Little Caesar's hands clasped into a prayer posture.

Pacarina clung to Lawrence and he held her tight, his left arm around her heaving shoulders, her head tucked against his shoulder. He kissed her and lowered his sword.

"Little Caesar, if you worshiped the true God I would tell you to thank Him that I won't kill you because you are unarmed and are not actively threatening me or my wife. But—" Lawrence drew back his foot, "—I have no scruples against doing *this*."

His toes struck home in one of the fleshy parts of Little Caesar's back and the pompous tyrant flailed over the pool and landed with the most satisfying splash that Lawrence had ever heard.

Wood splintered and an angry shout came from the doorway. The soldiers had broken down the upper half of the door and the first man was climbing over the statue. Lawrence raised his sword.

"Stand back, Dear."

"But Lawrence, you're not a fighter," Pacarina said.

She was right. It hurt—but it didn't sting like Bronner's words.

Lawrence kissed her. "No, Dear, I'm not a fighter, but I am your husband, and I'm not letting you go again. Now, stand well back against the wall. Knowing my skill with weapons I'm as likely to cut you as one of these Romans."

The first Roman shouted at Lawrence and sprang forward along the edge of the water. What did Chester say to do if attacked by multiple men? Throw knives. But Lawrence didn't have any knives.

Lawrence grabbed a pitcher of oil from the floor and flung it at the Roman, who received the pottery full in the face and lurched sideways, trying to wipe the oil from his eyes. His sandal slipped on the edge of the floor and he fell into the water. Lawrence leaped forward and struck downwards. The soldier's struggles ceased.

The next two Romans came on together, their eyes hungry for blood.

"Quick, to the next room!"

Lawrence pulled Pacarina through the doorway and slammed the door shut behind them. This was the first warming room in the baths, and the water bubbling in the center pool was definitely from a natural hot spring. Stone slabs piled with towels dotted the floor.

Lawrence motioned Pacarina to stay still, ran to the other side of the room, threw the door into the next chamber open, and ran back. The two soldiers' steps were just outside the first door. Lawrence lifted Pacarina onto the closest slab, lay down beside her, and shook a massive towel over both of them.

The door burst open and the click-clack of hobnails and raspy breaths of the soldiers overwhelmed the spring's bubbling. Lawrence inflated his chest and closed his mouth. Lord willing, the soldiers would rush through before he needed another breath. He clasped Pacarina's hands and pulled her tight against his side, their hearts beating together and sending tremors through Lawrence's stomach and wrists as his lungs began aching for air.

The bubbling once again was the only sound. Lawrence dragged a corner of the towel down until the wool was below his eyes. The room was empty and the two soldiers showed like shadows through the steam in the next room. Lawrence expelled a mouthful of old breath, helped Pacarina to her feet, and ran for the freedom of the open street—and met the fourth soldier.

The fourth soldier was leaning over the *frigidarium*'s water to help Little Caesar out of the pool. He turned as Lawrence charged and grabbed his sword from the floor. Lawrence held his sword out straight with both hands on the handle and leaped into his enemy. Both men toppled, the Roman undermost, and Lawrence tensed for the struggle, but there was none. He opened his eyes. The Roman was dead.

Lawrence forced his trembling knees into enough submission to raise him to his feet. The waters were dyed red with the blood of the first soldier, whose body showed dimly through the swirl, and the fourth, who lay at its brink. Lawrence blinked. He had seen violent deaths before, but he had never caused them. Chester did that. Lawrence was a writer, a scholar—now, a fighter.

"Come, Dear." Lawrence put his arm around Pacarina's shoulders. "Let's go."

Chapter 37

Huge white swirls of clouds filled the heavens. Below, the street outside the bathhouse was crowded with Christians and natives running from the amphitheater. Had the soldiers won? There was little screaming. Helmets lined the street on the other side of the amphitheater, but no faces showed. The soldiers had their backs turned, and they also were retreating.

Lawrence pulled Pacarina into a doorway and waited for the worst of the crowd to pass. There, at the fringe of the retreat, walked Chester, Nobody, Jacques, O'Malley, and Matthew, their faces still turned to the enemy.

"Praise God, they're safe!" Pacarina said.

Lawrence echoed the praise in his heart. Chester and Nobody were covered with blood, but they walked straight, so most of it was probably from the sheepskins.

"Chester!" Lawrence called.

Chester spun around. "You measly little professor. What do you mean by disappearing in the middle of a battle? I thought you were dead."

Chester gripped Lawrence and hugged him until his lungs began to feel like they had under the towel in the bathhouse.

"Don't do that to me, understand?" Chester blotted his eyes with his sleeve. "Terrible dust."

Lawrence smiled. Dust wasn't the only thing Chester was wiping from his eyes, and he felt a wet tug in his own eyes.

Nobody grunted. "I'm glad you're alive, Lawrence, but reunions must wait until we're over those mountains. We have a battle to fight, a battle the likes of which hasn't been fought since legionaries and citizens spilled each others' blood in the streets of Rome."

"What has happened?" Lawrence asked.

"Both sides are regrouping." Nobody's voice was husky from his cold. "They'll soon regret they gave us this chance."

The five sailors appeared out of the crowd of Christians.

"Found you at last!" Bill cried. "I thought you'd gone and gotten yourself killed without remembering your promise to get us out of this cursed place. I've never seen a 'tween deck as filthy as that bit of dungeon they locked us up in with these psalm-singing Christians."

"*Ma foi!*" Jacques said. "You are right. My soul shudders at zhe memory of zhat smell."

Nobody motioned for silence. "So here we are, all together for the first time. Squad One, you Stonings, and five sailors—our little party has grown since we first stumbled over those mountains."

The group paused at the end of the next street, which was full of milling Christians and natives, only half-armed, but beetle-browed and serious. Bishop Aulus, Otho, and Varius joined them.

"Have you seen my son?" Bishop Aulus asked. "I searched for him among my flock all last night, but he wasn't captured. Has he been fighting with you?"

No one spoke. A wind-gust raked the street and whipped Pacarina's hair around Lawrence's face. Colonel Nobody looked at him.

"You've a better way with words than me, Stoning number one. Tell him about the dwarf."

Lawrence licked his lips. How do you tell a father that his son is a traitor? How do you explain that all the Christians in Vallis Deorum were betrayed by a viper nursed in the bishop's own bosom?

"Your son has not been fighting with us," Lawrence said. "We met him in the palace."

Bishop Aulus clasped his hands. "They took the poor boy there? Why?"

"They didn't take him." Lawrence looked away. "Joktan went of his own free will."

"You mean—" Bishop Aulus's hands dropped to his sides. "My son—betrayed us?"

"I'm very sorry. Of course, he wasn't actually your son. I mean, he isn't your flesh and blood."

Bishop Aulus looked like an old man now. His skinny arms dangled limply, black smudged the semicircles below his eyes from a sleepless night, and the eyes themselves watered with unchecked tears.

Bishop Aulus shook his head. "The unbelievers will mock. They will ask if it was worth saving him as a babe, and tending his poor shriveled limbs, and rubbing that poor crooked back. They will ask why I did it. If I am sorry for it? No, I'm not. My duty is to save life as God commands. What becomes of that life is in God's hands."

The men stood silently with their heads bowed in respect of the old man's grief until he turned and slowly returned to his flock. Chester was the first to speak.

"I'm awfully sorry for the old fellow, but all this talk of traitors is reminding me of the whole reason we're in this place. Remember, Mr. Nobody—"

"Colonel!" Jacques and O'Malley said together.

"Right, sorry. Remember, Colonel No One, we came here so that you would know about the queen's ultimatum. Unlike these Romans, England rewards traitors with their just dues—a snug-fitting necklace with an awkward tail. Your friend Edmund is in mortal danger of the gallows unless you get back with these sailors, and your time is running out."

"I've thought of little else," Nobody said. "What date is today?"

Chester told him.

Nobody stared up at the white-capped ring that bound them to this land of blood.

"I don't know if we can do it. There is so little time—and the voyage—I don't know if we can make it in time."

"We can if we leave now," Chester said. "Look, the way is clear. All the guards have been drawn down to fight this battle. All of us are here. There's nothing to stop us from leaving now."

Otho must have understood Chester's gestures.

"You cannot leave us," Otho said. "You are a warrior. You must lead us or else we perish."

"Colonel," Chester said, "it doesn't take a science-lover like my brother to read that sky. That's a snow-sky, and in a few hours those slopes are going to be covered in snow. We can't cross the mountains until it melts, and that could be a week or longer. If we don't leave now, you're right—we won't make it back to England in time to save your friend."

Nobody's hands wiped vaguely at the blood on his tunic, but his mind wasn't in it.

"Otho," Nobody said, "it is my duty to return to my country—if I can call it my country—and save an innocent man's life."

"Are *we* guilty?" Otho waved his hand at the hundreds of Christians and natives crouched in the street. "You are the only man we have who can lead a battle. If you leave, our hope dies. We men will be slain, our women will be tortured, our homes will be destroyed—the last vestige of Christianity in Vallis Deorum will perish if you go."

Nobody grasped his temples. He no longer looked young. His face was worn, scarred by deep secrets and sorrows that Lawrence could only guess, weathered by war, loss, and betrayal. His features worked in agony.

"Edmund faces death because of me." Nobody's voice came through contracted teeth. "He was loyal to me when he knew it meant being outlawed, he followed me to regain our honor even when it meant being parted from the girl he loved. His life was in my hands—these hands!"

Nobody held out his hands. They trembled.

"His fingers slipped through mine."

Otho bowed his head. "Your friend is valiant and innocent, but look behind me. These people are innocent too. I won't say that the lives of we men are more valuable than your friend's, but think of our women. It is the duty of man to protect woman. I believe God has brought you here for a purpose. Your friend is in His hands. Trust him there, and help us here."

Nobody dropped to his knees. His head bowed, his hands clasped in prayer. His shoulders heaved with sobs. The clouds above darkened and swirled lower and lower while the cold wind swept the city streets and tore at the kneeling soldier's tunic.

When Colonel Nobody rose, his face was stern, but calm.

"I stay to fight. It is what Edmund would do. It is the duty of a warrior. I trust his soul to God. I can do no more."

Chapter 38

The wind was bitterly cold now, but Nobody scarcely bothered to think about it. He felt incredibly calm. He had made his choice, and Edmund was completely in God's hands. Was he happy? No, he couldn't say that. He tried to take joy in God's promises, but the flesh is weak, and sorrow formed part of the blanket of calm on his soul, but he squashed it down to deal with another day and turned to the business at hand.

"This is going to be a battle to remember," Nobody said.

"I hope we're around *to* remember it," Chester said.

Nobody strode down the street to inspect the available weapons. It was a motley group of swords, some made by Balbus, some captured from the soldiers, of scythes, hoes, flails, and homemade spears, of rocks, clubs, and fingernails. The men were farmers, shop-keepers, barbers, street-cleaners, scholars, and more. It wasn't exactly the 42nd, armed with rifles and mounted on the best horses in Siberia, but it would have to do. One of the tests of leadership is how much can be done with how little. In this case, 'how much' meant defeating a Roman army.

"Gather round," Nobody called. "Form around me." He jumped onto a box and waited for the crowd to coalesce below him.

"Today we fight the soldiers of Rome, not because we lust for power, but because we long for freedom. I have spent most of my life fighting men in a land far, far away, and I know the face of war. I was weaned on blood. The death-rattle was my lullaby. With God's help I believe that I can lead you to victory, but only if you give me implicit obedience. What say you?"

The men gave a great shout. Their upturned faces showed blind trust. They didn't know the limits of an Outsider's power, but they were willing to dream great things. Nobody forced a coating of saliva down his sore throat.

"Good. The legionaries are better armed and better trained than we, but they also have never been in war, and trust me—the only true preparation for war is war. Fight your hardest and pray harder."

Nobody jumped off the box and snapped his fingers at Jacques and O'Malley. Matthew wasn't in a condition to lead men.

"Jacques, O'Malley, take opposite sides of this street and search the shops and houses for anything that can be used as weapons. After that, post men behind each door and be prepared to lead each flank attack. We'll make these Romans think we're springing from the ground itself."

He gave orders rapidly, sending the crowd flying in ten directions. The Romans would not need long to regroup, and he expected any minute to see the first line of helmets turn onto the street. They would be furious at this insurrection and boiling to slit throats at once and be done with it. With that mindset they would simply march head on and slash at whatever was in their way, and that was exactly what Nobody needed.

He wanted to send the women and children away from this street but he wouldn't trust them unguarded to the tender mercies of the citizens waiting in the surrounding streets like vultures for a carcase, and he couldn't spare men to guard them. Instead, he gathered them in a villa at the end of the street farthest from where the soldiers would come and left them there with a few sentries to warn him in case of a surprise attack.

He set the main body to work building a barricade across the street. Tables, chairs, beds, sacks of grain, hides, and everything else movable or only slightly immovable was brought out and stacked as a breastwork against the enemy. The street wasn't wide, and the laborers were hearty, so an impressive work soon rose.

A scout ran in and reported that the soldiers were coming.

"Chester," Nobody said, "you're taking this battle to the roofs. Post men on each side and be ready to heave down tiles and anything else heavy you can find. From that height a tile will kill. Do you want your brother?"

Chester rubbed his hands together. "Thanks, but Law is safer with his feet on solid ground. Never fear, I'll have those Romans thinking the sky is falling before I'm done." He waved at a group of men. "Come along, laddies. I can't twist my tongue into your ancient language but I can show you how to drop a tile on a pig."

Tramp. Tramp. The measured tread of hobnails on stone grew steadily louder. Nobody reached for his sword, then remembered that his legs were his best weapon. But in a fight like this, kicking wouldn't be enough. He needed something else.

"Varius," Nobody called, "what happened to our pistols? The short wood-and-metal clubs that click which we brought from the Outside?"

"I hid them."

"Then unhide them and bring them to me with the leather bags. We're going to introduce these legionaries to the 19th century."

The soldiers rounded the corner and paused on seeing the barricade. Their line was perfectly straight, each man with his sword and shield at the regulation height, the legion's banners floating from a pole. Nobody shaded his eyes.

"Lawrence, I think your brother has influenced the enemy's fashions. That fellow holding the standard is wearing the head-skin of a dog."

"Actually, standard-bearers usually wear animal skins. Chester's idea isn't as original as he thinks."

Nobody grunted. "I only hope yonder fellow doesn't fight as well as your brother. Are you ready for this?"

Lawrence shook his head. "I'd rather be sitting down at a desk to write this as a past event, but I won't shirk my duty."

"Good man. Matthew!" Nobody motioned the soldier to him.

Matthew's face was gaunt, his eyes were ringed with dark circles, and the hand gripping his sword was white-knuckled. The sight chilled Nobody. He had brought Matthew to try to ease his misplaced guilt, but the craziness of these last days had left the remaining twin to his own devices. And they hadn't helped.

Nobody grasped Matthew's shoulders.

"Matthew, you can't go on like this. Forget the past. You're not the only man who has suffered pain before."

"How do you like kicking, sir?" Matthew said.

Nobody squeezed as hard as his bad arm allowed. "You're also not the only man who has made a mistake. It's God's will that I have this bad arm. I accepted it in the mines—you need to accept it now or the guilt is going to drive you mad."

Matthew grinned a ghastly smile. "May be too late for that. You keep kicking, sir, and I'll try drowning my memory in blood."

Nobody couldn't say anything more because the soldiers had come. They advanced in a tight body. The Christians and natives on the barricade tensed. This was the moment of destiny.

Tramp. Clash. Tramp—Clash. Tramp-Clash.

The soldiers' feet moved faster and faster until they charged the barricade at the run. Varius appeared panting at Nobody's side and handed him the four pistols.

"Do you know how to load these?" Nobody asked Lawrence.

"Yes, but not as efficiently as Chester."

"Start cracking your fingers, because you're going to do it faster than Chester ever dreamed."

Nobody leveled a pistol. The Romans were ten yards from the barricade. A deep battle-cry roared from twisted mouths and swelled to a scream of hate and disgust. Five yards. Nobody cocked the pistol.

"42nd!" he called.

Squad One crouched at the top of the barricade. Chester's head peered off a rooftop. Three yards.

"For your wives, your children, your sweethearts—now!"

The pistol cracked, the recoil tore at Nobody's arm, the smoke whisked away in the wind, and the first Roman fell with a bullet in his head. Battle was joined.

The barricade trembled at the shock of the armored soldiers. Steel clanged on steel and dying men groaned along the line as the soldiers' up-thrusting *gladii* met the downward sweep of scythe, club, and flail. Nobody shouted encouragement and scrambled across the barricade, firing his pistols as quickly as Lawrence could load them. Then, the storm broke.

The air thickened with falling snow. Snowflakes sizzled on Nobody's pistol barrel. That feeling of heat belching from a barrel into a world of cold brought back thousands of memories until he could almost see the screaming Romans below change into fur-capped Cossacks, and the war cry of the 42nd rang in his ears. But in those days Edmund was at his side.

"Now!" Nobody waved at the rooftops. "Unleash Fury!"

A shower of tiles mingled with the falling snow and crashed onto the packed soldiers below. The air filled with those horrible war sounds, so thrilling and yet so terrible to a soldier's ears. Nobody pulled trigger after trigger and with each contraction of his finger sent a messenger of death ripping through the mass.

"Retreat!"

A Roman officer dashed through his men and pulled them away from the barricade with curses on more gods than Nobody knew existed in the whole Roman pantheon. His missing helmet revealed bristling hair. As the soldiers drew back from the barricade, the Christians and natives shouted in triumph and began leaping down after them.

"No!" Nobody yelled. "Back, as you value your lives. Stay on the barricade!"

The battle could end right now. The barricade's height balanced the disparity of skill, but man to man Nobody's "rebels" couldn't match the armored soldiers.

The soldiers wheeled and charged into their pursuers and the tide of battle flowed back. Swords ran red. The Christians and natives tried to hold a line but they were swept back and fell in heaps. Those who remained rushed to the barricade where their comrades who had stayed back tensed to cover their retreat.

One scream out of dozens tingled Nobody's spine. It came from an English throat. There were sailors down there. He searched the running crowd over his pistol barrel and froze, pointing at three men in sailor slops at the fringe of the Roman pursuit. As he watched, one man fell to a soldier's sword.

Nobody blasted a bullet into the nearest soldier but another took his place and the second sailor fell. Nobody closed his eyes. When he opened them the soldiers' front line had engulfed the bloody spot and three crumpled heaps alone told the story.

Tiles rained like a stone blizzard, most shattering harmlessly on the street, but some splatting on soldiers' heads. Slivers of stone rebounded from the street like shells exploding on a pebbly beach. The only "rebels" left in the street were carcasses, and faced again with the hailstorm from above and the barricade towering in front, the soldiers retreated sullenly and crowded at the end of the street.

"Have we won?" Lawrence asked. He paused with a ramrod half jammed into a pistol barrel.

"Round one," Nobody croaked. "Barely."

He leaped onto the barricade's highest point, an inverted table with four legs pointing at the sky.

"Men, catch your breath and listen hard. If I'm to be your general then I must have implicit obedience. If I had wanted you to fight on the soldiers' level I wouldn't have wasted your breath dragging this furniture out, but I didn't. The mangled bodies down there tell you why. When I tell you to fight, fight, and when I tell you to stop, stop."

"I'd like to get my hands on that Eskimo mummer," said an English voice. Bill the sailor scowled at the carnage. "He tells us stories about a hidden land full of devils and gold, and we disbelieve the devils and follow him for the gold, and here we are in a land full of human devils and not a gold doubloon ready to hand."

Bill and Mr. Trumble the mate stood panting on the barricade.

"What are you doing here?" Nobody said. "I told you to stay with the women and children. Three of you just *died* down there."

"So I saw," Bill said. "They never was smart."

Nobody clenched his fist. "You fool, do you think I've risked everything to find you just to watch you die? Get back to guarding the women and children before I give you a taste of what the Romans taught me about discipline."

"Colonel, they're coming again!" Lawrence held out a brace of freshly-loaded pistols.

"Hello, down there," Chester called from the roofs. "These walking sign-boards for a tinker's shop called soldiers are giving us some new ammunition to throw down. If you start seeing metal-plated bodies falling from the sky, don't blame the blizzard."

A line of soldiers clambered over the roofs toward Chester, who bowed them on as if accepting a lady's hand for a dance and began somersaulting across the alleys between the rooftops.

Nobody looked at Lawrence. "Are you quite sure that's a relative of yours?"

"So I'm told. I wouldn't believe it if we weren't twins."

"Which of you is older?"

"I don't know," Lawrence said.

Nobody shook his head. "You are a strange pair. Well, get your ramrod ready, because we have our own problems down here on earth to attend to."

The second wave of the attack was better prepared. The front line rushed to the foot of the barricade, knelt, and stuck the edges of their shields into crevices, thus forming steps which they supported while the men behind leaped upon them and tried to scale the wall. The men on the roofs were too busy with their own fight to drop anything but dead bodies.

Three soldiers sprang onto the barricade's crest fifteen feet to Nobody's left. He toppled them with three shots in rapid succession and Otho leaped into the gap to stop the other soldiers struggling up. More helmets rose on the right, but Jacques and O'Malley rushed the spot and threw the soldiers off the barricade. Other soldiers kept coming.

Christians and natives sprawled on the street inside the barricade with horrible gashes from the *gladius*'s wide blade. The lack of armor was deadly. The battle must turn *now* or it was lost. There was still a reserve force hidden in the houses on both sides of the street, but Nobody only wanted to use these for a final rout, when an attack from an unexpected place could break the enemy's morale and send them flying. If the flankers attacked now they would be fighting at the same disadvantage as the men who had followed the soldiers' first flight.

The leader must die. Nobody searched the crowd for that bristling head and sneering face and quickly found his target at the front of the fight, cheering

299

his men on and cursing his enemies. Nobody sprang to the piece of barricade directly above him.

"Remember me?" Nobody called.

Bristle Hair looked up. "Ha, ha, Christian dog. You want to fight me again? This time there's nothing to stop my blade from drinking your blood."

Nobody leveled his pistol. Bristle Hair didn't flinch. Of course he wouldn't, because he didn't know the power of gunpowder.

"Should I find you a sword?" Bristle Hair shouted. "I would love to knock it out of your baby hands again before I kill you."

"If I read romances I would jump down and start hacking with you like a novel's climax. But I'm a practical man." Nobody pulled the pistol hammer back with his left thumb. "Goodbye, Roman."

The bullet flew true and Bristle Hair sprawled back into the ranks of his men.

"Squad One, drive them back!" Nobody shouted.

"Hooroo!"

"Vive la republique!"

On the right, soldiers shrank away from O'Malley's giant strokes like wisps of grain before the reaper, while Jacques danced from table top to bed post and darted down for quick thrusts before pirouetting out of danger again. On the left, Matthew Preston rained blows on his shrinking foes with the strength of a madman and splattered them with froth from his twisted mouth.

Dark forms whirled past Nobody and he thought for a moment that the men were disobeying him again and were charging the enemy, but it wasn't his men. The detachment of dog-handlers he had sent at the beginning of the fight back to the arena had returned, and a pack of war dogs scrambled over the barricade at eye level with the climbing soldiers.

The loss of their leader, the Outsiders' redoubled fury, and the vicious four-legged attackers turned the soldiers' appetite for blood into a longing for the safety at the end of the street. They retreated again, in better form than the first time, but still, they retreated. The war dogs were slaughtered one by one, but they had served their purpose.

Nobody scanned the rooftops. Lawrence was already watching them anxiously. Only a small group of soldiers remained. Bodies lined the street below. But where was Chester?

"There he is," Lawrence said.

One roof over from the main fight, two men grappled in each others' arms at the tiles' edge. The man on top wore the dog's head and skin of a standard-bearer. The man on the bottom was Chester.

"Can you shoot him?" Lawrence said.

"Pistol isn't accurate enough."

Both men's hands were locked on a knife which the Roman was trying to drive down into Chester's heart. Their bodies slid toward the edge.

"Goodbye, Colonel."

Nobody spun around. Matthew held out a folded piece of paper. Nobody took it.

"What is this?" he asked.

Matthew's eyes were wild. A dribble of foam from lip to chin sliced his square face. Blood dripped from a cut on his cheek and more flowed from his arms.

"I don't think I'll see Mark again, sir, because he's in heaven. But when you get up there, tell him something from me, will you, sir?"

"Matthew, what on earth—"

"Tell him I always loved him and I couldn't stand things without him. Goodbye, Colonel Nobody." Matthew snapped to attention and saluted.

Before Nobody could grab his arm the guilt-ridden soldier leaped from the barricade and charged the enemy.

"No! Matthew!"

Nobody tried to jump after him but arms locked around his chest and he struggled in Otho and Balbus's grasp.

"You're our leader, you can't die," Otho said.

"He's my soldier!"

Jacques and O'Malley did follow, but they were scarce halfway to the enemy when Matthew dashed into the ranks with an unearthly scream. The soldiers fell away from his fury for a moment, then their ranks closed, a dozen swords fell, and all was over. Jacques and O'Malley staggered back to the barricade with tears coursing their cheeks.

Nobody bowed his head. He had failed. He had tried to comfort Matthew, he had brought him to Greenland because he felt the responsibility of the man's grief, but he hadn't been able to do anything. Guilt and bitterness had turned Matthew's head. *Help me, God. You give, and You take away. Blessed be the name of the Lord.*

"There's only one," Lawrence said.

Nobody forced himself to follow Lawrence's pointing finger. Only one man lay on the roof where Chester and the soldier had been fighting, and that man wore a dog's head.

"No!" Lawrence said. His eyes mirrored the horror in Nobody's soul. "Lord, let him not be dead!"

The man rose, looked down at the barricade, and—grinned. A hearty, good-natured, devil-may-care grin that only an Englishman can give, followed by a bow and salute that only Chester can give. Chester lived, and he had a new hat.

The Romans advanced for the third time.

"We're low on powder," Lawrence said.

"Keep loading," Nobody said. "This is the last great attack. Either they or we will break."

The snowfall thickened until the roofs were all but invisible from the ground and the approaching soldiers were simply a line of black specters in a world of white. The line of men on the barricade was sadly gapped by the soldiers' swords, but Varius and Otho still stood, and with them was Balbus, finally fighting for his beliefs, and behind the barricade knelt Bishop Aulus with his hands lifted to the heavens in prayer.

"Stand strong!" Nobody shouted.

The wave struck. The crashes of falling bodies were muffled now, deadened by the mounding snow, but the death-shrieks were just as loud. The blizzard attacked in all its fury until Nobody could scarcely see the men he was shooting. Ah, that was why the battle hadn't felt quite right. He was used to fighting in a haze of smoke. Now that the falling snow was taking its place he felt natural again, and it's easier to kill a man when you can't see him clearly.

It was jump, kick, trigger-pull, shout encouragement, dash to Lawrence for freshly-loaded pistols, dodge, hold the hand of a dying Christian, stem a gap in the line, all motion, and blood, and whirling swords, and screams.

The soldiers were cresting the barricade now. Their ranks were made mostly of their best fighters and their cowards, as their bravest men had already died in the first two charges, except for the men skilled enough to survive. Nobody couldn't see the tiles falling from the roofs, but he heard the thuds, and the cries of the men holding back from the front of the fight. This was the moment.

"Now!" Nobody cried. "Jacques, O'Malley, to the flanks and release the reserves. Chester, you grinning monkey, if you can hear me up there then tear the very roofs up for one last shower of death, then join the final melee."

"All four are loaded, Colonel."

Lawrence had one brace of pistols in his hands and the other tucked beneath his arms. What? The fellow had tied himself a cravat over top of his tunic. Nobody shook his head. These Stonings were odd fellows.

"Keep two and use them." Nobody grabbed one of the pistol braces. "This is the last hurrah—the second or third last charge of my life."

"I'm not very good with pistols," Lawrence said.

"All you have to do is point and shoot. How could you miss?"

Lawrence's teeth showed white between powder-blackened flesh.

"I'd feel better if you weren't in front of me when I pulled the triggers."

"Then lead the charge. Your uncle led many a one and his nephew is no less a man. Christians, Dogs, to me!"

As the barricade, stressed and battered by the armored foes below gave way with a splintering rumble, its occupants dashed after Lawrence and Nobody and closed with the soldiers on their own ground. At the same moment an Irish hooroo from the right and a French caterwaul from the left announced that the reserves, hidden for the whole fight in the houses on both sides of the street, were finally in action.

The soldiers broke. Who could blame them? Stymied by the slaves and Christ-followers they despised the most in front, rained upon by destruction from above, scoured by strange death from the hands of the boy Outsider, attacked on all sides now by foes who seemed to spring from the earth—it was more than untested soldiers could stand. The army of Vallis Deorum broke into a hundred flecks of foam and the soldiers ran with no thought of return.

Nobody didn't call back his men now. The enemy was broken, the battle was won, the city was free. His duty was done. But oh, what a duty. Nobody looked past the dead and dying men, above the stripped rooftops, up, up, through the swirling snow to the mountain path he knew was there but couldn't see. It was impassable until the snow melted. How long would that be?

His right hand was clenched on something more than a pistol handle. He laid the pistol on a body and looked at the paper Matthew had given him, crusted with dried blood and blotted ink. He turned it over. The words scrawled like the serrations on a knife blade.

To my colonel, to my colonel, to the 42nd's colonel,
I have dreamt too long of madmen, I have steeped too long in guilt.
I have sought to drown my sorrows, but they've gored me to the hilt.

To my colonel, to my colonel, to the 42nd's colonel,
May you weep not at my loss, or may your tears be not as mine.
I have no more tears for weeping. I must end this last repine.

To my colonel, to my colonel, to the 42nd's colonel,
May your courage never fail you 'til you whisp your final breath.
I can't take it any longer—I will die the soldier's death.
Farewell, Colonel. Farewell, Colonel. Farewell, 42nd's colonel.

Nobody dropped to his knees, whispered a prayer, and fell prostrate in the snow. His duty in Vallis Deorum was done.

Chapter 39

The palace halls were safe now. Lawrence tucked Pacarina's arm under his and pointed out all the niches where once there had stood statues of gods and goddesses. The palace walls were a little empty now, but the palace rubbish heap was thriving.

Two weeks ago the mighty Barricade Battle, or, as Chester liked to call his part of things, the Snow of Death, had broken the Praetorian Guard and effectively overthrown the government of Vallis Deorum. The day after the battle plunged Lawrence into constant meetings with the Christians and the natives, whose perspectives differed as to how the new government should be formed, but who both agreed that the Outsiders should help.

Lawrence had spent both weeks secluded in a comfortable meeting room with Aulus, Otho, and leaders from the natives and main citizenry. After hours of arguing they had all basically agreed on a code of just, biblically-based laws.

Lawrence had scarcely seen his companions, except for Pacarina, for the whole two weeks . They had agreed unanimously that he was the man to create a new government and had then wandered off about their own pursuits. Colonel Nobody was training Varius as a general and watching the snow melt. Chester? Lawrence didn't know what Chester had been doing, which was always frightening, but rumors swirled of intense cooking competitions between him and Jacques. If so, that was a relatively safe occupation. One can do damage in a kitchen, but it's hard to destroy a nation by overcooking an egg.

Pacarina shuddered.

"What's wrong, Dear?" Lawrence asked.

"I don't like this place. I never can after being locked in that room upstairs."

"Logically speaking," Lawrence said, "there's nothing to fear now. Little Caesar is in prison and his friends are either with him there, waiting sentence for crimes, or they've slunk back into the population."

Pacarina smiled. "Do I always speak logically, Law?"

"Good point."

Lawrence pushed through a row of curtains and led Pacarina into the main throne room, where Colonel Nobody had ordered everyone to gather. He might have a surprise for Lawrence, but Lawrence definitely had a surprise for him.

Chester stood by the table's inside right corner.

"Morning, Professor. I always said you'd be running a university some day, I just didn't expect your pupils to be Ancient Romans."

Everyone was there. Bill and Mr. Trumble leaned on one of the windowsills looking intensely bored, while Jacques and O'Malley stood three feet away arguing about something. Chester organized piles of weapons and accessories on the table. Balbus and his family were there with the little boy Balbus rescued from the baby pit and a slave girl named Ennia, who seemed to know Colonel Nobody well. Colonel Nobody stood at the farthest window watching the path out of the valley. He turned as Lawrence and Pacarina entered.

"I'm afraid the rumors are true that married men are always late," Colonel Nobody said.

Lawrence raised an eyebrow. "I'm sure Lady Liana will be glad to help confirm your theory," he said.

Colonel Nobody smiled. It was only the second time Lawrence saw his lips curl up, not down. He seemed to possess better spirits than he had for many days. His top eyelids no longer drooped to ease head-pressure as they had during his cold.

"I say," Chester said, "it seems that everyone has or is going to have a wife except for me. Please, Jacques, tell me that you haven't been bitten."

Jacques fingered the fuzz above his upper lip. "A vife? Me? Bah. A vife would argue all zhe day long."

Colonel Nobody brought things to order with a snap of his fingers.

"Today we leave this place," he said. "I believe the snow has melted sufficiently. Everyone has their orders except you, Stoning number one, and your job is simply to come along and think of hare-brained schemes for your brother to risk his life on. Think you can manage?"

Chester laughed. "Trust me, he has experience."

Lawrence opened his mouth to announce his decision but Colonel Nobody wasn't finished.

"Now to business. I have two things I want to do before I leave this place. Ennia, come here."

The girl started and gripped the edge of the table where she had been standing. She stepped slowly into the center of the room, one foot after the other, like a bather testing the water's temperature.

"You don't have any family, do you, Ennia?" Colonel Nobody said.

She shook her head.

"I want to give you a family."

Colonel Nobody took the girl's hand. Chester's glance skewered Lawrence. His glabella—the hairless space between his eyebrows—creased with two vertical lines. What was Colonel Nobody doing? Lawrence's stomach knotted. If he had risked so much to help this fellow get back to Lady Liana just to watch him marry some pagan slave girl—

"Balbus," Colonel Nobody said, "will you take this girl as a daughter?"

Lawrence's stomach growled with relief.

"I'd take a war dog as daughter if you asked it," Balbus said.

"I trust she'll be a little less fierce." Colonel Nobody smiled like a father. "Ennia, you saw that I am different from the pagans. Balbus and his sons are the same because we worship the same God. Would you like to learn about our God?"

Ennia nodded so violently that her crown-plaited hair nearly flopped out of its braids.

Nobody gently laid her trembling fingers in Balbus's forge-scarred palm and closed his fingers over hers. Mrs. Balbus—Lawrence didn't know her surname—wrapped the girl in her arms and laid her head on her shoulder.

Colonel Nobody gripped Balbus's arm. "Love her as a daughter and honor her as a woman. She needs both badly. And, if God calls her as His child—" he looked meaningfully at Otho, "—she would make a good wife. Now, Jacques, O'Malley, you two Stonings, gather round."

Colonel Nobody swept some of Chester's rubble of weapons out of the way, took something from a bag, and rested his closed fists, knuckles down, on the table's surface.

"We've gone through much. Squad One has gained two members who have valiantly and intelligently honored their uncle's legacy. And we've lost a friend." His gaze fell to the table. "Matthew was a good and loyal soldier, but in the end, he couldn't trust his troubles to God. A bad man may be a good soldier, but the best soldier is the best Christian."

There was silence. Colonel Nobody, Jacques, and O'Malley were all tensing their faces against tears. Lawrence hadn't seen much in the glowering soldier to engender love and loyalty, but these men obviously had both for him. Perhaps he had been a different man in former days.

Colonel Nobody opened his fists and spilled two handfuls of something on the table.

"I don't know what is going to happen to us in the Outside, as the Romans call the rest of our world. I don't know if you Stonings will stay with me or move on to other adventures."

"Adventures," Chester said.

Lawrence bit his lip.

"But wherever you go," Colonel Nobody said, "I want you to bear a reminder that you are members of Squad One."

He pinched one of the objects on the table between his thumb and index finger and held it to the light.

"Balbus has made seven rings bearing the mark of our brotherhood."

The ring dropped heavy and cold onto Lawrence's palm. A gold band encircled a blue gem, but the gem was hollow. A letter and a number were carved through the gem's face, showing a fiery red stone below. A brilliant S and the number one showed like blood encrusted in a sea of blue.

"Squad One," Colonel Nobody said. "May we always stay true to God and each other. Two rings are for you, Lawrence and Chester. Two are for you, dear Jacques and O'Malley. Three are for Dilworth, Petr, and Thomas, who were blessed enough to escape this bloody valley. One is for me, and I trust to place the seventh firmly on Edmund's finger."

"We will be faithful by God's help," Chester said. He coughed. "Er, isn't this where you say the bit about anyone in need simply showing this ring and Squad One will assemble from anywhere in the world to help out?"

Colonel Nobody laughed. "Edmund would say that. You two have read the same novels. I don't believe that a ring is necessary to remind us of our commitment, but yes, if you send me your ring, I'll come to your aid if it's humanly possible."

"Splendid," Chester said. "Well, do we have any more emotional scenes to wrap up before we go mountain-climbing? I'm anxious to see dear old Banastre Bronner's face when he sees you walk in with your sailors in tow."

"I'm ready," Colonel Nobody said.

Lawrence sucked a breath.

"Actually, there is one more thing." He squeezed Pacarina's hand. "Pacarina and I have been married for close to three years now, but God has not blessed us with a child. I'll be frank with you—I don't know if He ever will."

Chester looked away. Everyone else stared with curiosity and a little embarrassment stamped on their features.

"We have already asked Balbus, who seems to be the only person who might claim the authority to answer us yes or no, and we have his permission, but I'd also like to ask yours, Colonel."

Colonel Nobody frowned. "You've used a great many words to *not* say what you're trying to say. Ask."

Lawrence took the little baby boy from Balbus's daughter. "We want to adopt this little fellow as our son."

Colonel Nobody folded his arms. "Would you tell people where he actually came from?"

"I don't know. Do you think it would be wise?"

Colonel Nobody drummed his fingers on his left bicep.

"I wish upon no child or man the weight of keeping his identity a secret from the world, but in this little fellow's case I'm afraid it would be best. You have my permission to take him as a son under one condition."

Pacarina grabbed Lawrence's arm. "What?"

"That you make me his godfather." Colonel Nobody's face slowly broke into a smile. "Now, does anyone else have anything to say?"

"I think Chester may," Lawrence said.

"Me?" Chester shook his head. "I'm not adopting anyone."

"But are you sure there isn't someone you would like to take with you out of this valley?"

Chester looked around the room and scratched his head.

"Well, I want to make sure Jacques comes with us so that I can find some proper ingredients to prove that his sauces are too strong. That's all. What are you blinking at?" Chester finally took Lawrence's hint and looked sideways at Balbus's daughter. "Oh, Law, you're hopeless."

"You'd make an excellent couple."

Chester grunted. "No, Colonel Nobody, we have nothing more to say."

"Then come, friends. We've done the duty of warriors in this lost settlement. Now we must do the duty of lawyers and get our witnesses to England."

He gripped Otho's hand.

"Farewell, friend. As an outlaw, I have no responsibility to claim this land for England, and I'm glad of it. May you rest in God's peace and prosperity for many centuries to come, and if I ever have need of a true friend and a brave one, I know where to search."

He slid a pistol into his belt.

"Farewell, bloody valley. We go to England."

Chapter 40

London looked the same.

Somehow, Nobody had expected it to have changed, but London never changed. The outside world might ebb and flow, triumph and fall, live and die, but the heart of the British Empire remained the same gob of corroded arteries and smoke-filled veins. Nobody shook his head. He was starting to think like Lawrence.

The voyage had been quick, but not quick enough to make back those last two weeks' delay in Vallis Deorum. The ultimatum date was three days past. But surely Lord Bronner—not Banastre, but his father—would have begged for an extension. His influence at court might be waning, but surely the government wouldn't have acted on time in this one instance when they delayed about everything else. That was Nobody's prayer.

His little group of adventurers threaded the docks, Jacques and O'Malley holding on to Bill and Mr. Trumble as if they feared they would drown in a barrel of fish or walk under a falling box of nails.

Nobody signaled a cabby. The fellow scratched the stubble on his chin and blinked at them.

"Wot's that?" the cabby asked. He pointed at Chester.

Chester's forehead furrowed. "It's a hat. Genuine, one-hundred percent wolf. Imported. Hand-killed. Not for sale."

"Take us to Buckingham," Nobody said.

"Wot? The palace? You want to tour the city?"

"No, we need to see the queen."

The cabby laughed. "That's a good 'un. But really, where d'ye want to go?"

"I don't like repeating myself." Nobody threw the door open, helped Pacarina inside, motioned the Stonings to join her, and sent Jacques and O'Malley to find another cab.

The cabby frowned. "You're not saying you've got an appointment wi' the queen, are you?"

This fellow was getting annoying. "Not an appointment," Nobody said, "but we're going to see her."

"Why, who are you?"

"Nobody."

"Well, the queen doesn't see nobodys."

"She'll see this one."

The two cabs disgorged their loads in front of the palace. It was all far more dramatic than Nobody liked, but it was also the quickest way to accomplish his purpose. He was done with delaying.

The cabby hung off his perch and watched with bulging eyes as the adventurers alighted.

"Are you about to do wot I think?" the cabby asked.

"Frankly, I'm not concerned with what you think," Nobody said. He led the way straight to the marble arch in front of the palace. "Chester, take off that hat."

"But those guards are wearing bears on their heads," Chester said. "What's wrong with a little wolf?"

"For one thing, their bearskins don't still have the teeth showing. Hat off."

The guards came to attention.

"Hello, fellows," Nobody said. "I'm here to see Her Majesty the Queen."

"Do you have an appointment?" the guard asked.

"No, but I think she'll see me."

The guard's expression blinked from surprise to supercilious annoyance.

"Go jump in a pond you little urchin. You should all be ashamed of yourselves, making a mock of the queen. Go see some other sights."

Nobody drew a paper from his pocket and unfolded it.

"Does this drawing look familiar?"

The guard squinted. "Yes, that's Colonel Nobody, the fellow everybody is wondering if he'll come back. What of it?"

"Look over the paper."

The guard's gaze topped the paper and studied Nobody's face, first with annoyance, then with a glint of gathering surprise. He looked at the drawing in the newspaper, then back at Nobody. His bearskin quivered.

"Yes," Nobody said. "I've come back. Take me to your officer."

Within five minutes a wide-eyed officer and six soldiers were standing beneath the marble arch.

"Colonel Nobody," the officer said, "it is my duty to arrest you as a traitor to Her Royal Majesty Queen Victoria."

Chester gasped. Nobody held up his hand. He had expected this.

"Quite right," Nobody said. "You will please inform the queen that I've brought the requested witnesses to prove my innocence. I hope she'll be good enough to hold a special trial very quickly, as I'm quite tired of being viewed as England's enemy. May I be put in the same cell as my lieutenant-colonel?"

"Your—lieutenant-colonel? You mean, Lieutenant-Colonel Burke?"

"The same."

The officer rubbed his hands together. "I'm—sorry about that."

"About what?"

"You, er—you haven't heard?"

Fear clutched Nobody's heart. He tried to steady his knees. "Heard what?"

The officer licked his lips. "About the trial. Lieutenant-Colonel Burke was sentenced to death."

Only sentenced. Nobody smiled with relief.

"I've brought witnesses to change that."

The officer shook his head. "I'm afraid you haven't. You see—he hung three days ago."

Chapter 41

Stone floor. Stone walls. Stone ceiling.

Nobody slowly realized that he was in a cell. He didn't remember fainting. He wasn't a fainter. But he didn't know how he came from the marble arch in front of the palace to this cell. It was all black, as if his memory had slept. The last thing he remembered was the face of the officer, respectful, half-embarrassed, speckled by pimples and a mole in the left corner of his mouth, as he said that Edmund was dead.

Edmund was dead. Hung. As a traitor.

His grin would lighten no more rooms. His laugh would puncture no more lonely nights of watching. Nobody would not stand by Edmund at his wedding, and Edmund would not stand by Nobody at his. Nobody was too late.

Nobody tried to kneel, but realized he already was. He folded his hands.

Father God, help me bear it. I gave him into Your hands and You took him. Blessed be the name of the Lord. Give me Your peace, Lord, help me bear it—and oh, Father, be with Elyssa. My heart is ravaged and I was only his brother by friendship. She was to be his wife. Be with her, and give us both peace.

Someone knocked softly.

He tried to crush down his reflex of anger, but drips of it strained through.

"If you wear a red coat you'd best stay outside," Nobody said. "I want to see no queen's soldier today."

"I wear a black coat." It was Lawrence's voice.

Nobody stood. "It's a fitting color. Enter."

Lawrence's eyes were deep with sympathetic sorrow, but he didn't say anything immediately. Nobody swallowed. He couldn't stomach commiseration right now.

Lawrence held out a piece of paper.

"The officer tried to give it to you, but you weren't yourself."

He didn't need to say who the letter was from. The paper was so thick that it hardly crinkled. Prison-stock. Nobody held the paper by his side, unable to open it at this moment.

"I should have known Lord Bronner wouldn't save him. Have you seen him?" Nobody asked.

"He came as soon as he heard you arrived, and he's incredibly sorry about— everything."

"Why didn't he save Edmund?"

Lawrence sighed. "He tried. I don't understand it all, but there are some deep political maneuverings going on right now, and Banastre has friends with tremendous influence at court. I don't think the queen wanted to pass sentence, but she was pressured into it. The government is sensitive about appearing just and firm at the moment. No one has quite forgotten the Luddites or the Swing Riots. The government wanted an example of justice, Banastre wanted him dead, and I'm afraid the army didn't give Edmund much support."

Nobody shook his head. "No. The army never liked us. We weren't traditional." He tried to hold the paper still. "When will I be tried?"

"Tomorrow. The queen has said so herself." Lawrence rubbed a thumb along the bottom of his chin. "I wonder—that is to say, I hope you can trust your witnesses."

Nobody's fingers tensed. "What do you mean?"

"Well, they worked for Banastre once before. I just wonder—but, I'm sorry, I'm just a croaker, as Chester would say." Lawrence shrugged, but it wasn't entirely convincing. "Should I go now?"

Nobody nodded. The door's clang washed him in a sense of loneliness such as he had not felt for years. He looked at the paper in his hand. It was a letter, folded three times, and addressed simply to "Noble." He forced his fingers to unfold the leaves.

My Dear Noble,

It appears we won't be seeing each other again. It's not that your face is particularly pretty, but it's much nicer than the dough-faced warden who brought me this pen and paper. There, you see? I'm still in good spirits. At least, that's what I'm pretending.

I always wanted to see a trial. I'm cured now. They're hanging me in the morning. Rather ironic, I think, considering how often you joked in the old days that I would be hung. Don't blame yourself, Noble. I knew what I was doing when I followed you onto Banastre's ship, and I knew what the cost might be.

I'm afraid you must be having a pretty bad time in Greenland, otherwise you'd be back. I know what you're thinking as you read this, but know that I knew that something unavoidable delayed you. I trust you implicitly, Noble, and if it was humanly possible to get back here in time, you would have. Or maybe someone else needed your help more. I don't know what's kept you, old man, but I know you're doing your duty.

I'm not afraid of death. I'm a little afraid of the dying part, but once I'm dead I have no fears. I'll be barracked in heaven, and that's better than any igloo and an awful lot better than this cell. I'm mostly sorry about Elyssa. Poor girl, she'll take my death hard, and I'm not just being egotistical. We love each other true, but apparently we were never meant to be one. Be good to her, Noble. But I know you will. Liana's already a sister to her, so you just be a brother, or a father, you old young fellow.

Short and sweet is the best rule in charges, poems, and dinner at headquarters, so I'll take my own advice here. I love you, Noble. You've been the best soldier-brother a man could ask for. And yes, I'm calling myself a man now. I've had an awful lot of time to think these past months, and a trial with a verdict 'guilty' at the end really helps sober a fellow. I've sent a letter to Elyssa, but I'm sure she'll read this one too, so I give her my love. Marry Liana and have a regiment of healthy babies, and if you'd want to name one of them a little Ed, I wouldn't take offense.

I die as I lived, your loyal-to-the-last friend:

Edmund

Nobody folded the letter and tucked it into the pocket closest his heart. A scene ballooned in his mind of a body swinging on a gallows at daybreak, with a sleepy gallows' guard blinking below, with the last fresh-eared reporter making a sketch for his evening paper, with Banastre Bronner smiling out of his coach window—he clenched his hands.

No. That wasn't the picture Ed would want him to remember. He would want him to remember the hundreds of women and children filing out of that street in Vallis Deorum, safe, happy, free, because of Edmund's sacrifice. It's hard to suffer oneself, but oh, so much harder to see your friends suffer and die and not be able to do anything. Helplessness in the face of tragedy is one of the worst feelings of all.

Nobody slipped his hand inside his waistcoat and pressed the letter to his heart. Edmund would never be forgotten.

He was still pressing the letter to his heart the next day as he sat in a private room in the palace next to Jacques and O'Malley and waited for the audience to file in. Queen Victoria would be there, and much of her court, but those weren't the faces Nobody was looking for. Only two faces mattered. One held a pair of hazel eyes and dimpled cheeks framed by jet-black hair. The other had a red nose and looked like a hawk.

Liana came first. They locked eyes, and that was all they needed. Nobody didn't need to tell her the pain of Edmund's loss or the joy of seeing her again. The eyes speak the most fluent language on earth. Liana swept past the first line of chairs and made for the table behind which Nobody sat, but a guard stepped in the way.

"No communication with the prisoner on the morning of trial," he said.

Nobody clenched his fists. "That is my future wife."

The guard wrinkled his forehead. "Fellow, I don't care if she's your wi—oh, she is. Well, I don't care. No communication with the prisoner."

"I haven't seen her for months."

The guard shrugged. "It's not my fault that you took a pleasure-cruise off to Greenland."

Nobody forced his knees to remain bent and his arms to stay on the table. "Are you a man or a machine?"

"Just doing my duty."

"Well, when you've seen the world a little bit longer you may realize that a man's duty is more complicated than it seems."

The second face walked in, and Lord Banastre Bronner smiled at Nobody. *Smiled.* Why would he smile? Was it because of Edmund? Or could it be— Nobody felt a twinge of some unsettled emotion and searched the room for Lawrence. He sat with Chester and Pacarina along the back wall. He didn't look comfortable.

"All rise for Her Majesty the Queen," someone said.

The rustle in the room was echoed by the rustle of the queen's voluminous skirts as she entered. Nobody gave her a glance. She looked like any young noble-born girl dressed up in expensive clothes. He respected her as his ruler, but it would take time and healing before he could think calmly of the woman who sentenced Edmund to death, even if it did seem the just thing to do.

Lord Bronner, Banastre's father, rose.

"Your Majesty, you were gracious enough to extend your pardon for the forcible action the accused took towards the officers of the Crown, namely the deceased General Tremont and Lord Banastre Bronner, if the accused produced witnesses attesting to his innocence in his first alleged crime, that of piracy against the merchant ship *Miriam.* Though sadly delayed by no fault of his own, the accused has produced the required witnesses."

"Thank you, Lord Bronner." The queen's voice was clear and inscrutable. "Please administer the oaths."

Bill stepped forward with Mr. Trumble in his wake. The old seaman looked as care-free as if he was tramping the deck on a calm day, but Mr. Trumble looked more like a Frenchman standing in front of a loaded cannon. His knees, which always looked weak and knobby, were threatening to clack together. He was probably nervous because of the queen's presence. Probably.

The oaths were given and Lord Bronner began the preliminary questioning to establish that the sailors had indeed been at the right place, at the right time, on the right day, of the right month, of the right year. Finally, it was all established. They were without doubt on the *Miriam* when Nobody supposedly attacked her. The question that had cost so much time and blood in answering was finally to be asked.

Lord Bronner cleared his throat. "Did the accused, Colonel Nobody, forcibly detain the ship *Miriam*?"

Everyone in the room leaned forward. Even the queen's dress rustled as she inclined her upper half.

"Yes," Bill said.

Lord Bronner dropped his cane. A flurry of powder shook from his wig to his shoulders.

"What?"

"Yes," Bill said firmly.

"Y-yes," Mr. Trumble said weakly.

"You mean to say—on your oath before God—that Colonel Nobody attacked your ship as a pirate?"

"That's right," Bill said.

Nobody laughed. He didn't know what else to do. He had found these men across the world, saved their lives, and brought them from torture to freedom, and they had sold their souls for Banastre's gold.

No one spoke. Lord Bronner's glass eye rolled helplessly in its socket and the powder accumulating on his shoulders looked like a minor avalanche. Liana— no, Nobody couldn't bear to look at Liana.

Finally, Nobody rose.

"Your Majesty, may I speak in my defense?"

Victoria nodded.

The pain from Edmund's death had turned into a crisp perception, a sort of extra-vivid reality in which Nobody didn't want to die, but the thought was no longer so strange or final. For a fighting colonel he had certainly made many speeches in his life, but this last one trembling on his lips didn't feel like a speech. It was simply the overflow of the blood pounding in his forehead.

"I was raised by the army," Nobody said. "The army was my family. It was my waking hours, my sleep, my food, my drink, my friend, my comrade, my life. I didn't know a father's firm hand or a mother's loving arms, but my general and my colonel became my father, and raised me to be the man I am, and Britannia was my mother, and for her I spent my blood, my tears, and my years."

Nobody pressed the back of his hand against his face and forced his lids against the burning in his eyes. It passed, and he looked out over the small audience.

"When I found it my duty to leave the army, God had granted me a brother in my lieutenant-colonel, Edmund Burke, and a future wife in Lady Liana. I left the army, but I still had a family. Then came General Tremont and Lord Bronner, and they wanted to destroy that family. They tried to take my betrothed. I fought them, Your Majesty, as I would fight any snake, and Edmund fought beside me. For that act Edmund is dead and I will soon join him."

Nobody turned to the queen.

"I don't blame you for carrying out what seems to be justice, by hanging Edmund and me, but I solemnly declare that I never attacked the *Miriam*. We fired one shot across her bow in accordance with common naval practice as a signal to hove-to. We boarded her, did her no damage, and returned in her to Rahattan Island with the full agreement of Captain Mathers. I am not a pirate. I do acknowledge that I fought General Tremont and Lord Banastre Bronner, not because they tried to falsely arrest me, but for the protection of my betrothed. I make no apology for that, and I would do it again."

Nobody locked eyes with a sneering Banastre Bronner.

"Lord Bronner, I forgive you. If I were to survive this day, and you were to once again seek to harm my family, and I could do so in righteousness before God and man, I would kill you. But I forgive you. May you repent, and may God forgive you also."

Nobody pointed at Bill and Mr. Trumble.

"I have spoken. All I request is that you ask those two wretched liars to deny my innocence once more."

He sat down and lowered his face into his hands. Silence reigned until Queen Victoria made a small noise.

"Ask them again," she said.

Someone else made a noise, and suddenly Lawrence was talking.

"Your Majesty, may I please ask one of the men four simple questions?"

Nobody looked up soon enough to see Banastre Bronner pop out of his seat.

"This is highly irregular!"

"This entire process is highly irregular," Lawrence said. "I trust that the queen's grace will extend to such a simple request. Your Majesty, may I proceed?"

"You may," Queen Victoria said.

Lawrence pointed to Mr. Trumble. "Kindly answer me these questions. First, where were you taken yesterday after arriving in London?"

Mr. Trumble looked like a trapped rat. "W-w-we went t-to a house."

"Did anyone come to see you in that house?" Lawrence asked.

One of the sailor's trembles took the form of a nod.

"Did Lord Banastre Bronner see you in that house?"

Mr. Trumble thrust the fingernails of his right hand into his mouth.

"Did Lord Banastre Bronner offer you money?" Lawrence asked.

"The insolence!" Banastre Bronner shouted.

"Now, Your Highness," Lawrence said, "please ask this man again about that day on the *Miriam*."

Mr. Trumble shrieked. "All right! All right! He's right, I'm a liar, *he* made me do it!" He shrank away from Bill. "Curse me, hang me, do anything, I don't care, I can't bare it. Colonel Nobody isn't a pirate. He saved our lives, he's brave, and noble, he's not a pirate. He didn't attack us. Lord Bronner bribed us to say he did, and Bill made me do it."

For a third time the silence in the room was thick enough to drown a fly. The queen rose. Her young face twitched with emotion.

"Colonel Nobody, you are acquitted, and may God forgive me for the death of your friend. You are a free man, and one of the bravest Englishmen ever to draw breath. Your country is proud of you."

Thank you, God.

It was all that Nobody could think to say, and he meant every letter of it. No guard could stand between him and Liana now. She was in his arms in a moment and the blood, loss, sorrow, despair, fear, and betrayal faded. Faces he loved and hands he had fought beside pressed round, beaming their congratulations and gripping his own hands. Now that the verdict was passed all the courtiers would line up to soak him in good cheer, but he didn't care a grain of powder about them.

Lawrence hovered at the edge of the crowd, smiling. Nobody shouldered through and grasped his hand.

"You saved my life, Lawrence."

Lawrence shrugged. "It was only a few simple questions. I happened to place myself in some strategic locations yesterday and apparently failed to communicate that information to some of the concerned parties. I don't think it could be called spying—not quite. I hope not."

"You're a good man, Lawrence Stoning." Nobody let go of Lawrence's hand and reached for Liana's. "Will you lend me your brains for one more plan?"

Chester's head appeared on the other side of Liana. "An adventure?"

"No, a wedding."

"Oh." Chester shook his head. "A good thing, but not quite an adventure." He snapped his fingers. "I say, isn't there some tradition about kidnapping the bride?"

Nobody wrapped his good arm around Liana's shoulders and grinned wider than he remembered doing since Rahattan Island.

"I wouldn't try it if I were you," he said.

The End

Epilogue

Greetings,

My name is Lawrence Stoning. When I wrote my book detailing our experiences in the Amazon, Chester convinced me to let him write the epilogue, and if you have read it, you will remember that he expressed great interest in future adventures. In this epilogue I do not express the same interest.

Now that I have a wife and a son I'm very much hoping that we can settle down in a quiet country estate full of the smell of old books and new ink. In addition, if we were to have another adventure, I would find it challenging to survive an upgrade on Chester's wolf-hat.

Men often ask me if all that we went through in Greenland was worth it. It was. We saved the lives of hundreds of innocent men, women, and children, and reclaimed the honor of Colonel Nobody and his men. I wish I had known Edmund Burke, but Nobody says that he has many similarities to Chester. He did have the good sense to try to get married, so I'm hoping that Chester has at least that similarity.

In most of the novels Chester reads, the final chapter ends with the hero getting the girl and the loyal friend beaming as they walk down the aisle. But life isn't a novel. Yes, Colonel Nobody and Lady Liana are to be married soon, but Edmund is gone, and Elyssa, the poor girl he was betrothed to, is heartbroken.

The real question of 'is it worth it' should be directed to Nobody, not to me, and I've asked him. He says that he made the right choice. There isn't always a good choice and a bad choice, but it's a Christian's duty to make the best choice, even if it hurts. That's the duty of Christians, and the duty of warriors.

So, I am often asked, any more adventures? In my flesh I answer in the negative, but with God as my God and Chester as my brother I really have no idea.

Until we meet again, I am

Your obedient servant,

Lawrence Stoning

To learn more about the author and other books in the Men of Grit series, visit
www.johnjhornbooks.com